W9-ATK-684

Praise for Mackenzie McKade's *Black Widow*

"Like the infamous spider, BLACK WIDOW draws readers in and won't let you go until you've read every fascinating word. ...an all around thrilling plot full of all the suspense you could possibly want and you have a story that you'll definitely be adding to your keeper shelf!"

~ *Chrissy Dionne, Romance Junkies*

"Black Widow is a must have book for any paranormal buff. The story line is intriguing and it draws the reader in until the very end. The story is well thought out and the world that is created is absolutely fabulous. This is the kind of book you have to read more than once so you can appreciate all of the nuances of the characters and plot... Black Widow is a must have novel. It is definitely a highly recommended read."

~ *Kimberly Spinney, Ecataromance*

"Black Widow is an intriguing novel. The dynamics between the characters both primary and secondary kept me turning the pages and completely entertained throughout. Black Widow has a bit of everything -- angst, emotion, a touch of humour, explosive love scenes, some sweet endearing moments, and plenty of action both in and out of the bedroom."

~ *Abi, The Romance Studio*

"Mackenzie McKade has written a fast paced adventure that will surely steal the reader's breath away. Hold on tight while you read this story. The tension between the three main characters runs hot with not only Roark and Marcellus attracted to Tammy, but Marcellus does a wee bit of seducing Roark as well."

~ *Valerie, Love Romances and More*

"Mackenzie Mckade creates truly enthralling characters that I quickly came to love. Tammy is a delightful mix of vulnerability and strength while Roark and Marcellus are simply divine Alpha's. The Ménage sex scenes in this book a scorching hot with the primal instincts of the werewolf and the playful wickedness of the vampire leaving me more then satisfied. ...This book is for anyone that loves Alpha's and hot sex."

~ *Midnight Minx, Literary Nymphs*

Look for these titles by
Mackenzie McKade

Now Available:

Six Feet Under
Fallon's Revenge
Beginnings: A Warrior's Witch
Bound for the Holidays
Lisa's Gift
Midnight Summer Steam: Take Me
Lost But Not Forgotten
Second Chance Christmas
Bound by the Past

Print Anthologies:
The Perfect Gift
Beginnings
Midnight Summer Steam: Sins of Summer

Coming Soon:

Take Me Again
Merry Christmas, Paige

Black Widow

Mackenzie McKade

A Samhain Publishing, Ltd. publication.

Samhain Publishing, Ltd.
577 Mulberry Street, Suite 1520
Macon, GA 31201
www.samhainpublishing.com

Black Widow
Copyright © 2008 by Mackenzie McKade
Print ISBN: 978-1-59998-990-7
Digital ISBN: 1-59998-856-9

Editing by Angela James
Cover by Scott Carpenter

This book is a work of fiction. The names, characters, places, and
incidents are products of the writer's imagination or have been used
fictitiously and are not to be construed as real. Any resemblance to
persons, living or dead, actual events, locale or organizations is entirely
coincidental.

All Rights Are Reserved. No part of this book may be used or
reproduced in any manner whatsoever without written permission,
except in the case of brief quotations embodied in critical articles and
reviews.

First Samhain Publishing, Ltd. electronic publication: January 2008
First Samhain Publishing, Ltd. print publication: November 2008

Dedication

For my readers who support me and who have given me so much in return with their emails and letters. To my critique buddies, especially Sharis Mayer, who stepped up and helped me during my time of need. Thank you.

Chapter One

For the umpteenth time Tammy Ryan's long blonde hair fell before her eyes. "Where's a hair tie when I need it?" She tucked the errant lock behind her ear, before continuing to flip through the stack of papers verifying page numbers. *"Un...deux...trois..."* She counted in French. Everyone had a fantasy. Her dream was to visit Paris someday. Everything about the city on the Seine was seductive—including the men. The thought put a short-lived smile on her face as she raised her gaze and looked around. This place was a far cry from her dreams. The grind of the printer spitting out the rest of the packet was the only sound in the large room. It was a cubicle maze. One of fifty people, she spent her days trying to find a way out of the humdrum routine that had become her life since she'd left Boise, Idaho.

No family to hold her there, Tammy had come to Phoenix three months after her father's death. She'd never known her mother, because the woman had skipped town shortly after Tammy's birth. She sucked in a breath, then released it slowly. Damn. She missed her father.

The heavy smell of ink rose overriding the various scents of the day, except for the stale cup of black coffee and half-eaten tuna sandwich she had placed in the trash can at her feet.

"*Aie!*." Tammy squirmed in her chair, trying to relieve the tingling in her right leg. It was a wonder every extremity wasn't numb. What did she expect, sitting too long behind a desk?

A sudden *clunk*, the printer halted signaling the last of her job was finished. "It's about time." She set the pages she was reviewing down on the desk before her. The carpet muffled any sound as she slid the chair from beneath her desk and rose. Lucky for her the printer was only three cubicles down, just enough time to work the feeling back into her leg.

Almost midnight, the two-story building was empty, except for the security guard. George was seventy-two, past retirement, but held on for the sake of benefits. Around nine he had checked in on her, but if she knew him, he was probably slumped over his desk fast asleep. Not much happened on a Monday night. Hell, who was she kidding? Not much happened in the life of an underwriter. Long hours meant no social life. It was the nature of the beast. She wasn't really complaining.

The hell she wasn't.

Tammy worked twenty-four/seven, ate dinner at her desk, and couldn't remember the last time she'd left work when the sun was still up. Each night when she finally made it home, her apartment was empty. But what was worse—her bed was cold. If she ever did take a day off, she spent it alone.

Last week she had sworn things would change. She hadn't planned on working late tonight. A trip to Home Depot to pick out a Christmas tree had been on her schedule. Yet the Emerson's mortgage papers had to be on her boss's desk first thing tomorrow morning. Just her luck to have inherited the most screwed-up deal in all of Arizona—or at least Phoenix.

A drawn-out yawn confirmed the late hour. Even her steps took on a lethargic pace as she stepped into the printer room. The copies were still warm when she picked them up and thumbed through the pages. "All here." A breath of relief met the final page.

A new bounce rose in her step as she headed back to retrieve the rest of the packet. Carefully, she added the remaining pages to the stack and headed for mahogany row. Where her desk was made of cold steel, her boss's was the richest of wood, dark and expensive. Usually off-limits, he had left the door unlocked for her. Now all she had to do was deliver the mortgage papers and she was out of there. Tammy set the package square in the middle of the desk and turned quickly to leave. As she pulled the door closed, she listened for the click to ensure it locked, and then padded back to her cubicle.

Without delay, she swiped her mouse over the pad and shut down her computer. Her purse was already on her desk, it had been sitting there since five o'clock when Mr. Cox informed her that her night wasn't over. She grabbed the bag, swung it over her shoulder, and headed for the elevator. Stopping before the shiny gray doors, she hesitated. Pressing the down button, she wondered whether she should turn off the lights.

"Nah..." That would leave her in total darkness. The guard could take care of it. Besides, she was tired and for some odd reason the skin on her arms was prickling. Even the moan of the elevator opening put her on edge. Call it intuition or just plain silliness, but something didn't feel right tonight. Maybe she was just worrying about the quality of her work so late at night. One page out of order and she'd hear about it tomorrow. Should she go back and re-count the pages?

No. No. No. Tammy stepped inside and pushed the lobby button and the doors closed. She was through for the night. A sudden jerk had her grasping the rail. When the elevator pulled to a halt and opened, she stepped out. George was just where she knew he'd be, slumped over his desk and fast asleep. She smiled, moving quietly not to disturb him. The glass door was heavy as she pushed it open and stepped outside into the cool air. The door swung shut, automatically locking as an iridescent glow surrounding the full moon caught her attention. She'd never seen anything like it. Eerie, yet beautiful.

Umph!

From out of nowhere something struck her, hard. With the speed and impact of a semi-truck, the thrust ripped her off her feet and sent her flying through the air. Street lights and the surrounding buildings were a blur distorted by the force.

When she hit the ground, her vision darkened. Teeth scraped teeth, jarring to make that skin-crawling, grinding sound. Stars burst behind her eyelids. She couldn't breathe. Every place on her body ached as she lay face down on the cold sidewalk.

Tammy didn't have time to think—to move—before her assailant pinned her with his weight. He was big, covering her tall frame with ease. The pressure of his fingertips against her back felt more like nails digging into her flesh.

Raw fear rose quickly, tearing through her like a cyclone. Legs kicking wildly, she attempted to roll over—face her attacker—but she was helpless in her current position.

Terrified, a scream crawled up her throat only to be snuffed out as something sharp clamped around her waist. Intense pain blinded her. She couldn't find her voice. Desperately she swung balled fists behind her, connecting with a furry mass and hard bone. A pang exploded in her hand, but that didn't stop her. Tammy fought with everything she had.

In retaliation her assailant raised her into the air, shaking her as if she were a rag doll. It didn't matter that she weighed one-thirty. The ease with which her body was slung around was frightening.

Air stripped from her lungs. She went rigid. Tammy had

never felt such excruciating pain as he shook her unmercifully. The result was a million sharp knives thrusting into her waist and ribcage.

Frantically, she continued to pummel whatever had her in its grip. Like a rush of fire ants, a scream burned up her throat. But when it released, the strangled sound came out a weak cry, almost a sob.

Before rational thought returned, her assailant began to move. Each step pushed the blades deeper into her sides. Held in what only could be described as a demon's embrace, the glow of Christmas and street lights were ribbons of color blending together as he increased his pace. Fast and furiously, he headed toward a building that would hide them away from the traffic. If he succeeded, Tammy would have no chance of being rescued.

Her lips parted again on a scream. But still nothing emerged except a gurgle. The taste of blood filled her mouth.

Between patches of scenery and the haunting moonlight, she glimpsed the sidewalk and thought she saw paws, sharp black claws, and fur-covered legs.

Was she hallucinating? Her attacker couldn't possibly be a dog.

Tammy tried to rationalize what was happening to her. Costume? It was two weeks before Christmas, not October. Halloween was over. Still it had to be a costume.

Even as she pushed the irrational thought from her mind an odd scent touched her nose. Wild and musky, the aroma was almost pungent.

Tammy wasn't a little woman, five-nine and curvy, which meant she had meat on her bones. A Saint Bernard, even a Great Dane wasn't large enough to grip her waist with its mouth. Oh God. She'd heard of wild animals coming down from the high country when there wasn't enough food for them. Could it be a mountain lion or a wolf? Whatever carried her behind the four story building they approached did so as if she weighed nothing.

Again, the sharp sensation of a steel trap tightening around her mid-section made her scream. But her cry was suffocated, lost somewhere between her diaphragm and her quivering lips.

Tremors rippled through her, shaking her until her vision blurred. Like a hot slice of steel the burn was penetrating. The agony that followed felt as if her belly was being ripped apart.

She was going to die tonight and there was nothing she could do to stop it.

With a jolt, her assailant came to an abrupt stop. She tumbled from its jaws. The sudden release sent another wave of pain through her body as she collapsed in a fetal position on the asphalt parking lot. The scent of oil rose up to meet her.

Tammy tried to rise, but it hurt too much to move. A trembling hand placed below her breasts confirmed what she already knew. There was no way she was going to make it out of this alive. Whatever had attacked her had nearly torn her stomach wide open. Her hands were wet. Bloody.

Scuffles, grunts and cries of what sounded like a fight came from beside her. Odd animalistic noises ripped through the night like they belonged in the jungle instead of the streets of Phoenix, Arizona.

Through a haze she glanced toward the scuffling and her mind froze. The shadow of a man flew through the air—not leaped or jumped—but flew, crashing into the largest wolf Tammy had ever seen. The wolf's eyes glowed red; his jaws wrenched wide, his teeth dripped with saliva as he growled and then he lunged.

On impact the two creatures molded together, hitting the

ground to skid across the unforgiving asphalt. Twisting and turning, the man pushed from the wolf just as its razor sharp teeth snapped the air, missing him.

An acute ache radiated through Tammy's abdomen. She shook, closing her eyes, trying to bear the agony as she heard bones snapping—breaking.

Whimpers and growls and a passing car funneled through her head. A bang—something fell making a tinny noise. She opened her eyes to see a trash can rolling across the parking lot.

In an exhibit of strength, the man raised the wolf and tossed him through the air to collide against the building. The animal released a sickening cry as it fell to the ground. The metallic scent of blood filled the air.

Hers—theirs? God, she couldn't think right.

The throb in Tammy's chest and abdomen was becoming unbearable. She struggled to remain conscious. Her eyelids felt heavy as she fought to keep them open. She was so tired. Cold.

For a moment silence reigned. Man and beast faced each other. Their chests rose and fell rapidly.

Tammy fought for another breath. A gasp. Wheeze. Another gasp. Her blood felt thick, sluggish, as if it were forced through her veins. Yet she knew it was flowing freely as she looked down at the red soaking her shirt. She held her shaky palms to her mid-section and prayed for help before it was too late.

A dangerous hiss similar to the sound of a semi's airbrakes pushed from between the man's lips. The wolf returned a series of threatening growls before he jumped to his feet and attacked.

Thud—crunch!

The fight began anew.

The heavy breathing and grunts that had rung in Tammy's

ears were beginning to grow dim. Sounds were muffled, almost gone now. Even the pain was lessening as her eyelids slid closed. A quiet roar rumbled in her head, building to a crescendo before the last note of life was sung—her life.

She was dying.

"My pet, do you want to live?" A French accent broke through the haze her mind had become.

Tammy tried to lift her eyelids, but they refused to open. Her mouth slightly parted, but no words emerged.

She didn't want to die.

"I'll take that as a yes." His laughter was a gentle caress, as he took her limp body into his arms. If she had wanted to fight him she couldn't have—no energy remained.

Pain lanced her neck, and then it was gone with everything else.

Chapter Two

"He has arrived." A female voice caressed Marcellus Donne's ears as he glanced over his shoulder. Dressed in tight leather pants and a matching halter top, Sasha swayed seductively toward him. The woman was petite, tiny but with full breasts which usually set his body on fire, but not tonight.

Close behind her was Deirdre, so different from the other woman. Tall and slender, the white gown and turban she wore was a stark contrast to her dark skin. She reached out to him, her touch warm beneath his shirt as she stroked his arm.

Sashas's lashes lowered as she took his other arm. Her gaze swept over him like a caress. "Do you have time to play, Master?" The tips of her fangs pressed into her bottom lip as it curved into a smile.

Marcellus looked at both women, and then stared into the flickering flames of the hearth. "Not tonight, my loves." Truth was, he dreaded speaking to the leader of the lycanthropes. Their already stressed relationship hinged on Roark Lanier's reaction to the death of his friend and pack-mate.

Regret? Yes. Yet Marcellus wouldn't allow the lycanthrope to see his sorrow. The events of the night had been inevitable. Grady had attacked a human. When Marcellus tried to intervene, the werewolf turned on him. Rationalizing with Grady had not been a choice. Death had shown in the wolf's eyes.

Marcellus inhaled the smoky scent of mesquite and listened to the pop and sizzle of the fire.

Concern pulled at Deirdre's forehead. "Let us ease your mind." She leaned into him, pressing her lips to his cheek.

If only it were that easy. "Thank you, but I am fine." He forced the tension from his body, replacing it with a smile he didn't feel. There was more than the wolf's death that bothered him. Something silent and indescribable slinked beneath his skin. The sensation continued to nag him without mercy and that alone perplexed him. The attraction he experienced when he laid eyes upon the battered woman had been irresistible. When her blood had flowed through his veins, he had felt a bond develop that had never happened between him and another soul. His composure slipped—something that rarely occurred. He had distanced himself from her, left her in the care of several of his people. But the truth was he wanted the woman.

His loins tightened with the thought of her long legs. Legs were his favorite part of a woman's anatomy, that and a woman's scent. Soft and feminine. Even injured and covered in blood her musk had called to him—drew him like a lodestone.

In short, she was stunning—and deadly, as his men discovered when they had attempted to satisfy her needs. She had attacked and now they lay beneath the earth recuperating.

Sasha frowned. Her eyes narrowed as she pushed her brunette hair from her face. "She must be destroyed." Words said with a certainty he should have felt but didn't share.

For some reason the woman he had saved from dying made him feel alive again. Something he hadn't felt in centuries. A gust of air squeezed from his lungs, when he finally yielded. "I know." The idea of her death shouldn't have brought him distress, but his stomach knotted just the same.

Deirdre moved between him and the marble fireplace in the study of his mansion. She pressed her palms against his chest. Their eyes met. "Marcellus, you know what you have to do." Shadows danced across her face and flickered off the walls lined with books from all time periods. A collection he treasured almost as much as his art, but tonight they were just pages of the past—paper.

Without answering her, Marcellus moved away, heading toward the window. He pushed back the drapes and looked into the star-studded night. Even though Sasha and Deirdre remained quiet, he felt their disapproval and anxiety. Both women had been with him for the past two centuries. Friends. Lovers. Yet tonight neither of them was on his mind. He didn't crave Sasha's touch or Deirdre's kisses, but that of another.

Mentally, he attempted to shake his wayward thoughts. His desires were of no matter. He had the future of his people to think of. "Leave me." He needed a moment to prepare and gather his thoughts. His guest had waited long enough and the night was not over.

Roark Lanier's host certainly had an odd sense of humor. Pristine white walls and floors graced the chamber he had been led to await Marcellus Donne. Several sets of chains and D-rings were strategically placed, which probably accounted for the lack of windows. From the doorway he eyed the room's single inhabitant, an unconscious woman. Her wrists, manacled in iron, were connected to chains hanging from the ceiling while her splayed ankles were bound to the tiled floor. She even wore a black leather collar around her neck. Golden waves of hair fell forward, hiding her face and parts of her body. Her naked body.

The scene was shocking and strangely arousing. Desire slammed into him. Blood rushed to his nether region, creating

19

an ache between his thighs. He swallowed hard and retraced his steps. What the hell was Donne up to?

Although the room was clean, Roark's keen senses picked up an acidic scent of antiseptic, beneath it a trace of blood. A whiff of lingering fear revealed a struggle and the musky aroma of sex mingled. The last thought thickened his cock more. Another familiar aroma rose that didn't belong—lycanthrope. He brushed the ridiculous thought aside. Drawn by the female, he took another step into the room. His gaze traveled up the length of the blonde's shapely legs. His beast woke with a jolt. The animal within rippled beneath his skin. The sensation that he knew her made the pit of his stomach flutter.

Anger rose on swift feet that she, or any woman for that matter, would be held in such disregard. Even more disturbing was the sudden urge to protect her—take her into his arms. He didn't, realizing that he knew nothing about her or the situation. For all he knew, she could be a willing participant in some kinky game his host enjoyed. The idea only served to arouse Roark more. He stroked his gaze over her slender neck, frowning at the bite mark marring her tender skin. Donne's handy work no doubt.

Damn vampire.

Through lush hair the glimpse of full breasts pulled Roark's attention away from Donne's pinprick signature lying below the collar. Roark adjusted his hips to relieve the growing pressure in his jeans. Somehow he knew her eyes would be blue, bluer than the sky.

Now where the hell had that thought come from? He shook his head to erase his curiosity. When that didn't work he attempted to focus on why Donne dragged him out tonight or more accurately early morning? It had to be around two a.m., no longer Monday but Tuesday. When the vampire had called,

Roark had been running with the pack. A full-moon always put the lycanthropes on edge. Nights like this one were for running and hunting and making love. The thought drew his attention back to the woman.

A rosy nipple peeking through a web of silky hair made Roark catch his breath. The urge to taste her and run his tongue around the taut bud consumed his thoughts. Would she be sweet like honey or spicy like her perfume? His mouth salivated.

Drawn to her, he stepped nearer for a better look. Through breaks in the thick strands of hair, pink, angry scars were visible on her flat belly. Roark saw red. This was *not* a consensual act. Someone had attacked her.

Moving closer, Roark used his animal senses and inhaled deeply. She carried the stench of several vampires, but undeniably there was another presence he recognized. Wild and earthy and most definitely lycanthrope.

"Grady." His dearest friend's name came out a whisper. But it couldn't be.

The slightest of movement from behind had Roark spinning on a dime to come face-to-face with the leader of the undead.

"What's this all about?" It had taken Roark several hours to trek through the rugged mountain range to make it to the city, but it had been his choice. He'd had a bad day and felt the need to stretch his legs, run in his wolf form. Bad decision. His feet hurt and the trip hadn't improved his mood. He should have driven, but hindsight was worthless. He tugged at the collar of his red flannel shirt. Instead of running amongst his clan on this night, he was clothed in jeans and uncomfortable shoes that he kept hidden just outside the city for sudden visits like this one.

One shoulder propped against the wall, Donne stroked a

toothpick around one sharp canine. Dark hair tied back by a leather thong flowed down to touch his waist. Wearing a black silk shirt, dress pants and leather shoes, the vampire could easily pass as a prominent business man. But the fangs were a dead giveaway he was not human.

"You recognize one of your wolves' scent?" He pushed away from the wall, flicking the toothpick into a nearby trash can, as he came to stand beside Roark. "Lovely isn't she?" His words came out on a purr of appreciation.

Hell yes, on both accounts. But that didn't answer Roark's question. He had recognized Grady's presence on the woman, but why? No self-respecting werewolf would share a lover with a vampire. Besides, this woman had not been loved but abused. Another question rose swiftly. Why was she healing so fast? Bruises were fading before his eyes. The odd sensation that he knew the blonde kept nagging him. Had he met her through Grady?

Roark pushed his fingers through his hair, the ends brushed his shoulders. Vampires and lycanthropes didn't commingle. He wouldn't say vampires and werewolves were enemies, exactly. Hell, who was he trying to fool? They couldn't stand each other.

Centuries of conflict in a world where both species were the minority had gotten them nowhere. Instead of fighting to establish dominance over each other, they should be working together to solve common issues, mainly how to live amongst the human race. Lycanthropes and vampires dwindled in numbers. More and more of Roark's people were losing their lives in hunting and trapping incidents. Vampires had a different problem. They needed the humans to sustain life, at least the undead kept human conversions to a minimum.

Roark and Donne thought much alike. They were the leaders of their races. Through extensive negotiations and hard work, they had come to a gentleman's agreement. The metropolitan areas of Phoenix and Tucson were vampire territory. The outskirts and Northern Arizona belonged to Roark's people. Occasionally their paths crossed, tempers flared, but to date all had been rather calm, unlike in the past.

Grady's participation here—in this room—was inconceivable. Not to mention the woman was held captive and apparently ravished against her will. But the evidence before Roark said his friend had stepped beyond the limits of lycanthrope law.

Roark's jaws clenched. He berated himself for not taking action sooner. For weeks he had seen it coming, but because of his relationship with Grady he had turned a blind eye. No longer. Friends or not, Grady would have to pay for dishonoring this woman.

"Where is he?" Roark spoke no name. Donne knew who he referred to. The vampire leader was as familiar with Roark's pack as Roark was with the vampires. Both believed in the philosophy of keeping your friends close, your enemies closer.

"Dead," Donne announced calmly. Only a twitch in his jaw gave away his anxiety.

So much for peace between their people.

Heat crawled up Roark's neck consuming his face and ears. The muscles in his neck crackled as he resisted the change and his instinctive need to strike out at Donne and shred him to pieces.

The vampire had the good sense to back away as he held up an outstretched palm. "Now don't go furry on me, Lanier, hear me out."

Roark's nose twitched, his skin itched to transform. The

beast within him paced, roared for revenge, begging to be released. Saliva formed in his mouth. "Where is his body?" The words came out garbled, caught between a demand and a growl.

"My people are preparing him for your return to the mountains." The cavalier attitude Donne usually held onto slipped. Roark could have sworn he saw something close to regret flicker in the vampire's eyes. "I swear I'd never seen him like this. He attacked not only the woman, but me. I only defended myself."

Grady had been Roark's best friend from the moment their fathers had introduced them as children. They had played, hunted, and caroused together, and then something had changed. Several weeks ago, Grady had come home mangled and beaten. He had not revealed what had happened to him, but he had never been the same. Quiet. Despondent. His temper volatile—he was a powder keg, on the edge.

An invisible fist squeezed Roark's heart. Emotion pricked his eyes making them burn. His gut was a twisted mass. How could he tell Grady's father? The clan would want an eye for an eye. Even now Roark fought the need to taste Donne's blood, rip him apart from limb to limb. He struggled to center himself. The only calm he found was in the chained beauty before him. "And the woman?"

"Well... That's another problem." The hesitancy in Donne's voice rattled Roark's control. He clenched his fingers, nails biting into his palms as he resisted reaching out for the immortal. Donne watched him cautiously as he continued, "I felt sorry for her, so..."

Damn vampire. The undead were unscrupulous—they took what they wanted without permission or thought of consequences. Lycanthropes lived by strict rules—humans were not on their menu.

"You were attracted to her," Roark stated the obvious. What man wouldn't be—she was perfection—a piece of art?

Donne shrugged. "Well, there was that. But it was your brethren that robbed her of life."

Just like a vampire. Disdain struck Roark hard. Donne refused to take responsibility for his actions. "So, what? You felt so sorry that you saved her life by turning her into a vampire, chaining her to the ceiling and floor as a trophy?" Bitterness oozed from Roark's mouth.

His friend was gone. Grady was dead.

Donne strolled toward the woman, stopping more than twenty feet away. "Not exactly."

Roark pinched the bridge of his nose, closing his eyes briefly. He released a heavy sigh. "I tire of this game. Show me to Grady. I wish to take him home." Roark wouldn't have believed it if he hadn't smelled and seen Grady's devastation.

"Ah, yes. But the woman?" Donne gave him an inquisitive glance.

Roark took one more look at the luscious blonde. What had happened was indeed a shame, yet he didn't see how her becoming one of the undead was his concern. He had bigger fish to fry—like how to convince his clan not to kill every vampire that walked the earth.

"Not my problem." He turned and headed for the door. His fingers wrapped around the doorknob when Donne said, "It seems she is."

As Roark slowly pivoted, the tautness in his stomach drew tighter. "She's lycanthrope?"

What the hell had Grady done? He knew the law. Anger exploded inside Roark once again. "Why is she chained? Have you so little respect for my people?"

Donne shoulders squared. His pupils darkened as his voice grew serious. "Like I said *we* have a problem."

The hair beneath Roark's skin prickled, tingling to be released. The beast inside him was demanding his attention, pushing against his will. His gums ached, his canines threatening to expose themselves. By a thread he held onto his human form, even as he felt his fingernails grow, curling into sharp claws. "Explain, Donne, and do it fast. My patience has come to an end."

"Do you recall the tale of the Lamia?"

Donne's absurd question forced a huff of disbelief from Roark's mouth. He brushed his fingers through his hair. It was a nervous habit, but God he was tired. His heart and eyes felt heavy and he had a long trip back up the mountain. Not to mention the vampire was fucking nuts.

"You must have sucked the blood from one too many loony humans. Still that doesn't explain why she is bound like an animal." Donne didn't expect Roark to believe the innocent woman chained to the floor and ceiling was the mythical creature that had brought destruction upon all mankind? But the gravity upon his host's face gave him pause.

"It appears the combination of our races is very dangerous," Donne stated frankly.

No way could the woman be a hybrid, half wolf-half vampire. The bloodlust of this creature was legendary. Roark assumed the myth was a childhood story meant to retain the purity of their races.

"You're kidding right?" Roark asked. "She's lycanthrope and vampire?"

Donne slowly nodded.

There had to be some explanation. Roark tried to calm the pounding in his head. Just the idea that such a monster existed made him ill. "Have you seen her change?"

Donne shifted his feet. "Not personally, but my people have. That's the reason for the collar."

Grady, what have you done? The conversion of human to lycanthrope was nearly unheard of. There were stiff penalties for a wolf who disobeyed the law.

Okay, let's be rational here. Lamia don't exist. Vampires and werewolves don't mate. Donne had to be wrong. Roark glanced toward the peaceful woman and felt another jolt to his cock. Rays of electricity zapped him hard enough to steal his breath. His beast answered with a roar. It paced restlessly beneath his skin.

Donne and his people were confused.

Roark thought for only a moment, his resolve firmly in place. He would take her home and make up for what Grady had done to her. As leader of the Mogollon Rim Pack, she would be his responsibility. If he had addressed Grady's problem before now this wouldn't have happened.

The hardness in Donne's stance relaxed, he gazed upon her with something close to appreciation. "Perfect is she not?" He took another step closer, stopping just out of her reach. "When awake she draws men like honey..." he paused before adding, "...to their deaths."

"What?" This was ridiculous.

"Yes. She is a veritable black widow. She almost killed two of my men, Titan and Darta. They only meant to feed her, but she can be very seductive when she's awake. And well, they also wished to accommodate her lustful needs, after which she turned furry and nearly took their lives."

Roark couldn't believe what he was hearing. "There is no

way an injured woman could take on one vampire, much less two. Not in her weakened condition." Yet Roark knew a lycanthrope's sexual needs and hunger were always an issue with young female wolves when they came into their first heat. There was no telling what would happen during the heat cycle of a converted wolf.

He had witnessed a human's transformation once. The life-changing hormone lycanthropes released during a bite that altered a human to wolf caused unstable results.

"My pack stopped turning humans several centuries ago. It has been outlawed. Grady knew this. He wouldn't—"

But evidently his friend had. It did Roark no good to keep trying to ignore the obvious.

"Your man was not in control," Donne interrupted. "The truth lies before us."

"If what you say is true, you should have let her die." Roark regretted the words the minute he said them. But it was true. How would she live? The human race would not welcome her, nor would she be accepted by the wolves or vampires. And if what Donne said was true—that she was dangerous—they had no alternative but to end her life. His beast screamed in protest.

"How was I to know the abomination she would become? So, what are we going to do?" Donne asked.

"We?" *Damn Grady.* What the hell was Roark to do?

"Yes, we. She will not be welcomed in my world." Donne confirmed what Roark already knew.

An uneasy chuckle pushed from his tight lips. They faced each other. "And you think she will be in mine? The only solution is—"

"Release me now." A female's disgruntled voice finished Roark's sentence with a recommendation that was far from what had been on his mind. She could not live in this world. He jerked his attention to where she hung.

His breath caught.

She was the most incredible creature he had ever seen. And he was right. Her eyes were sky blue.

Chapter Three

Tammy was trapped between sleep and that moment when her conscious mind begged for control. *Sleep.* That's all she wanted. Just ten more minutes before she had to face the day, rise and go to work. Was it Tuesday morning? She had no idea as she fought the threads of wakefulness threatening to pull her from slumber. Maybe she'd call in sick. Hard as she tried, sounds and smells began to seep through the mental wall she had erected.

The first to break through was the scent of male musk. *Dream,* she rationalized. Tammy slept alone. What she would give for it to be real. She'd turn over and slowly licked her way across the man's body, every succulent inch. A tightening fluttered in her belly. A moan parted her lips as the ache in her stomach grew. Need made a lousy bed partner and so did hunger. When was the last time she ate? With the thought, something clawed at her insides. A craving rose so quickly she groaned.

Chocolate? *No.*

Meat? Her mouth began to water.

Blood? The pain inside her sharpened.

Okay. Now that's odd, she thought even as visions of her body entwined with two strange men popped in her head. Now this was a dream made in heaven. Not one, but two men.

30

Yummy. The warm smell of the heater kicking on dissolved the image. Her eyes open on a sigh. She blinked once, twice, and then again.

A cry of distress stung Tammy's throat. This wasn't her room. Panic rose swiftly engulfing her like a wave pulling her under. For the love of God, she was naked and bound.

She jerked her head up as she fought her bindings. The shuffling of feet drew her attention across the room. She wasn't alone. Fear washed over her a second time. At the same time her senses jumped like live-wires striking different polar ends. A million questions assailed her. The most acute—how was she going to escape?

The men seemed unaware of her existence as they argued. Testosterone rolled off them in sheets. For some unknown reason their fervent scent made every nerve ending inside her come alive, heating her body like a furnace. She had to taste them, feel them against her skin and between her thighs, now.

Tammy tensed. What was wrong with her? She should be concerned for her life, not fantasizing about fucking her kidnappers. But try as she did, she couldn't erase the need that screamed to be fed.

In her sexual frenzy, Tammy thought she heard the auburn-haired man say something about letting her die. Her breath caught. Panic took hold once more. Quietly but firmly she pulled against her bonds. When she heard the dark-haired man call her an abomination it was like cold water dousing a fire. She went rigid with anger that quenched her arousal but did nothing for the hunger gnawing in her belly.

"Release me now," she growled, low and menacing. The tempered voice was not her own. Just as fast as her anger had risen memories flashed, snatching her breath away.

A wolf. The attack. She remembered the pain, the fight—

dying. A kaleidoscope of scenes continued, making love to two men, a wolf, then blood—the men's blood. God it had tasted so good.

Her stomach pitched. For a moment she thought she would vomit. Instead acid rolled like an angry sea causing a burn to develop in her chest and throat. A whimper squeezed from her parted lips.

When both men's stares scanned across her skin, her mind froze, but her body responded. Her nipples drew tight. An ache developed between her thighs, the result a flood of desire she couldn't control.

Mixed emotions assailed her. Her immediate reaction was to free herself, run and hide. At the same time she wanted them next to her, to feel their strong hands roam her body, to feel their cocks buried inside her, and to taste them upon her tongue. The hunger was so great her spasms ignited a chain reaction that overtook her. She groaned, a raspy sound, washing away the mental conflict. Here one moment and gone the next, she felt the muscles in her body relax. Some freaky-ass thing was going on inside her—she didn't feel right, and then a noise like a kitten's purr slid off her tongue.

Her fingers splayed wide, her wrists held firmly by the manacles. *"Venez à moi." Come to me*? She mentally translated the words as she spoke them. Her French lessons were paying off. Yet the sexy voice belonged to someone else. She should have been frightened, but for some reason wasn't.

Almost as if he were in a trance, the buff man in jeans took a step toward her. His face was absent of all expression. As he drew closer excitement filtered through her. She shuttered her eyelids. *"Venez à moi, mon prince."* My prince. She liked how it rolled off her tongue. French was a beautiful language.

Her breasts filled with need, heavy and ripe. She couldn't

wait for the moment of contact. She craved him like she had craved no other's touch. Thick eyelashes swept her cheekbones. Her body undulated, her hips swaying, invitingly.

What is happening to me? But the thought didn't linger longer than a heartbeat. She wanted this man and his friend.

A shiver of need made her next purr staccato, distinct breaks, so it came out an alluring mating call. Heat flared across both men's faces. The man in black didn't move, but the other one stepped closer, as if he couldn't resist.

Tammy's back arched as teasing rays of her arousal shuddered through her body. Rattling chains stopped her from reaching out, seeking her pleasure.

"Lanier, I wouldn't get any closer," warned the tall, lean man. "She's hard to resist. I know." He reached down and cupped his erection.

Still the auburn-haired man called Lanier stepped nearer—

If her hands were free she could have touched and savored him. "Are you afraid of me?" Her mouth drew into a pout. She tilted her head from left to right needing to be free of the collar around her neck. "All I want to do is play. Won't you please release me? I promise you won't regret it."

Where this teasing, sexual woman came from Tammy had no idea. All she knew was that she needed to satisfy the lustful ache in her body. Not to mention, she was hungry. She cocked her head, listening to each stranger's heartbeat. Healthy and strong.

Her fingers splayed, curling as if to emphasize her long fingernails. "But I can't touch you," she whimpered. "And I want to touch you both so badly." Her hips swayed side to side enticingly.

Again, Tammy's breath caught. Sanity briefly surfaced once more as she wondered what was happening to her. This wasn't like her—not that she hadn't secretly wanted to be seductive and charming. Looks? Yeah, she had them, but experience—zip.

Tammy wasn't promiscuous, just the opposite. Yet her body felt more in control than her mind. She desired these men more than anything she'd ever wanted.

"Kiss me." Her voice was a plea.

Lanier appeared caught in her web. His pupils were dilated as he stepped close enough she could feel his masculine heat. It warmed her blood like a fire was set beneath her. She couldn't wait to feel his embrace, the caress of his hands against her flesh. Couldn't wait for the moment his cock parted her folds and filled her.

Suddenly a spasm clenched her belly and threw her body into convulsions. Pain splintered in all directions as a drawing sensation like a knot being pulled tighter and tighter twisted inside her.

A sharp, breathy cry pushed from her mouth. "It hurts. Oh God, it hurts." She jerked against her bindings, the metal biting into her wrists and ankles, as a fiery burn raced through her body.

She couldn't quiet the involuntary muscular contractions pulling and pushing on her insides, threatening to rip her in two. She squeezed and released her vaginal muscles, attempting to lessen the throb between her thighs. But it did no good.

"Shit," Lanier cried as he ran to her.

The minute his hands touched her waist the pain inside Tammy eased, but not entirely. She brushed against his body as he folded his frame around her.

The rapid pulse in his neck called to her. Her mouth salivated. But it was the bulge pressing into her belly that made her cry out. "Please help me."

Donne glanced at Lanier.

"Her needs are sexual. It happens to all the young wolves as they come of age. Her transformation must have thrown her into a heat," Lanier said.

Heat? The thought disappeared as her stomach growled and the sound of Lanier's blood flowing through his veins became a symphony in her ears. She could hear the swish of his life essence as the chambers of his heart opened and closed. His breathing seemed to melt into hers, almost as if they were becoming one.

Donne's eyes widened. "Are you telling me she needs to be bred—fucked?"

Lanier held her firmly against his body.

Blood. Tammy sucked in a breath, fighting to think of something other than sinking her teeth into the vein pulsing in his neck.

"Fucked." He watched her guardedly. "And thanks to you, fed."

"*Oui*— Please—" Tammy purred, rubbing her body against his. Each caress stoked the flame of desire flickering across her flesh with pleasure /pain tingles. "Fuck me. Both of you." A moment of sanity peeked through the cloud of lust fogging her senses. A battle warred in her mind. Yes, her body wanted both men buried inside her, pounding into her with a ferocity that bordered on madness, while her head cried out in defiance. This couldn't be happening.

The men's expressions went blank. Their glances snapped to one another.

Donne cocked a brow. "Share her—with you?"

Lanier began stripping his clothes off. "If her needs aren't met immediately— Well, let's just say you already know what she's capable of."

Buttons popped as he ripped his shirt off, displaying a sculptured chest, lightly covered in auburn hair. Her palms itched to touch him, caress the trail of hair that disappeared beneath his jeans. He was working on the button of his pants when Donne slipped off his silk shirt.

Lanier's broad chest rose and fell as he sucked in a breath. His eyes glistening pools of gold that made every one of her nerve endings cry out. His voice thickened. "There's nothing as persuasive as a young wolf in heat. I believe your men discovered this earlier. Look at the way she tosses her hair; the poutiness in her lips, the slow dip of her eyelashes, and the sexy arch of her body—all serve as an enticement to lure a mate into her arms." Each of his words only drove her need higher. The ache in her belly clenched to make her push closer to him.

Where Lanier was bronze and bulky with muscle, Donne was less tawny, lean like a runner. Each man so different—

Tammy's burning need and the sight of the half-naked men sent her into meltdown. Moisture dampened her thighs. An unmerciful tightness formed in each of her nipples. She ached from head to toes as she pulled at her bindings.

"Even restrained, her sensuality is overpowering. Smell the release of her sweet pheromones? They call to your inner beast to be released." A hoarse growl rumbled in Lanier's throat. "A female wolf caters to her man's desires—she is insatiable. There isn't anything she wouldn't do to quench the craving churning inside her."

He had that right. They weren't moving fast enough to extinguish the burn racing through her body. Tammy squeezed her eyelids together as the whisper of zippers falling made her insides shiver. As the next slice of pain tore through her, she threw back her head and screamed.

Masculine cologne mingling with pine and earth surrounded her like an embrace. Another male scent, spicy, closed in on her from behind. Yet, it was the firmness between her thighs moving hard and fast, parting and entering her pussy with one thrust that quieted her raging desire. It was magical—heavenly. When her eyes opened she stared into eyes hot with desire.

"What's your name?" His smile was gentle, but the edges of his lips tensed.

"Tammy," she answered weakly, moving against him to feel his thickness fill her completely. Each penetrating stroke helped to ease the pang that made her tremble and release a sigh.

"That's it, breathe," Lanier coaxed as he withdrew his cock and slammed into her again, striking her cervix to send tremors throughout her body. "I'm Roark Lanier."

"More," she groaned as someone's fingers stroked her labia. They weren't Roark's fingers because his were digging into her hips.

"Careful, Donne," he growled. His eyes simmered even more, but this time not from desire.

"*Pardonnez-moi.*" the man behind her chuckled. "I must prepare her for my entry."

"Just watch where you stroke, buddy." The heaviness in Lanier's tone leaked his subtle warning.

"Of course, but I thought your kind was bisexual." Another growl from Roark made the man behind her laugh again. "It is a pleasure to meet you, Tamanen." He pronounced her name with a sexual French accent. "Marcellus Donne at your service." Marcellus must have deliberately caressed Roark's cock again, because he released a low, menacing growl.

The pressure against her ass as Marcellus spooned her back should have been disconcerting, but it wasn't. Instead she found herself leaning backward and gasping as a single finger penetrated her virgin entrance. There was an immediate sting, a burning sensation overridden by the fullness of Roark in front of her, heightening her arousal so that another wave of moisture released from her body.

Again, Marcellus brushed his fingers across each side of her slit, eliciting a growl from Roark. "My pet, you are so wet." Marcellus's words hummed in her ear. Two fingers slid between her ass cheeks, filling her.

She flinched. Her breaths were short, fast pants. Her body a flame raging into a fire as a wave of heat surged across her skin. The tightness—the pang in her entrance began to accede with each careful thrust. When Marcellus replaced his fingers with his erection and slowly began to enter her, Tammy tensed.

Her face must have shown discomfort as Roark whispered, "Relax. Let us take care of you." He cupped her cheeks, tenderly pressing his lips to hers. "Let us take you to paradise."

"It will hurt less if you push as I enter you," Marcellus instructed as he slowly penetrated her ass. "You are so tight."

And it hurt so good.

Tammy released the air in her lungs as Marcellus pushed past the first tight ring of muscle. Stars burst behind her eyes. Roark captured her mouth in a kiss so demanding it took her breath away, erasing the stars behind her eyelids. He didn't give her time to think of the sharp pain as his tongue mimicked the movement of his body. But it was the fullness of two cocks buried deep inside her body, moving in unison, that threw her over the edge of sanity and into the hottest mind-blowing orgasm she had ever experienced.

Her climax was an explosion of hot and cold rushing through her veins at the same time. In rapid succession every muscle in her body clenched and released. Her groan echoed in

Roark's mouth as his tongue continued to duel with hers.

With a pop, the suction between their mouths broke. His nostrils flared. "Mine," he growled, sending chills up her spine.

Sandwiched between two men was something she had dreamed of, even fantasized about, but this was so much better. They both slammed into her at once, rattling the chains and driving her higher up the scale of sensation to ignite another orgasm that forced her mouth open with a cry of ecstasy.

The next thing she realized, her teeth were piercing Roark's throat. The first taste was an aphrodisiac, balmy and savory. Even the metallic scent filling her senses was arousing.

"Fuck. That's unbelievable," he moaned, arching his neck to give her better access. She closed her lips around his skin and sucked. Rich blood filled her mouth and trickled down her throat. It was heaven—it was life's nectar. It was hell. She had no idea what she was doing—instincts drove her.

Roark's fingers dug deeper into her hips, grinding their bodies together as his warm seed shot to the back of her pussy.

Unexpected pain lanced Tammy's neck just below the leather collar, but faded quickly into a sultry heat. A rush of rapture filled her with such intensity she clamped down harder on Roark's throat and sucked.

He moaned, as if the sound was pushed from the very depths of his soul.

The sensual sensation against her neck ended abruptly, leaving her bereaved for Marcellus's touch. But it didn't stop her impending orgasm. Her body was a rage of emotions. Like a drug straight through her blood stream it hit, burning with a delicious fervor that sent her mind soaring. Even when Marcellus said, "Release him, Tamanen," she knew she couldn't stop—not now. She wanted more.

Two fingertips pressed hard into one of her carotid arteries reversed the erotic high to send her plummeting downward. It was like falling down an elevator shaft with no hopes of stopping. A wave of nausea struck hard. Then everything went black.

Chapter Four

Roark stumbled back, weakened by the blood loss, but more sated than ever before. He felt intoxicated. The roar of the ocean rolling over a sandy beach and then back out to sea filled his head. His hand rose to his neck cupping Tammy's mark, a bite that had nearly robbed him of life.

As with Donne's signature on her neck, the two pinpricks on Roark's neck had not closed and disappeared like he had seen happen when vampires fed. Instead the area continued to throb with shooting rays of sensation that made his body burn. He felt himself drawn back to her side. His cock stiffened, hungry for more.

Fucking amazing. He swayed, trying to say upright.

Tammy's body hung listlessly from her bindings around her wrists, ankles and neck. She was unconscious again thanks to Donne's knowledge of the pressure-sensitive artery that constricted and lowered her blood pressure until she blacked out.

Roark brushed strands of hair out of her face. The heat wouldn't be so hard on her next time. With each mating the contractions would subdue, until finally she was pregnant or out of heat.

Pregnant? The thought of being a daddy, of seeing a child grow in her belly, made him smile. Gently, he outlined the curve of her jaw-line and smoothed his palm across her soft cheek. He had dreamed of the day he found his mate and began a family. The tenderness that filled his chest was dashed when he heard Donne moving from behind her. She was half wolf—half vampire. Was a child even possible?

Anger replaced the moment. If he had found her before Grady had then there might have been a chance for them. What life laid in store for them now?

He'd heard stories of humans who would sell their souls to lie with the undead. The vampiresses who had approached him on occasion, although sexy and beautiful, had always been a turnoff. They were walking corpses, thirsting for the blood of those who were unlucky enough to encounter them.

But this woman—

Roark couldn't keep his hands from caressing up and down her slender waist. Her full breasts and rosy nipples were a beacon enticing him to taste and fondle. Damn, if she didn't send his body into meltdown. His balls throbbed. His cock firmed beyond comfort.

Given half the chance to fuck her again while she took his blood, he'd do it in a heartbeat.

Yes. Lycanthropes nipped and bit their mates during mating, but never took blood. The suction of her mouth on his neck was the most sensual thing he had ever experienced. It had torn the orgasm from his cock. Talk about a pleasure/pain moment.

Donne extracted a white handkerchief from his pants on the floor. He stood before Roark, gently patting his lips. "Would you like for me to lick your wound clean?" He didn't smile, but Roark could see the hint of a grin that sparkled in the vampire's dark eyes.

"Hell no." Roark cupped his neck, feeling the stickiness of

his own blood against his fingers. Many of his people indulged in ménages, were even bisexual, especially during heat cycles when the pheromone levels soared arousing the entire pack. But if Donne even thought of nibbling on his neck—

"Exquisite." Donne's voice was full of male satisfaction, which immediately raised the hairs on Roark's neck. The vampire extended him the handkerchief. Roark snatched the linen from his hand and wiped his neck. Donne's gaze drifted back to the woman. "Ahhh... She is a treasure indeed. I think I shall keep her."

"Fuck that—" Roark roared. He swayed trying to keep upright. "She's lycanthrope."

"Yes. But she is immortal as well," Donne stated as if Roark needed the reminder. If Roark had had the energy, he would've knocked that cocky grin right off the damn vampire's face. He embraced Tammy possessively. The truth was he held on to her to keep from falling. His legs felt like rubber beneath him.

"Your people will not welcome her." Roark gazed at Tammy's delicate features. Her bondage had added another layer of sensuality. He had never taken a woman chained by her wrists and ankles. Not to mention the collar around her neck turned him on. The scent of leather rose to caress his nose. By God, the whole thing had been heady.

"And yours will?" Donne asked with a haughtiness that said he already knew the answer.

No. Neither werewolf or vampire wanted their race tainted by the other. It simply wasn't heard of.

"They will once they realize we are mated." It was true. The minute their bodies had come together, Roark had realized what it was about her he recognized. Her beast called to his. He'd lost blood before—lots. It was the added factor of their beasts mating that had drained him so thoroughly.

"Mated?" Donne couldn't hide his surprise, before a grin took its place. "Then it is so between the three of us."

Roark's stomach tightened into one big knot. No way in hell. It was true that in his pack mates were often shared. But never the leader's—never his father's or grandfather's and definitely not his. He took a step toward the vampire. "You sonofabitch—"

A ripple of dizziness washed over Roark stopping him in his tracks. *Whoa.* This wasn't going to happen every time he fucked his mate, was it?

"Easy, Lanier." Donne went to him, linked his arm around his shoulders. "I felt the connection as well."

"It isn't possible." Roark wanted to shun the vampire's help, but he was too weak. He chose to overlook the fact that both of them were stark naked, hip to hip.

"It is so." Donne began to lead him toward the door, but Roark planted his feet firmly on the ground. "Let me help you to a room where you can rest."

Roark glanced over his shoulder. "No. I don't want to leave her."

Donne glazed followed his. "I shall have her cleansed and she can join us."

Roark jerked away from Donne. "Us?" His arms flailed as he caught his balance. He pinned the vampire with a glare.

"She is vampire. We must shield her from the sun. This room does not provide the safety we will need while we rest. Come." Donne started toward the door and opened it. "We will sort everything out tomorrow evening."

Roark hadn't thought of that little complication—sunlight. So, what did that mean? Would he have to wait until the evening before he could be with her once again, never seeing the light of day? What kind of a life would that be for her?

"What about the lycanthrope part of her?" he asked before passing through the open door. Roark thought of her bound to the night and something twisted around his heart. No sunshine against her skin, filtering through her hair.

"It is a dilemma." Donne shook his head. "Until she is past the sexual frenzy your kind has brought upon her, we will not know what her limitations are. For now she can be bedded above the earth, but in a room void of any light."

"This room has no light." Roark stated the obvious.

Again with that grin, Donne said, "But it has no bed."

What the hell was the damn vampire up to? Roark's stamina was fading fast. If he didn't sit down soon he'd fall. He swayed. "Take me to this room."

"There are no manacles down there. Unless we tie her hands to the bed she will be free," Donne stated.

That was a chance Roark was willing to take. He didn't want to leave his mate alone and he sure didn't want to leave her alone with Donne.

The vampire led the way toward a bookshelf filled with ancient writings. Just how old was Donne? He pushed and then pulled on one of the shelves and the bookcase sprang open, revealing a hidden passageway. Clever. Roark would have never thought that a whole living space was hidden behind the wall.

Slowly, he followed Donne down the stairs, grasping onto the railing to assist him. With each step Roark's legs grew more leaden. Did he have the strength to fight Tammy off if she woke? Would he even want to? He could do that pressure-point touch if he needed to disengage her.

At the bottom of the stairs was a maze of hallways. Flickering candles aligned the walls. The scent of wax was oddly removed. The air felt damp and cool as Donne led him down a corridor, stopping in front of one of the closed doors. With a turn of the knob his host opened the door and stepped aside, allowing Roark entrance.

Light flooded the room as Donne flipped the switch. Roark blinked hard, adjusting his vision. The room was large and spacious. Walls painted bleached white blended in with the white marble floor veined in pinks and reds. Classic art hung from the walls. Roark recognized one piece as a Van Gogh by the dark brown and olive colors and heavy, slashing brushstrokes creating the image of a peasant woman. Of course the signature at the bottom of the picture helped.

"Did you know Van Gogh?" Roark asked as his gaze slid across the massive bed covered with a red velour comforter. When Donne jerked back the coverlet, Roark saw there were red satin sheets to match.

"Brief encounter only," Donne said. "I'll leave you now and see to our mate."

A growl rumbled in Roark's throat. Donne met it with a chuckle.

Did Roark trust the vampire? Hell no. But he didn't have much choice since he could barely stand on his own two feet. Damn. He was weak.

As Donne headed for the door, Roark climbed in bed. The sheets were cool against his bare skin. He was tired. Still he couldn't wait to feel Tammy next to him.

His troubled gaze swept across the room, taking in its contents. A small, intimate table and two chairs sat in the corner of the room. Offset from it was a marble fireplace with an intricately carved mantel. The workmanship was breathtaking, giving him the sense that this single piece of wood had seen many, many years of history. Before the spotless hearth lay a large bearskin rug, as white as the walls and floor surrounding it. There was a dresser and a nightstand on each side of the bed that matched the mantel. Two additional doors were off to the right that he assumed led to a bathroom and perhaps a closet. He glanced at the pillow next to him.

How would Tammy accept what had happened to her after the effects of her heat was gone? And how would she react when she discovered that she belonged to him and one ever-irritating vampire?

The smile on him face grew as he pulled the door close. For a moment he leaned against the wall. Amazing. After years of searching, he had found his mate and something more. He couldn't explain it, but an attraction for the lycanthrope existed. Perhaps it was an illusion. Power was heady, but the wolf's primitive nature went beyond that—it was sexy and alluring. Marcellus couldn't resist touching Lanier. The wolf's reactions aroused Marcellus.

Many of their people, both Lanier's and Marcellus's, were bisexual. At rare times he had indulged in ménages consisting of males and females during bloodlets—feasts or soirées.

He chuckled, "The more the merrier."

Although exhilarating—the forbidden always was—he still preferred the hand of a woman, especially the one awaiting him. His mate. Try as he might there was no ignoring the facts; something lay between him and Lanier. Something Marcellus planned to investigate further.

Besides, harassing the wolf thrilled him.

With just a thought Marcellus dissolved in the way of his people, molecules shifted, shrunk, until nothing of his existence was left. He reappeared inside of the room where his mate still hung unconscious from her bindings. The scents of their loving hung in the air, stirring his cock. She looked more like an angel than the creature his people feared. He didn't even want to think about what would happen if after her heat ran its course she was still dangerous.

Once more he breathed in her scent. She was his, well, his and Lanier's. The fact he shared a mate with the lycanthrope didn't bother him, which was strange in itself. For some odd reason he found their triangle provocative and intriguing, a chance to experience life from someone else's eyes.

As he moved silently across the room, a moment of regret stung him. The need to exert force upon Tamanen had bothered him, yet she had left him no choice. If he hadn't stopped her from feeding, Lanier would have perished. Marcellus had to admit feeling envy for the wolf. There was nothing like a woman's bite. His cock hardened with the thought. *Mine*, whispered through his mind. He brushed a lock of her hair from her face as his thumb caressed her lips. He couldn't wait to feel her mouth all over his body. Blood rushed his groin, creating a sweet ache between his thighs.

Tamanen did something no other woman had—made him long for things he never thought possible since his conversion. A home. Family. Yes. His people where his family now, but it wasn't what he had envision in his younger years—his human years.

The dream of children had died that stormy night his carriage lunged from the cliff and he met his Maker. Marcellus shook his head. He hadn't thought of his loss in ages. Not that he could father children, but maybe through Lanier—

Marcellus's chest tightened as he caressed Tamanen's delicate features with his gaze. No one knew the secrets that lay within his heart, not even Sasha or Deirdre. He had kept that part of him private and hidden. After his conversion, he had surrendered to a world of darkness. Each night was a test of survival which led him to where he was today—leader of a vampire clan. His word was law. No one crossed him without paying dearly.

Marcellus laughed at his frivolity. With one hand he steadied his mate, while he unlocked her chains. "Will bindings hold you, my pet, once you discover your strength?" Or would the wolf part of her be predominant? Lycanthropes had preternatural strength, but even they could not break free of the heavy metal.

Scooping her up into his arms, he padded toward the door. Marcellus thought of asking Sasha for assistance, but he looked down at his sleeping beauty and decided against it. It would be his pleasure to see to her needs before he shared her once again with Lanier.

In less than thirty minutes Donne returned, Tammy cradled in his arms. A surge of jealousy burned inside Roark seeing her naked body pressed to Donne's equally bare skin. When the vampire laid her beside Roark, she turned into him, cuddling close. With a brush of his hand he moved her hair out of her face and stared down at her.

She was so beautiful. Angelic. Yet she was a picture of deception. The cross of lycanthrope and vampire had truly made her a formidable force. Would she overcome this after her heat cycle? He prayed so.

With his fingertips, he traced the scars on her abdomen and chest that were almost gone. Her hair had hidden them from his sight before, but now he could see the damage Grady had inflicted upon her. Shadows existed where other injuries had been on her knees and the side of her cheek. She was healing more rapidly than a werewolf did. They could only achieve this speed of healing in the wolf form. Did that mean that the vampire part of her was more predominant? The thought sent a chill through him.

Donne watched him curiously. A dimple touched the corner of his mouth as if he fought a smile. Gracefully, he slid in beside Tammy so she lay between them.

"What the hell are you doing?" Roark roared, jerking into a sitting position that sent a wave of dizziness over him.

"Take it easy, Lanier." Donne spooned his length against Tammy's like he'd done it a million times. "Should she awake you may need my assistance."

"No." Roark was confident he could handle her. Well, somewhat confident.

"Then let me say that I am protecting my interest." Donne's fingers slid over her thigh, forcing a growl from Roark.

"She's my mate," Roark insisted as he brushed away the vampire's hand.

Donne released a drawn out yawn. "Must we argue this point again? I'm tired. Rest." His eyelids slid closed.

Roark turned his attention to the woman beside him. He eased back down, wrapping his arms around her to draw her closer. "Mine," he growled. His affirmation fell on deaf ears. Donne's chest stopped moving. He slept the sleep of the undead and wouldn't awaken until the sun dipped in the sky.

That didn't stop Roark from refusing to fall asleep. Heavy eyelids and the need for rest failed him as he held her close.

That evening as the veil of slumber began to rise, Roark woke to the thick ridge of his cock nestled between Tammy's thighs. Moist, warm folds cradled him, while something else slid back and forth against his hardness, taking him further into heaven.

He bathed in the sensual feel, continuing to push past the haze and become more aware of his surroundings. It was pitch-black. Donne must have risen and extinguished the light sometime during the day. He didn't think vampires rose except at night. Roark could see perfectly. Wolves had excellent vision in the dark. But knowing the vampire walked about while he slept was a little disconcerting. The thought vanished as he looked down at the woman before him.

Golden hair fanned the satin pillow next to him. Her eyelashes lay like crescent moons against her skin. Full lips enticed him to sample their nectar. Her pussy was hot and wet, as his hips thrust back and forth. Heat built against the underside of his erection with the increased friction.

"Holy shit!" Like a bullet shot from a gun, he jerked into a sitting position, moving quickly away. It was another cock rubbing along his.

Donne's cock.

Roark's pulse sped. His embarrassment faded to anger when the fucking vampire grinned from where he lay snuggled to Tammy's back.

He nailed the bloodsucker with a fiery glare.

Donne stretched the arm he wasn't lying on. "*Bonsoir.*"

"What the hell do you think you were doing?" Roark grumbled, trying to mentally shake off the fact that the vampire's dick had touched his.

"Staying warm, as you were." Donne palmed her firm breast. She arched, leaning into his hand. "Is she not the perfect bed partner? Even in slumber her body is responsive."

Mackenzie McKade

Her nipples were taut buds of delight. She moaned. Her lips parted on a gasp as her eyelids rose, revealing beautiful blue eyes.

Chapter Five

Through the curtain of darkness surrounding Tammy, her sight began to focus on a set of haunting eyes. They were so intense, magnetic, pulling her into their magic. As if she had infrared vision, a handsome face and hard, muscled body materialized to go with those eyes. For a moment, she lingered on the sexual heat they emanated.

The dream continues, she rationalized. It was the only logical reason she didn't lunge from the bed she was lying upon and run screaming from the room.

Naked, Roark sat beside her, his cock jutted from the nest of hair between his thighs. She ached to touch him—feel him inside her. What the hell was she thinking? There had to be a legitimate explanation why her body called to his. It was ridiculous, but he made her feel as if they belonged together, like two halves of a whole. Of course, there was another part of her that screamed for Marcellus's touch. This was crazy.

"Tell me I'm dreaming." Her smoky voice turned quickly into a breathy groan when her belly clenched tight. Blades of sensation splintered in all directions.

No. Not again.

She blinked, willing herself to wake. This had to be a dream. She couldn't go through the pain she had experienced before. When her eyelids rose, Roark still remained and so did the contractions.

"I wish I could, baby." Regret rang in his voice.

Another pang shot through Tammy. She curled into a ball, holding her knees against her chest. Pictures flashed before her eyes.

Wolves.

Blood.

Vampires.

Sex.

Not that she was complaining about the dream man before her, but she couldn't help but associate him with pain like the currents tightening her belly. Of course, sex usually followed. Yet some of her remembrances were violent. In her nightmarish state she had even imagined she had drunk his blood. Just the thought increased her heartbeat and another spasm bore down upon her. But it wasn't the pain that had her tied up in knots. She pinned her gaze to his throat. The blue vein throbbed invitingly, awakening her taste buds. Mouth salivating, she licked her lips.

Oh shit! Her mind screamed out in protest, trying to hold on to whatever saneness remained, but her body and the hunger gnawing at her stomach didn't agree, forcing the thought from her head. Heat simmered across her skin. She had never craved anything like she did this man or his blood. "*Venez à moi, mon prince.*" Again with the sexy voice she didn't recognize. Not to mention her body sliding against the length that spooned her from behind, each movement carnal and lustful. She patted the area next to her to entice the Adonis closer. Beneath her hand she felt the cool satin sheets. A strong palm smoothed down her ribcage, dipping along her waist and down her thigh. Slow and sensual, he retraced his path until he cupped and gently caressed her breast again.

Tammy glanced over her shoulder meeting the most charming smile she'd ever seen. The man who introduced himself as Marcellus was drop-dead gorgeous. Slowly and thoroughly, she scanned his length. He pressed his erection against her ass and a whimper slipped from between her lips. A chortle met her cry.

He cuddled up to her back, continuing to stroke her breast, stoking the fire inside her, while Roark looked at her as if someone had just rung the dinner bell.

His hungry stare warmed her blood, but intensified the crazy things going on inside her. Nothing made sense, except that she wanted—no needed to taste him.

Grasping onto a little sanity, she asked, "Where am I?"

Before either man answered, her control slipped, again. She leaned willingly into the hand that kneaded her breast, rolling her nipple between his fingers. Sharp, penetrating sensations shot through her heavy globes.

Why wasn't she terrified?

Instead, her body felt foreign as she wiggled her ass against the firmness behind her. She couldn't help herself. His cock was wedged between her thighs and pressed so close to her sex she could angle her hips and take him within her body.

He bowed his head, a lock of hair falling across his forehead. "You are a guest in my home." He pinched her nipple.

"How did I get here?" she asked, even though she bathed in the ecstasy washing through her body.

"So beautiful," Marcellus whispered in her ear. "I brought you here, Tamanen." His thumb rubbed back and forth over her sensitive nub sending heat waves to shimmer across her skin. She turned to look at Roark.

He didn't speak, but she heard him all the same. A

mournful howl filled her head. His suntanned skin rippled over hard muscle causing a tickling sensation to sweep over her arms. She needed to rub against him—to fuck him.

"Are you real?" She glanced between the men.

A twinkle sparked in Marcellus's eyes, while concern burned in the depths of Roark's.

A brush of his hand, he pushed his fingers through his hair. "Yes. We're real." Roark's voice released a flood of moisture between her thighs. Her pulse jumped. "Do you remember anything about last night?" he asked.

"Last night?" Time seemed elusive to her. "What day is it?"

"Tuesday evening." he answered. "You slept throughout the day."

"I remember you." How could she forget someone who set her body in such turmoil? Before she glanced over her shoulder to say, "And you," intense pain sliced low in her belly. A groan pushed from her diaphragm. "Something's wrong with me." She drew her knees to her chest and fought to catch the breath that squeezed from her lungs. "I hurt."

Roark moved closer and slipped his hand between her folded body to begin massaging her mid-section. "You're in heat."

Tammy looked up at him. Disbelief surfaced in a huff. "If that's a pick-up line, you've got to do better." Still, his touch was magical as the tightness subsided.

He hesitated before extracting his hand. A frown creased his forehead as if troubled. Immediately a cramp resulted, and then another, followed by another. In seconds, her body felt like a bundle of nerves.

As she reached for him, he turned her, guiding her on his lap facing away from him, her back to his chest. "Easy baby," he said.

She wanted him in her arms, to fuck him and take his blood as she climaxed. "I need to touch you. Taste you."

"No. It's safer this way."

Something close to a hum vibrated in her throat. "Please." She began to rub her ass across the bulge beneath her that lengthened with each caress.

Yes. That's what she really wanted. She raised her hips, moved so his erection stood firm and hard between her thighs and nestled against her moist folds.

Her fingers folded around his thickness. He groaned. A triumphant smile slid across her face.

Marcellus lay on his side, head resting on his palm, watching them with a half-grin. A pearl of pre-come eased from the slit at the swollen head of his cock. Her mouth watered. She wanted to taste him. Feel him at the back of her throat, while Roark's cock filled her pussy.

Her tongue made a seductive path along her bottom lip, tempting.

His smile grew wider, while hers faded. Her tongue made another swipe, coming into connect with long, sharp canines that pressed into her lip.

Fangs?

She was contemplating the possibility when her hand lost its grip on Roark's erection. Her gaze fell to her hands.

Panic iced her veins. Her fingernails were sharp black claws slowly curling as they lengthened. *Thud.* Her heart crashed against her breastbone, as hair pushed from her pores.

"Oh God." The words were garble. Her mouth twitched, as she felt a pull against her jaw and the snap of bone. "Help me."

"Fight it, Tammy. Fight the change," Roark growled.

Marcellus's eyes widened. But he didn't say a word, nor did he approach them.

Every place on her body itched as soft down swept across her skin. The room felt too small. Her chest constricted. Raw fear choked her.

Mangled thoughts were wild and frightening. Flashes of her fangs buried into the throat of one man, while another fucked her. Then popping tendons and breaking bones, both men beneath her snapping jaws. Her fur matted in their blood.

Fur?

Tammy freaked. Her arms and legs flailed. She tried to jerk away from Roark, but he held her tightly against him.

She screamed—the bloodcurdling cry torn from her throat.

Her vision blurred as tears filled her eyes. Like a river they raced down her cheeks.

"Ahhh...baby. Stop or you'll hurt yourself." When she didn't immediately obey she felt Roark's teeth pierce her shoulder. Instinctively, she knew it was an act of dominance to still her fight, but it didn't slow the racing of her heart.

When he released his bite, he began licking the wound with long, wet strokes. His actions should have disgusted her. Instead they sent electricity shooting through her. It was turning her on.

"Close your eyes and slow your breathing. Think of me. Our bodies—human bodies—mating." His voice was a whisper against her ear. "I can't wait to taste you, lap the cream between your legs."

Her eyes squeezed shut. No matter what she tried, her breaths were short, quick pants. She could feel the hair lengthening on her arms—her legs.

"Breathe, Tammy," he encouraged.

She tried to focus on his voice, his earthy masculine scent, and his touch. Fingertips slid across her abdomen, threading through the curly patch of hair to settle between her thighs.

She trembled as he stroked her folds, spreading them wide so the air in the room caressed her intimately.

"I bet you taste like honey on a warm summer night." Roark nipped her ear playfully. His sexy words made her hotter, eased the itch that covered every inch of her body.

"Yes. Fuck me," she whimpered, squirming against his body. "Fuck me, now." Something moved beneath her skin, sexy and decadent. Yet something wild and untamed existed too. What the hell had she become?

His breath tickled her neck. "You must learn to subdue the need for immediate gratification." His voice dropped an octave turning gravelly. "We are animals by nature, but we live in the human world. Control and patience is a virtue you must obtain."

"I don't understand," she cried, as a spasm rippled throughout her. *Damn. That one felt good.*

"I think you do." His fingertips circled her clit, causing a burn in her belly. "The world as you knew it is gone. You feel the need to change, to mate, to hunt and run free. Let your instincts guide you."

She moaned as he slid a finger deep inside her wet, aching channel. With a slow, steady rhythm he began to finger fuck her.

Her head lolled back against his shoulder. "Yes. But why?" Tammy's hips rose to meet each thrust of his finger.

"You are no longer human—you are immortal." Marcellus's French accent made her eyelids fly open. She jerked upright echoing his last word. "Immortal? A vampire? But he said—" Nothing made sense. Clearly she wasn't human any more. What exactly was she?

Marcellus still lounged upon the bed. His lids half shuddered, his nostrils flared as he watched her. She could smell his lust—his hunger. Hear blood rushing through his veins. Nectar she craved to taste.

With the lithe movements of a predator, he crawled across the bed toward them. The easygoing veneer he wore was a pretense. Sexy and dangerous—most definitely dangerous. It screamed from every one of his pores.

When he opened his mouth to speak again she swore she saw fangs. Honest to God fangs like her own. "My pet, you will never die or grow old."

His palms slid up her legs, to settle on her thighs. His finger joined Roark's thrusting in and out of her pussy.

These men were friggin' crazy. But damn! They knew their way around a woman's body. She'd worry about the other stuff later.

Chapter Six

Tammy was hot, burning in Roark's arms as he and Donne pumped their fingers in and out of her moist, swollen folds. She cried out. Long fingernails, now human, dug into his outstretched legs as he held her in his lap, her back against his chest. Their sitting position on the bed was the safest he could think of to control the situation. He could pleasure her, ease her heat-induced spasms, without the fear of falling beneath her seduction and allowing her to take his blood. No matter how he longed to do just that.

Donne lay casually on his stomach between their splayed legs. He inhaled, the rapture on his face said he enjoyed the perfume of her desire. Roark watched the vampire closely, uneasy with his proximity to his erect cock.

The discussion of her immortality seemed to be forgotten in the moment. Soon she would believe. She had no alternative.

"Fuck me." Her voice was pleading. When that didn't work she quickly changed her tactics, crying out, "I hurt. Please help me."

Dammit. Roark knew he should deny her, make her wait longer before satisfying her. Against his better judgment, he extracted his finger from her heat and knocked Donne's hand away.

"What the hell—" Roark brushed off Donne's disgruntled outburst as he grasped Tammy's hips, raising and angling her so his rock-hard erection entered her pussy.

A sigh of ecstasy pushed from her lips. He knew that his fullness inside of her would immediately ease her cramps, at least for awhile.

"You're so tight and slick." Covered in her liquid heat, he easily pushed deeper. Her inner muscles latched on to him, squeezing. He ground his teeth and held her motionless while he breathed, quieting the raging need being inside her had created.

If their relationship was going to work, he had to establish some semblance of control. As a wolf or a man, he could command her by dominance and satisfy her needs until the heat cycle passed. But her overpowering blood lust could kill him, not to mention others in the pack, if it got out of hand. Above all, he had to protect his people.

When Donne dipped his head to taste her juices, she arched, going wild in Roark's arms. He tried to ignore Donne's warm breath caressing his cock and the whisper of the vampire's silky hair tickling his balls and thighs. Still, his testicles drew taut against his body.

"Let me go. I need to touch you." She tried to squirm, to thrust her hips against his erection and Donne's mouth. Roark held her stationary. She had to learn control. Besides if he moved he'd explode. "You're killing me," she whimpered.

A grin touched the corner of his mouth. He knew exactly what she was going through, because waiting for fulfillment was tormenting the hell out of him. Visions of throwing her to her belly, fucking her from behind, crossed before his eyes. "You love it, don't you, baby?"

She threw back her head, striking his shoulder. "Yes. God,

yes."

When Roark felt the warm, wet brush of Donne's tongue at the base of his cock, swirling around his balls, sensation shattered through his groin. What was meant as a threatening growl turned into a moan. There was no way in hell he would reveal that Donne had affected him, even as a shiver shook him.

Donne tilted his head and through dark lashes he shot Roark a devilish grin. The vampire's tongue flicked across Tammy's clit, causing her to writhe against Roark, but her eyes were pinned to where their bodies came together. Donne playfully wagged his tongue several times as he held Roark's glare with a lustful one of his own.

"Don't do it, Donne," Roark warned, even as the heat in his body soared. Like Tammy, he felt the need to thrust, but he steeled his jaw and remained composed. As composed as a man could be perched on the edge of insanity. Only his fingertips sinking deeper into her hips gave him away.

"Yes. Do it again," Tammy cooed. Her silky voice deepened. "I want to see him suck your cock."

Her words released a penetrating burn down Roark's shaft. Holy shit! He ground his teeth together, his fangs emerging so quickly they pricked his bottom lip. Two beads of blood formed on his bottom lip. *Damn. Damn. Damn.* He licked the drops away, hopefully before she noticed or smelled the metallic scent. He felt trapped, unable to move except for the tremor that assailed him.

The temptress inside her must have felt him shudder, because she laughed. Not a high-pitched giggle, but a low, sexy sound that was nearly his undoing. "Take Roark to the back of your throat, drink as he comes."

Her fluids released with a warm rush, anointing Roark. Her breaths were becoming choppy pants. From the gleam in her eyes when she glanced back at him, she was turned on by the thought of Donne going down on him.

Before Roark could say, "Hell no," Tammy's body contracted around him. She uttered a shrill sound of agony, stolen from the intensity of the spasm clenching and releasing.

As Roark began to push in and out of her pussy, Donne wrapped his lips around her clit again, sucking the nub deep into his mouth. He released her and flicked his tongue over the sensitive flesh.

Roark growled. "Donne."

Tammy's gaze had fallen once again to where their bodies joined. With every lick across her swollen clit, Donne also ran his tongue up and down Roark's firm cock. When the vampire sucked one of Roark's testicles into his mouth, gently applying pressure, Roark nearly lost it.

Every muscle in his body drew taut, ached under the pressure to ignore Donne. He needed to stay focused—his mind on helping Tammy. He squeezed his eyes closed, stars bursting in the darkness, as his toes curled with the throbbing in his groin.

Again, Donne's tongue bathed Roark's cock as it slid in and out between Tammy's fold. The combination of being fucked and licked at the same time was driving him friggin' crazy. And now the damn vampire seemed more interested in pleasuring him than the woman pounding her body frantically against Roark's hips.

He tried to breathe, but it was useless. He strained to hold on—fought to draw out the storm building inside him. *Fuck.* At this rate Roark would be the first to climax. After he had the orgasm of a lifetime—he'd kill Donne.

But not now. He was too engulfed in sensations to do anything other than feel as he gave in and let the fiery orgasm wash over him.

Red-hot flames consumed him. With a sudden jerk, his head rose toward the ceiling and he released a strangled howl. He could feel his beast moving beneath his skin, begging to be freed, needing to throw Tammy on her belly and enter her from behind—take her in the most dominate fashion between a man and woman or animal.

Roark was lost somewhere between heaven and hell when Donne cried out.

Tammy snarled, her fingers woven tightly in the vampire's waist-length hair as she yanked him up and against her mouth. Before Roark knew what was happening, her fangs pierced Donne's throat.

Her body clamped down on Roark's spent cock as she came violently. The tautness upon Donne's face said he followed her down the same path of fulfillment. But the growls and animalistic sounds pushing from Tammy's mouth revealed she had once again lost control.

Ecstasy swam in Donne's eyes as he willingly let her rob him of life. Roark knew he had to stop her and now.

His hands were shaking as he wrapped his fingers around her neck and applied pressure.

With a gasp, she tore her mouth from Donne's neck. Fury filled her eyes as she glared at Roark. He could smell the bitter scent upon her skin. Like a rabid animal, she snarled and growled, snapping her teeth together rapidly. For a moment, he was afraid the change would engulf her. Instead, she twisted around and attacked.

For a woman, she was amazingly strong. The impact knocked both of them off the bed and onto the cold marble floor. As they wrestled, he yelled, "Tammy. Stop."

Adrenaline pumped through his veins as he dodged her

teeth. With a thought, he let the change come over him. Tendons popped and bones snapped as his body morphed from man to wolf.

A shiver raced across his thick coat as he faced her. His ears lay flat upon his head.

The sight froze Tammy, but did exactly what he had expected, beckon her beast. A helpless expression stole the color from her face. He saw fear in her eyes as hair eased from her pores, fingers curling as claws appeared. The bones in her mouth popped, elongating into a muzzle, while the rest of her body twisted and transformed. In seconds the prettiest blonde bitch Roark had ever seen appeared before him.

He stood erect on all four legs, his tail aloft, and the points of his ears up and forward. His upper lip rose in a snarl, showing teeth to establish dominancy over her.

She mimicked his stance, taunting him as she moved her bushy tail to the side to entice him.

With a leap, he knocked her off her feet. His powerful jaws locked and pulsated around her neck, threatening.

A whimper came from her parted muzzle. Her ears lay docilely against her head as she rolled upon her back. The dominance hierarchy in their relationship had been established.

Roark was basking in his triumphant when he remembered Donne lying crumpled upon the bed. A warning growl rose from Roark's diaphragm. He nipped Tammy lightly, sending her a mental command to remain still. Quickly, he changed back into human form and moved to the vampire's side.

"Too much—blood loss." Donne's voice was weak. "I need to feed."

This was a helluva dilemma. Donne needed blood. He couldn't leave him in the same room as Tammy, because he had no idea what would happen. Tammy couldn't be the donor because it would throw her back into a sexual frenzy. That left only one other person.

With a heavy sigh, Roark said, "You know, Donne, I should let you die for that earlier exhibition."

A small smile pushed to Donne's thinning lips. "Admit it. You enjoyed my attention."

"Fucking bloodsucker." Roark extended his arm to Donne. "Drink."

"Are you sure?" Donne asked.

"Wipe that grin off your face and do it before I change my mind," Roark grumbled.

The moment Donne's canines broke skin a rush of heat flowed through Roark's veins. His semi-hard cock lengthened. It took everything he had not to come—not to admit that the vampire had aroused him yet again.

Donne raised a haughty brow as he continued to suck. Each pull felt directly attached to Roark's unfaithful cock, making it jerk again and again. He felt the vampire's smile firm against his arm.

"Fuck you," Roark rumbled.

Donne's tongue stroke once, twice over the wound, closing it. "It would be my pleasure," he said, licking his lips.

They heard a strangled gasp and pulled their attention to the direction it came from. Tammy stood before them. All color drained from her face. Her cute little chin trembled. She was once again in human form. She shook uncontrollably.

"I'm not hallucinating, am I?"

Marcellus couldn't stand the helplessness in her voice. He pushed to his feet and crossed the room taking her into his arms. She trembled and he pulled her closer feeling the chill that swept over her body. Tamanen had no idea the power she possessed and he couldn't wait to show her. She could control the temperature of her body as well as a million other things. The elements were at her beckon call. That is if the vampire within was strong.

It was at that moment he recognized his own strength had increased. Lanier's blood transfusion had invigorated him. The lycanthrope was indeed a powerful man. His essence surging through Marcellus's veins would make the bond between them stronger.

"No, my pet, you are not hallucinating," he whispered against her ear. "There are things in this world the human race isn't ready for." He doubted that even she was ready for the life that lay ahead of her. She looked at him with such disbelief. Marcellus couldn't stand to know she hurt. He escorted her back to the bed. The mattress squeaked as Lanier scooted over making room for them.

"I can't believe—" She choked on the words unable to complete the sentence. She swallowed hard and her chin quivered. "How? Why me?"

"I'm afraid that's my fault," Lanier readily took responsibility for his pack-mate's actions. "The man—wolf who attacked you was my friend."

"Friend? I don't understand," she said.

"Several weeks ago, Grady returned home beaten, a broken man. He chose not to confide in me regarding the details, but I knew he wasn't stable." Lanier's features were unreadable as he explained what he knew of the event. "I didn't encourage him. I thought he just needed time to heal." When his backbone straightened, a flicker of regret flashed in his eyes. "I was wrong. This is my fault." He reached out and placed his hand on her bare thigh. "I'll do whatever is necessary to make this up to you."

Silent tears rolled down Tamanen's cheeks. Blinking several times, she attempted to dash them away, and then she swatted at them with both hands. "Why me?"

"I don't know, baby." Lanier's voice softened.

Marcellus smoothed his palms up her arms resting them on her shoulders. "Wrong place—wrong time." He shrugged. "We'll never know why he chose you." He inhaled her feminine scent. "Perhaps even he could sense that you were special."

"Special?" Her eyes narrowed on Marcellus. "He almost killed me."

"But he didn't." He reclined against the headboard.

"Maybe he should have." She wiped her tears away.

"Don't say that," Lanier stated adamantly. "Like Donne said, you *are* special. Half lycanthrope and half vampire, you are the fulfillment of a legend."

Of course Lanier conveniently forgot to tell her that the legends made her out to be a monster. Nor did he tell her that neither of them knew just how dangerous she might be to all mankind. Marcellus brushed the thought away.

Right now all he wanted was to ease her discomfort. Help her to accept what had become her fate. There was a world out there she had no idea existed. He wanted to be the one who showed it to her. And, he wanted to get to know the woman who had become his mate. Perhaps he might also discover what made Lanier tick. He had already discovered what excited the wolf. When his blood had flowed into Marcellus's veins he had felt Lanier's arousal, known the bond between them would be strong. But it had been so much more. A smile slipped across Marcellus's face, and then faltered when a shudder raced through her.

Tamanen looked so lost—so unhappy. He wanted to take her into his arms, tell her everything would be fine, but one thing he refused to do was lie to her. Neither he nor Lanier had any idea what the future held.

One thing he knew—their path would not be easy.

Chapter Seven

There was no need for lights. Tammy's new predicament allowed her to see clearly in the darkened bedroom. It was early morning. She was a werewolf—or lycanthrope—as Roark had called her. Oh and how could she forget the twist in this situation—she was also a vampire. Her life had officially become a drug-induced hallucination. Too much proof existed for her to continue to hold on to her disbelief. Things like this—werewolves and vampires—didn't exist outside television. She wasn't just trapped in a nightmare. Hell no. She was actually living it.

Like in the movies, she was a freak of nature—even worse, because she didn't belong in either the lycanthropes' or the undead's world. She didn't need them to tell her their people would shun her. As in the human society, she was sure prejudice was alive and well in their realm.

Tammy felt numb as Marcellus finished the story of how she came to be. Mentally exhausted, she leaned back into his hands as he rubbed her knotted shoulders. Like three kids at a pajama party, without their pajamas, they sat naked on the bed, casually talking as if things like this happened every day.

A new set of taut muscles twisted, joining the others. "So are you saying that I'm dangerous?" Marcellus's fingertips danced over the newfound tightness. Patches of memory came

71

back to her. Roark saying something about letting her die, while Marcellus called her an abomination. Their opinions had changed. Now they thought she was unique, special?

Who were these men trying to fool? Her—or themselves?

"What I'm attempting to explain is the heat cycle and blood lust has broken down your control." Roark's blank face said he was trying too hard to appear unconcerned about her plight.

Tammy's pulse sped. "And my desire *not* to eat both of you miraculously returns when the cycle has been completed?"

"Well..." Marcellus paused. His usual sexy voice seemed to be lacking something. "We don't know for sure."

Oh God. This just keeps getting better. "And what about sunlight?" A host of other questions rose in her mind.

Silver bullets?

Wooden stakes?

Coffins?

She shivered. No way could she lie in a casket.

Roark turned, avoiding eye contact. "We're not sure about that either."

"I'll live in the dark for the rest of my life?" Her tone rose to a strained shrill. "And for how long?"

"You're immortal," Marcellus explained.

Tammy's blood pressure shot up. Her heart pounded like a war drum. "I could be stuck like this forever?" Her question went unanswered. She shook her head. "Well, boys, it sounds like you're not sure about a lot of things."

Roark placed a hand on her thigh. Their gazes met. "You're my mate. I'll protect you."

"Now doesn't that just make everything peachy-keen?" Her voice dripped with sarcasm. "Will you also make sure I don't kill you next time I get a heat-attack?"

"That's why I'm here." Marcellus's attempt at humor fell short.

She shot a hot glance over her shoulder. "Oh yeah, you're doing a great job. Weren't you the last man I attacked?"

Silence.

"Exactly." Tammy turned back around and tried to grasp on to her control that kept evading her. She dragged in a breath. "I don't know what to do." Then she began to ramble. "I've never hurt a soul. I'm good to children, the elderly, dogs and cats. I donate to United Way. Drop change in the Salvation Army's bell ringer's pot. The last time I was at the store I bought a turkey and a gift for a family in need." She spoke more to herself than the others.

"I'll take care of everything," Roark promised.

Just like a man. She shrugged away from Marcellus's hands. "What? You'll fuck me every time my eyes open?" Okay. Maybe that was a little harsh, but she was frightened.

"I'll help," Marcellus added with a chuckle. He reached out to touch her, but she slapped his hand away. She doubted anyone had ever done that to him because he raised his brows and leveled his gaze upon her. Who cared? What did she have to lose—her life? That wasn't such a big loss. If she thought she was lonely before, she just took a huge step off the cliff of isolation. Still, there had to be a bright side to all this. If vampires and werewolves were real, perhaps Santa Claus was too. Maybe he could take her to the Island of Misfits. Oh God. She was losing it.

Roark's Adam's apple slid up and down his throat as he swallowed, hard. "With each mating you become more lucid and aware of what you're doing. We just need time."

"Time?" She released a burst of disbelief. "Why me? Why

did you save me?" She confronted Marcellus with a cry in her voice. "Why couldn't you let me die?"

"I wanted you." He admitted it without shame.

Tammy closed her eyes. Tears burn hot against her lids, but didn't fall. Dammit. She wouldn't cry. What was she going to do?

Rapid pounding jerked their attention to the door. When it burst opened, she startled. A group of angry-looking men and women pinned their glares on Tammy.

"Time's up," Marcellus muttered.

A tall, slender man stepped from the crowd. "The black widow is still alive." He clutched his neck with his hand.

Roark immediately sprang from the bed. A menacing growl rumbled. His beast visibly rippled beneath his skin causing some of the vampires to gasp and move backward. But more importantly, her beast answered his, making her antsy.

The intruders' animosity slithered up Tammy's back. She pulled the sheet over her nakedness like a shield.

She mates—then kills. That's what these people think of me—and they're right.

Guilt clawed at her very soul.

Calmly, Marcellus rose to step next to Roark, both of them standing sentry before her. Neither appeared concerned about their state of undress as they faced the mob.

"She is not your concern, Titan," Marcellus addressed the vampire glaring at her with menace.

The blond-haired man huffed. "She nearly killed Darta and me." He removed his hand from his throat to reveal scarred tissue that had yet to heal, which meant the damage had been substantial.

Tammy cupped her mouth. *Oh my God. I did that?*

"She is an abomination," Titan snarled between bared teeth. "You promised that the Lamia would be destroyed."

Destroyed? Tammy bit her bottom lip to still the tremor overtaking her. This man wanted her dead and maybe he was right. Her skin began to itch as her fingernails curled into long black claws. Instinctively, Tammy knew she would fight to live. Even now her inner beast grew anxious, ready for battle.

Marcellus's shoulders firmed. Dominancy and strength shimmered around him. His presence became bigger than life as his easygoing demeanor vanished.

"Enough!" His sharp warning made Titan stumble back into the crowd. There was no doubt in Tammy's mind, or anyone else's, who was in charge. "This woman has had her life ripped from her." His voice dropped dangerously low. "I will kill the vampire who brings harm to my mate."

"Mate?" several whispered before they fell quiet enough to hear a pin drop. Surprise and alarm stole the color from their faces. In disbelief, they looked toward the individual standing to their left or right. Tammy could sense the undercurrent of discontent. But no one spoke or stepped forward.

"Leave us now," Marcellus ordered in a menacing tone that sent a shiver straight to Tammy's soul.

Every tendon and muscle in Roark's body stretched taut when the crowd didn't make a move to depart. His beast roared, preparing for the throng to attack.

Suddenly the air in the room thickened. It was like sucking in water, making it difficult to breath. Omnipotent energy radiated off Donne as he raised his arms and released an ominous hiss. Roark could have sworn he heard the warning sizzle and snap through the room, forcing him to take an unconscious step backward.

Donne's eyes blazed the promise of death, dark and unmerciful. Someone gasped, and then all at once the vampires reacted. Some made haste for the door. Others like Titan vanished into thin air. If Tammy learned that trick they were in big trouble. The door slammed, shaking the hinges, as the last person to leave pulled it closed.

Roark could smell the vampire's fury. Donne trembled as he drew his arms to his sides. His mouth was drawn into a cruel line. His people had thought to disobey him. Something a leader could not afford.

Heat waves shimmered around Donne as he narrowed his eyes on Roark. "Titan has had over twenty-four hours to work against us." The vampire's long fingers curled into fists. "I'll need time to mend what he's done. Prove to my people that Tamanen is not the resurrection of the Lamia—that after the heat runs its course she will not be dangerous." He pivoted to face Tammy, successfully masking his fury behind a smile. She attempted to return the gesture, but the result didn't make it to her eyes.

The sheet had fallen to her waist, exposing her full breasts. Her breathing was erratic. She looked pale and drawn. Roark wasn't sure whether the redness that rimmed her eyes was from fear or anger. He had sensed her battle to restrain her beast. She'd done well.

Donne strolled to the bed, climbing upon it to take her into his arms. "Do not worry, my pet. Their bark is worse than their bite."

Roark doubted that, but he remained silent. Vampires were deadly. They lived by their own set of morals and beliefs, another reason why werewolves and vampires didn't mix well together.

"I must leave you." Donne stroked her hair as he pressed

his lips to her forehead. "There is much I must attend to. Lanier will keep you safe until I return." He pinned his gaze on Roark. "*Inside the nightstand drawer is something to assist you in my absence.*" Roark was taken aback as the vampire touched his mind. Of course, he should have remembered they were now tied by blood. Donne's concerned expression was easy to read. It wasn't only Tammy he was worried about. Roark's respect for the vampire grew.

"We'll be fine," he assured Donne.

"I will stake guards outside the door. Anton and Henri are trustworthy." He kissed Tammy tenderly. "Call my name and I will return immediately." Without another word, he released Tammy and pushed to his feet. "I will have something prepared for your dinner." He blew her a kiss as he crossed the room and reached for the doorknob. "Until tomorrow night." For only a moment he hesitated and then he yanked the door open and closed it behind him.

"What day did you say it was?" Tammy sounded so forlorn. Sorrow rolled off her in waves. The wild look in her eyes was gone, instead she appeared tired.

"Tuesday, no it must be Wednesday morning by now," Roark responded, closing the distance between them. The mattress moaned as he crawled to her side. He wrapped an arm around her and pulled her to him. She shivered.

"My boss will be looking for me. I need to go home."

"You know you can't leave here."

She appeared so lost as she looked up at him. "I'm a prisoner?"

He brushed his palm up and down her arm, wanting to warm and reassure her at the same time. "Ahhh...baby, it's not like that."

Her voice shook. "How is it then? Are you afraid to be alone with me?"

"Afraid?" he huffed. "Of course, not." Even as the words left his mouth he knew he wasn't fooling her. The guards Donne had posted outside were for his benefit as much as for hers. Just a shout would have them running to his aide.

"The cramps are coming back. I'm terrified what I might do to you." She nibbled on her bottom lip. "I don't understand what's happening to me. It's like there are two individuals inside me."

"Lie down." He released her, moving out of the way before he guided her upon her back. "You are vampire and werewolf. It's natural that you would struggle with your beast and that of the temptress within. We are sensual creatures." His hand guided her head up so that their eyes met. He tried to smile reassuringly. "When the time is right they will merge and you won't feel torn between the two of them. I know it's confusing, but trust me—it's normal." As normal as this situation was going to get.

For a second Roark hated Grady. He had taken so much from this woman.

"If I were afraid would I being doing this?" He stroked his palms up her calves, tickling the sensitive area behind her knees. She jerked, a tight giggle revealed what he had already guessed—she was ticklish.

"Your skin is like silk." He caressed her thighs, parting her legs to move between them. Her sex, swollen and pink, glistened. What he would give to taste her, lick up and down her folds and then suck her clit into his mouth. His cock hardened, his balls firmed. Bad idea. That would put him at a disadvantage to protect himself.

Her chest rose and fell rapidly. "Roark." She raised her hips, enticingly. "I'm afraid." Concern laced her troubled gaze, even as her body began to take over. The scent of her desire was like a magnet. Damn. She was a sexy. Her body writhed beneath him, rubbing against his erection as she released a staccato purr from deep within her throat.

When he stroked a finger over her flesh she trembled. "Now. I need you, now." She reached for him, but he grasped her wrists, pulling them above her head, anchoring them with one hand. Her parted lips begged to be kissed and he was willing to serve her. He bent over, capturing her mouth with his. She tasted of heat and passion as he stroked his tongue against hers. He drank her mewling cry.

Some day he would explore her body, discover the places that drove her to the edge of madness, but he couldn't chance it, not tonight, not while her heat was so new, and definitely not alone. The knowledge was disconcerting. He thought of Donne and his loins tightened. Angrily, he pushed the thought away as he reached over and slid open the nightstand drawer. Inside was a veritable toy chest—vibrators, dildos, butt plugs, whips, anything one needed to spice up their sex, including a set of handcuffs. He extracted the cuffs and held them up for her to see.

"Would you feel better if I used these?" he asked, the tingle of excitement raced through him. Just the thought of binding her drew his balls close to his body. The ache between his thighs became a throb.

"Yes. But hurry."

With a click the first shackle folded around her wrist. He looped the free end through the wrought iron headboard. When the second one snapped into place he sat back on his haunches. Donne's kinky world held more allure than Roark wanted to admit. "You're beautiful." Seeing Tammy bound for his pleasure was beyond arousing—it was fucking hot.

"Roark, please." He didn't wait for her to ask again as he moved between her legs. With a single thrust of his hips, he parted her folds with his cock and sank into the warmth of her chamber. She was so tight, fitting him perfectly, it stole his breath.

Tammy shuddered beneath him. Her body clamped down on him, as if starving for what he offered. He fucked her slow, with long drawn-out strokes, only to drive inside her over and over again. Her breasts swayed sensually, her peaks too hard to resist. He cradled one in his hand and then leaned forward.

"Mmmm..." He hummed around the nipple he'd sucked into his mouth. She arched into his touch, her eyelashes crescents against her cheeks. As he fondled her globe, he teased the peak with his tongue and teeth. "You taste like heaven."

A light sheen of perspiration made the rocking of their bodies glide in harmony. She cried out his name. The moment was almost poignant, piercing his heart. He had waited for someone like her all his life.

Yet he couldn't help wondering how he could fall so hard for a woman he had only known for mere days? The time they had spent together was not getting to know her—her dreams—her wants and desires. His beast had recognized her from the beginning. The only irony was that he shared her with the leader of the vampires.

Tammy bucked beneath him. "I need to touch you." She yanked her wrists, scraping her bindings against the iron. Her body writhed and shuddered. He scented her arousal. A growl rumbled in her throat as she locked her ankles around his hips driving him deeper. Her mouth parted on a gasp. Sharp white fangs peered from between her lips. Beneath her shuttered eyelids the glow of hunger raged in her eyes. *"Mon prince."* The sultriness in her voice thickened. "Release me and I will make love to you like no other woman has done before." Her words were flames flickering across his skin. The temptress had returned.

Roark fought the urge to lean forward, bare his neck, and give in to what she wanted. He had never felt anything as seductive as bloodletting while he made love to her. The feel of her mouth on his skin, the piercing sting as her teeth penetrated his flesh, and the mind-blowing suction of her mouth, her body—

The elbow he had been propped on gave. The jerky movement brought him chest to chest with Tammy. Her warm breath caressed his neck.

"Mmmm..." she moaned. "Release me so that I may taste you."

He yanked back, nearly rolling off the bed. What the hell was he thinking?

Surprise and disappointment flittered across her face. "Please. I need to touch you." Her tongue slid sensually between her lips. "Release me. *Libérez-moi,*" she repeated in French.

Damn. She was sexy. He wanted what she offered almost as much as the next breath he sucked in between clenched teeth. His self-control wavered as he refocused his attention off the pounding of his heart, the ache between his thighs, and the throb that appeared in his neck where her signature mark lay.

Roark's breathing was labored, raspy, as he leaned into her, driving deeper into her core. At least he could satisfy one of her needs. He pushed his hand between their bodies and found her engorged clit, wet and ready. A single pinch had her whimpering, her hips rising off the bed. In slow, tantalizing strokes he circled the bundle of nerves, watching her pupils dilate, her breaths becoming quick and shallow pants. She was exquisite in the throes of passion. He wanted to hear his name on her lips as her body became his.

Roark began to fuck her hard and fast. His finger took on the same pace. He needed to kiss her, capture the small cries she released, but he couldn't chance getting any closer. When their gazes locked he saw something powerful, alluring, in the shimmering glow of her eyes. It was mesmerizing as she smoothed her heated vision across his skin as if her hands caressed him, urging him closer. He closed his eyes, breaking the connection. Her pussy clamped down on him and she shattered, screaming his name.

A fireball exploded down his shaft. It shook him from head to toe, hot sensations splintering in all directions as his seed released and bathed the walls of her sex. Her chamber rippled around him, squeezing and sucking his cock into her warmth. The steady pulse milked him, turned him inside-out. By the grace of God he resisted giving in to her and pressing his throat to her mouth.

They were both breathing hard in the aftermath of their orgasms. He wanted to hold her close, but the red haze in her eyes made him keep his distance. Her body was satisfied, but her hunger remained.

As he moved from atop her, she snapped. The high-pitch wail she released slithered up his backbone. In a fury he couldn't have ever imagined, she began to fight her bindings. Iron skidded across iron. She yanked, the handcuffs biting into her skin, but that didn't stop her. When he heard the creak as the headboard gave he moved closer, wanting to comfort her. His heart ached for what she was going through.

"Tammy. Baby, please." He tried to touch her leg, but she kicked out at him, pulling herself into a tight ball before turning away from him. "Leave me." Her command caught somewhere between a growl and a cry.

Shit. Roark didn't know what to do. His hand hovered over her shoulder. He wanted to console her, but that just might be her breaking point and he didn't know whether the bed could contain her.

A knock on the door made her head snap up. Her upper lip curled into a snarl, baring her teeth as she released a slow, tense hiss. "Don't let anyone come in here." The desperation in her voice was evidence that she fought her hunger. Tears raced down her face.

Roark moved quickly off the bed and toward the door. It wedged open as he caught the doorknob. "Don't come in here," he warned as he held the door partially ajar.

A black woman with a turban wrapped around her head and dressed in a flowing white gown stood before him holding a tray, several robes hung in the bend of her arm. Roark could smell the meaty aroma of steak beneath the silver dome. Two glasses balanced on the platter.

The female vampire appeared a little distraught as two guards moved up beside her. "The glass on the right is *hers*." She said the last word with distain. "My master said to make sure she gets it." She pushed the tray into his arms, and then the robes.

The glasses teetered, the liquid nearly sloshing over the side as he tossed the robes over his shoulder and gripped the tray firmly in both hands. "Thank you." But his appreciation was lost to the vampire making quick strides in the opposite direction. He glanced at the guards, their expressions unreadable, but he could smell the pungent scent of their unease.

When he closed the door, Tammy swung her head around to face him. "Get out of here. Now." Her eyes glowed a haunting red. Her breathing was labored. "I don't know how much longer

I can hold on." The cry in her voice made his chest tighten. Once again, he cursed Grady for what he had imposed upon Tammy.

He crossed the room, set the tray on the small table in the corner and picked up her glass with the heavy metallic scent of blood. He padded across the marble floor, careful not to spill a drop.

Tammy was shaking like an alcoholic under withdrawals. Her expression distorted as he approached. Her fingers curled into fists. The closer he came the more agitated she became, making whimpering sounds as her fingers grasped thin air.

"Drink this." He pressed the crystal to her lips and tipped the glass before she could resist him.

"Oh God." There was desperation in her cry. As he drew the cup away, she gasped, "More." Her body shook. He was afraid she might be going into shock. She took another sip and an expression of ecstasy softened her face. "Yes." He tilted the chalice and she chugged the remaining liquid. When she was through, he set the glass on the nightstand. If the situation wasn't so volatile he would have laughed. She had what he had heard referred to as a milk mustache, but red not white. As her eyelids closed, her tongue slid over her top lip. She appeared calm, appeased, at least for the moment.

Chapter Eight

Tammy leaned her head against the now-bent wrought iron of the headboard. She'd almost lost it again. If Roark hadn't handcuffed her to the bed would she have killed him? Drank every ounce of his precious blood? She felt cold to the bone, a broken woman, and her wrists chaffed beneath the manacles. There was no way she could go on like this. It was only a matter of time before she killed someone. She couldn't live with herself if that happened. The thought of it being Roark or Marcellus made her tremble harder.

Gentle fingertips brushed her cheek, but how? Roark stood beside the bed watching her.

"You did well, my pet. Do not chastise yourself." Tammy's eyes widened as Marcellus's voice stroked her mind. Her gaze darted to Roark. "Did you hear that?"

"Yes. It's the blood-bond that allows him to speak to us telepathically." Roark shook his head. "Damn vampire. I'll never be rid of him now."

Marcellus's laughter was like a caress. *"You did not think that I would leave you two completely alone?"*

"We had hoped," Roark mumbled beneath his breath.

"I'm glad I was able to dash that reckless thought. Eat before your dinner gets cold. I will return when I can."

Beneath Roark's frown, Tammy could see a smile forming. For all the banter that went between these two men, she got the feeling that they actually liked each other.

Roark rose and moved around the bed to slide open the nightstand drawer. When he turned, he held a key in his hand. Without a word, he reached for her wrists and released her.

Tammy rubbed her wrists, but already the soreness, redness that had circled them was beginning to dissipate. The healing process of a lycanthrope was remarkable. Or was it the vampire powers that flowed through her veins? She still couldn't believe such creatures existed and that she was one— or was she a half-breed—Lamia?

Roark extended her his hand. "You are remarkable, baby. Donne was correct. You did great."

Her brows pulled together. "You can read minds too?"

"It is a gift of our people. It aids us when we are in wolf form. You should have the ability as well." He helped her off the bed guiding her to the rug before the fireplace. It was soft beneath her feet. "Sit, I'll start a fire." As he began to stack kindling in the hearth, he continued. "The part of you that is vampire can adapt your body to any temperature, but I thought you'd like a fire."

His consideration touched her. Even if she had all these different abilities, something familiar was appreciated. The scent of sulfur filled the air as he struck a match. In minutes a fire blazed. The snap and crackle of the popping flames reminded her of her childhood, snuggled close to her father as he read to her. It seemed so long ago. The thought saddened her. Life as she'd known it was gone. What was she going to do? How would she live? Exactly what abilities did she possess? She needed to learn more about her situation if she were to survive.

The rattling of dishes pulled her out of her stupor. As

Roark uncovered the plates, the scent of charbroiled steaks rose. Her stomach growled. He must have heard it because he glanced at her and smiled. Holding a fork and steak knife in his hands, she watched him slice the blood-rare meat into bite-sizes.

Handsome. Muscles rippled beneath his skin. She had never seen a man with such a broad chest, powerful arms—and an ass that any woman would appreciate. A fluttering low in her belly made her look away. She tried to concentrate on something other than running her hands all over his body.

"Here." He handed her a red satin robe. The one he slipped over his shoulders was black, but just as silky. "I think our host thought it might curb our desire, to be covered up." He ran his fingers through her hair. The heat in his eyes made the flip-flop in her stomach turn into an ache.

"I don't think it's working," she admitted, staring at the rising bulge beneath his robe. He laughed. The throaty sound whispered across her skin straight to her pussy. "Maybe we should eat." The tingle made her rub her ass against the fur beneath her. Visions of him kneeling before her, the salty taste of his cock upon her tongue, made her groan.

"Baby, don't look at me like that if you don't want me to take you right here—right now." There was a gravelly tone to his voice that tugged on her strings of desire. His nostrils flared and she knew he scented her arousal, because she could smell his musky aroma. The apex of her thighs grew moist. Each step he took toward her made her pulse leap. When he bent his head to press a kiss over each eyelid, she snaked her arms around his neck, pulling him down to her lips. Gently he uncoiled her arms. His mouth teased across hers. "You need to eat something."

Disappointment clenched her chest as he released her and

walked back to the table. Picking up the tray, he returned, setting it on the floor as he sat beside her. He stabbed a piece of meat with a fork. His eyes simmered with heat as he placed the offering to her lips. She accepted the bite, her eyelashes sweeping the top of her cheeks as she savored the steak.

"Mmmm... That's delicious." She chewed as he took a bite.

"I was afraid you wouldn't be able to consume food." He must have realized her confusion because he began to explain. "Vampires only eat food to appear human. They have to purge it from their system afterwards or they become ill."

Roark slid his hand beneath her hair, cupping the nape of her head to pull her to his lips. The kiss was chaste. He smiled as if discovering she was more lycanthrope than vampire pleased him. He offered her another bite before he asked, "Are you married? Have children?" Even though his voice was unmoving, she saw a flicker of unease flash across his eyes.

"No children, no family, no man in my life—actually no life. I just moved here from Boise, Idaho about three months ago. I'm an underwriter for a mortgage company." For some reason that sounded pitiful to Tammy. There wasn't an interesting thing about her or her life, except for the fact that she went from a workaholic to a Lamia within what—two days? Two days if she counted Monday night and it was now Wednesday morning. Her tired body seemed to know it was time for bed. "What about you?"

"Me?" He offered her his glass of wine and she took a sip. "As Donne is the leader of the vampires in the metropolitan areas of Phoenix and Tucson, I lead the lycanthropes in Northern Arizona."

"So you really are a prince or king?" she asked, handing him back the crystal.

His eyes twinkled as his smile deepened. "I guess you could

call me that. Now you are my queen." He placed his hand on her knee and squeezed. If she didn't know better, she'd say his expression was filled with pride.

How could that be? She was a half-breed and a dangerous one at that. They barely knew each other.

"When the heat is over and your control is more manageable, things will change." Was he trying to convince her or himself?

"What if it doesn't? What if I end up killing someone?" Just the thought made her nauseated. Acid swirled in her stomach. "I can't go back to my old life. Marcellus's people hate me—they fear me. What makes you think your people will be any different?"

His slight hesitance was all the confirmation she needed.

She was screwed.

He set the wine glass down and drew her into his embrace. "I don't have all the answers. Honey, we don't even know what your abilities or limitations are, but I can promise you I will be there for you, Donne as well."

"I'm scared." It was the second time tonight she'd openly admitted her fear. She buried her face into the warmth of his chest. His arms held comfort and assurance, but for how long? If he had to make a choice between her and his people she had no doubt what his decision would be. He was their leader. She was a mistake, a freak of nature even amongst the vampires and lycanthrope.

He circled her waist and pulled her upon his lap, rocking her like a child. "I never want to hear you refer to yourself as a freak."

"But isn't that what I am? Lamia? A black widow?" she insisted.

Instead of responding, he shifted her in his arms so that he could capture her lips. Roark's kiss held the bittersweet promise of a future. In his embrace she felt like anything was possible. Yet, was she fooling herself? Tammy didn't want to think about it any longer. All she wanted was to snuggle closer and feel the stroke of his tongue against hers, the sensual pressure of his mouth as he deepened the caress and made her forget.

Marcellus had chosen to forgo sleeping beside Tamanen during the day. The previous night had ended badly and he didn't want her sensing his anxiety. Hell. This evening's rising had not gone any better. Tension crept across his shoulders as he watched his people filter from the conference room located in the left-wing of his home. A select few dared to challenge his decision to take Tamanen as a mate. Prejudice played a huge part. It seemed no one wanted to see the line between lycanthrope and vampire blurred, while others feared the legend which painted her as a monster.

Titan had been the most vocal, stating Marcellus was letting his dick speak for him. A Lamia's sensuality was hypnotic, bewitching the strongest of men—even a powerful leader. Beneath a placate expression, Marcellus had held onto his fury—barely.

When the room was almost empty he laid his palms on the oak table before him. With an ease he didn't feel, he leaned back in his chair, his gaze swept across the remaining people.

From across the room Sasha smiled and sashayed to his side. "You are tired, Master." It wasn't a question. They were close enough that he knew she sensed his frustration even behind the wall he had erected for the rest of his people. She placed a gentle hand on his. "Perhaps you need time to sort this out." She intertwined her fingers around his. "Until you do, let me ease your mind with my body." Eyelids half-shuttered, she gave his hand a tug. The musky scent of her arousal rose, caressing him like fingers across his skin. Yet it didn't affect him as it used to. No. He wanted the touch of one woman and only one woman, which was surprising in itself. Marcellus usually never took a single woman to his bed. He enjoyed a variety of bedmates. Sex was something to share and enjoy.

Before Marcellus could respond to Sasha's invitation, Deirdre turned around from where she stood nearby. She flashed him a smile. Her gown swept the floor as she drew nearer. "It would be my pleasure to join you."

Marcellus knew everyone left in the room had heard Sasha's and Deirdre's invitation, one he had never refused. He uncurled his fingers from Sasha's and scooted his chair back so that its wheels slid easily on the wooden floor.

"Tamanen is my mate." He pushed to his feet. "Time will not change that."

As Sasha opened her mouth to speak, with a single thought he disappeared, leaving without another word.

Tamanen was still asleep in Lanier's arms when Marcellus materialized next to the fireplace, looking down on them.

Lanier shook his head. "You know that little trick is going to be a problem, if she learns that particular ability," he whispered, obviously trying not to wake her even as he shifted his position. She moaned softly. He pressed his lips to the top of her head and Marcellus wished it had been him holding her— kissing her. He had missed not waking in her arms this evening. Lanier had been there to comfort and love her, while he had been occupied with his people. He felt as if he was getting nowhere with them. They were a superstitious bunch. They

91

couldn't see Tamanen as he did.

They were lucky Grady had chosen a woman like Tamanen, because the combination of both races could make her nearly unstoppable. By the furrow of concern etched in Lanier's forehead, he must have been thinking the same thing. Somehow Marcellus knew that after her heat she would settle down and accept her new life. The thought of killing someone sickened her. He saw the guilt in her eyes when she realized the damage she had inflicted on Titan. But what if he was wrong?

Marcellus didn't want to think about that. The evening had divulged one thing. "She ate and did not feel the effects as my people would. Perhaps she is more lycanthrope than undead." He tugged at his black slacks as he knelt beside them. The silk of his shirt sleeve breezed against Lanier's skin, and their gazes met. Marcellus was the first to break the connection, smoothing his knuckles across her cheek. "I missed you," he said even though he knew she didn't hear him.

Roark resisted releasing the growl that vibrated deep in his throat. Instead he focused on the subject at hand. "The drink you supplied last night quenched her thirst."

"Yes, but it is a poor substitute for the real thing." The heat of Donne's stare on the pulsating vein in Tammy's neck made Roark shift her in his arms, drawing her closer to his chest. Donne glanced up at him. "It is natural for us to feed upon each other. As you are aware it is very sensual. It heightens the climax. Besides, she is sweeter than anything I have ever tasted." A hint of devilment sparked in his dark eyes. "Except for your essence, of course. It—how do the human's express it? Turned me on." The damn vampire had the nerve to wink.

"Fuck you, Donne," Roark mumbled trying to rein his temper in. All the while his cock began to harden. Memories of the man's tongue caressing his balls and his shaft made him pull in a terse breath.

"With pleasure." Donne wasn't prepared for the quickness of Roark's fist, which swung out, connecting with his jaw and tossing the vampire back right on his ass. Surprise turned to something amusing. There was no animosity in Donne's laughter, even as he cupped his jaw and made a see-saw action with it. "Nice sucker-punch. I'll be ready for the next one."

"If you two are through playing around, I'd like to get out of this room." Tammy stared up at Roark as she pushed from his arms and then off his lap to rise.

Damn. She was beautiful. Golden hair draped down her back. A matching patch shaded the apex of her thighs show through a part in the red robe she wore. Luscious breasts pressed against the satin causing his erection to grow firmer. But she wasn't paying attention to him.

Tammy turned in a circle looking around the room. He could smell her anxiety rolling off her skin in sheets. "If I have to stay in here one more minute I'll go stir crazy. Please?"

Donne and Roark exchanged glances. He reached out for the mind path he shared with Donne. "*The wolf in her wants to run. She has been confined too long.*" He knew the feeling. The last days and nights had been difficult on him as well. The wild called to his beast.

"Don't do that." Tammy raised her palms to rest on her hips. She narrowed her eyes on both of them, daring them to lie.

Roark wondered if his expression matched the one of innocence that masked Donne's face as he asked, "Do what?"

"Use that mind thingy. Talk behind my back," she corrected. With quick steps, she began to pace. "I don't know how but I can feel you, sense the energy going between you two." She whipped her gaze over the room again. "I need some clothes."

Both Donne and Roark pushed to their feet at the same time. Donne took a step toward her. "My pet—"

"Don't *my pet* me." She ground her teeth and tightened the sash around her waist as if she pulled a blanket of courage around her shoulders. "I think I've been pretty compliant with both of you. Now it's time for me to take control of my life. I need to know everything about what I've become. I will not be the enemy here any longer—nor the victim," she added. Tammy squared her gaze on Donne. "Your people don't like me. I can accept that." She raised her chin and pride once again filled Roark. "I will not stay where I'm not wanted." Now that didn't sound good. "Last night I realized that if I have sufficient—" She hesitated, before clearing her throat. "Blood. Then I can manage the hunger."

"But—"

She held up a hand and Donne fell quiet. "Help me." Roark could tell she was in control, but still he heard the plea in her tone. Her essence reached out and wrapped around him. "I have become what I am. But I need your help to know my strengths, as well as my weaknesses. If you won't assist me then I will do it on my own."

Roark was seeing a whole different side of this woman, a side which he admittedly found arousing. The beast inside him woke and began to pace. An alpha bitch meant a challenge.

"Now, Tamanen, you can't just leave here," Donne stated matter-of-factly as he approached her. He reached for her, but with lightning speed she dodged his grasp. Shock radiated through the vampire. Already Tammy was beginning to discover her abilities, preternatural speed, or was it unconsciously?

Her rigid stance left no doubt in Roark's mind she meant it.

"I can and I will." A stubborn streak screamed in the way she positioned her hands back on her hips and once again raised her chin. Her mouth was drawn into a thin line.

Damn. How he wanted to kiss that defiance right off her lips. Blood rushed his testicles. His hands itched to take her into his arms and show her who was dominant.

Donne speared him with a sharp glare. "Some help here?"

"She's right," Roark stated frankly.

"What?" A huff pushed from Donne's lips. "*Ahhh...*I see. You think to steal her away from me." An ominous air surrounded the vampire as his eyes darkened. "Do not try to deceive me." The warning was a threat that made Roark's beast spring to attention. It growled, perched low on its haunches, ready—willing. But they had much more at stake here than petty jealousy. If either of them misstepped, didn't handle the situation right, they could lose her. There was an even larger danger. If she went rogue on them— Roark didn't want to think of the consequences.

"Donne, she has awakened without hunger or need this evening." Was it already Wednesday night? They had fallen asleep before the fire and slept the entire day away. Donne had never joined them, which meant he had spent the day sleeping elsewhere. For some strange reason that bothered Roark, but he pushed the thought away and continued. "This is good—very good." He sent what he hoped was a comforting smile toward Tammy, even though he could sense her beast close to the surface, needing to be stroked, caressed. "All she's asking for is a little bit of her life back." The freedom he knew they couldn't allow.

"She cannot return to her old ways," Donne insisted. "Her picture was all over the television. In my haste I forgot her purse and ID. The night guard discovered it and called the authorities."

Tammy pressed her hand to her chest. "Oh my God. I need to call my employer. Tell him I'm alright."

"I've taken care of that and the police," Donne announced.

"How?" she asked.

"Glamour." Donne didn't explain further. Vampires could make people see and think what they wanted. With just a thought, a suggestion, Roark knew Donne had easily made the police as well as her boss think they'd seen and talked to her even though she was never in the room. Had he even tendered her resignation?

"*I did. I'll take care of her apartment and belongings later.*" Donne shared his mental answer with Roark only.

"It's true she can't go back to her old ways, but she deserves to know our ways and begin to live again." Roark spoke aloud as he stepped behind her and trailed a finger up her arm, before he embraced her, pulling her close to quiet the stirring inside her. She visibly trembled at his touch. Her feminine scent wrapped around him like invisible arms. A tight breath squeezed from between her lips as her body melted against his. "Baby, Donne just needs reassurance that you don't want to leave us," he whispered against her ear. *I need to know you'll never leave me.* Anxiety gnawed inside him as he awaited her answer.

Roark felt the minute Tammy's heartbeat began to race. Every muscle in her body stiffened, as she jerked her attention toward the door leading into the hallway. "I feel their hatred, their fury and fear. I can't live here knowing that they want me dead." An emotion that sounded like it was caught between anger and agony choked her, and then she fell silent.

In the hush that followed, Roark tried to shake off the crawling sensation that raised the hair on his arms. There was something more going on here. He couldn't put his finger on it, but it felt as if they had come to an impasse.

Tammy drifted out of his arms, moving back so she faced both of them. She stood erect, regal. Even in a robe she looked like a queen standing before them. "You know I won't go down without a fight." Her expression was dauntless. "I feel my strength growing." She leveled her eyesight on Roark. "Last night," she paused, "I felt stronger than I have ever felt." Her gaze snapped to the headboard, which protruded where the handcuffs had once held her. "I did that."

Shit. This wasn't good—not at all. But Roark should have known it was coming. Time was all she needed to adjust to her new life and discover that she wasn't the victim anymore. The question was what was she capable of?

Shooting a glance in Donne's direction, Roark suggested, "Maybe it would be best if I took her to the mountains." Honestly, he wasn't sure if that was the best alternative, but what did they have to choose from? He had been gone too long from his home. It wouldn't be long before the clan came looking for him. He brushed his fingers through his hair. He couldn't let her go.

Donne took a step forward and then paused. "Is this your wish?" he asked Tammy.

"I don't want to feel like a prisoner any more, to be around people who want to harm me, force me to defend myself." She licked her lips, drawing both Donne's and Roark's eyes to her mouth.

Roark's cock jerked, firming. He wanted to kiss away her troubles. Tell her that he would take care of everything, but he sensed that would only anger her more.

A strand of hair fell before one of her eyes. She didn't bother brushing it aside. "There's a part of me that doesn't want to know what I'm truly capable of, another part that hungers for it. I can feel the wolf and vampire within me starting to merge. They want to become one. I'm confused, but determined to take hold of my life. I can't...won't—" she corrected before continuing, "—live caged, standing behind your protection." Roark heard resolve in each of her words.

The sudden opening of the door jerked all their gazes around. A small brunette dressed in tight leather pants and an even tighter corset that showed off her full breasts entered the room. Roark began to growl, low and deep. His steely glare pinned on her.

"Bag it, fur ball," she snapped. "Donne, a constituent of mangy wolves is here to see their leader."

Donne glanced at Roark with an uneasy smile. "Your turn." He drew his gaze back to the sassy vampire. She strolled up to him and gave him an intimate kiss. "Thank you, Sasha."

Roark raise an eyebrow as Tammy shot Sasha a look that would kill a lesser woman. But Sasha ignored her. The woman lowered her eyelids, and then gave Donne a quick wink before heading to the door and pulling it closed behind her.

Not good—not good at all.

Chapter Nine

Jealousy was something Tammy wasn't prepared for. It burned red-hot across her skin, heating her blood to a slow burn. She forced herself not to lunge at the prissy vampiress dressed in leather who slinked through the door as if she were completely unaware of Tammy's presence. Instead, she jerked her glare toward Marcellus. "Who is she?" The need to remind the vampire who he belonged to simmered low in her belly.

She realized for the first time her position held some power. These men belonged to her and she would fight anyone who stood between them.

"Damn you, Donne," Roark muttered, cupping Tammy's face to pull her from her anger. "I can feel your need awakening."

Awakening? That was an understatement. Her arousal was like pinballs pinging through her, causing every nerve ending to stand and take notice. She needed to be sandwiched between Roark and Marcellus, needed to have their cocks deep inside her body.

"Who is she?" Tammy repeated firmly, holding onto her anger, until a shuddering spasm gripped her.

"Shut up and breathe," Roark demanded. As he inhaled with her, Tammy sensed that he, too, searched for his center of gravity. She felt his apprehension of facing his people.

A series of sharp raps against the door made Roark glance over his shoulder. "I've got to attend to my clan." Concern shadowed his eyes as he asked, "Will you be okay?"

"Yes," she responded, even as a fist closed around her stomach. A mass of heat threatened to engulf her. She focused on the air filling her lungs, slowly pushing it out. Over and over, she repeated the process until the contractions were bearable.

"Donne, stay with her while I speak to my people?" Concern brightened Roark's eyes. He squeezed her arms before releasing her.

Marcellus stepped forward and wrapped his arms around Tammy. She wasn't ready to forgive him, but the temptress had other ideas. Even through the red satin robe she wore and the black silk shirt and pants he wore, Tammy could feel him surround her with his warmth when he pressed his length to her back. "Sasha is nobody to me, my pet." He nibbled on Tammy's earlobe, sending chills up her spine.

She spun around in his arms, capturing his lips, determined to make sure it was so.

Marcellus was taken aback by the fever in Tamanen's kiss. She was jealous. Her possessive caress was proof as she branded him with a soul-shattering mating of their mouths. Before they parted she captured his tongue in her mouth, sucking long and hard, making sure he understood who he belonged to.

Belong? That meant she cared for him—didn't it?

Like a teenager instead of the man he was, Marcellus fell into her web of seduction. Hell. He was the leader of the vampires; shouldn't he be able to resist her? Yet when he stared into her eyes his knees went weak and a grin pulled at the corner of his lips. He hadn't felt this giddy in ages, make that centuries. Happiness squeezed his chest, made his heart beat rapidly. There was no hesitation as her hands slipped down his back, smoothed across his abdomen, and slipped into his pants to cup his firming groin. He leaned into her touch. Each stroke was magical sending red-hot sensation to every nerve ending in his body.

"*Je vous tu.*" I want you, she whispered in that sexy temptress voice that shook him to the core. When she moaned, "Fuck me," blood rushed his groin.

Not a good idea without Roark, but fucking her was just what he wanted. He needed to make love to her alone—the two of them. It was important to prove what was beginning to develop between them was real and not just his imagination. She was like a craving to him—he couldn't get enough. But did she feel the same or was it the lycanthrope's heat masking her true feelings.

Even as Marcellus attempted to rationalize the dangers of mating with her alone another wave of heat flared across his skin. When her finger glided around the crown of his cock, paying special attention to the sensitive rim, he sucked in a breath. Fire raced down his shaft as she found the small slit and bead of cum that she rubbed, spreading over the top. He barely held on to his senses as he grabbed her wrist to restrain the movement of her hand rocking up and down.

"My pet, this is not wise."

She glanced up at him, her eyelids heavy and the cutest pout pinched her lips. "Please, I need you."

His resolve trembled. He could almost hear it begin to crumble. Of course, his guards were just outside the door. *Not a good idea*, he reiterated, holding his breath as she wiggled a finger against a particular sensitive spot that made Marcellus throw caution to the wild. A growl vibrated his throat. He took her mouth in another passionate kiss. He was just about to strip them both naked when he felt a reverberation in the air around him. It began as a soft rumble with the undertones of a storm about to be unleashed.

Marcellus's people needed him and so did Lanier. Without another thought he turned to Tamanen. "I've got to go. I am needed in the courtyard."

He could see her disappointment and the war she fought with her temptress as she attempted to push aside her arousal. Confusion overtook her expression as she skimmed her gaze across the room. "What is it? I feel—" She placed her palm against her chest. Her brows tugged inwardly. "Something's wrong." Then her eyes widened. "Roark. I need to go to him."

As Marcellus prepared to vanished, she grasped his arm. "Take me with you."

Marcellus's pulse began to race. Still he took a moment for Tamanen. "Lanier would not be happy with me if I let you go. You must stay here. I will return shortly."

Her grasp tightened. "*No*. You can't leave me here. This is about me—what I've become. I have the right to face those that accuse me. I have to get them to understand I mean them no harm."

Marcellus couldn't argue with her logic. He grabbed her hand and headed for the door.

Holy shit! Had the whole damn pack followed him to Phoenix? Beneath a full moon, three dozen or more lycanthropes in human form shadowed Donne's artfully decorated grounds. With the events of the last couple of days, he had nearly forgotten that Christmas was only a week and a half away. Donne had a blue Christmas theme going on, but Roark didn't have the time to revel in its beauty. As soon as the pack sniffed the air and caught wind of him, their gazes tracked him down. Alert, they moved cautiously between the polished marble statues that adorned the grassy area. Cascading water from a large fountain in the center of the courtyard could be heard above their footsteps. No one spoke, but Roark heard and felt their discontent and animosity toward the vampires.

Members of the vampire clan were strategically positioned around the perimeters of the eight-foot block wall and the entrances of the gothic mansion. Their unease matched that of the lycanthropes as they nervously shifted from foot to foot, while others were as still as statues as they scanned the throng.

Roark had found the clothes he'd arrived in several nights ago. His red flannel shirt was lacking its buttons and lay open, baring his chest. He secured the button on his jeans as he stepped barefooted out of the manor.

Several of the personal guards Roark had left behind when he decided to make the trip to Phoenix drew to his side. Manny, Stephen and Franc each shot him a worried expression as they gave quick bows. Each of their astute gazes swept over the masses as they moved into place beside and behind him. Built like line-backers, Roark knew these three men would never let anyone near him without serious injury.

"Roark, you should have never left without us," Stephen chastised. "You could have at least told us where you were going."

Franc, Stephen's twin brother, was an exact copy of the tall, barrel-chested man with wavy black hair. They were even dressed similarly in dark shirts and slacks, the color helping them to blend into the moonlit night. A handful of stars graced the sky, others shielded by the growing clouds.

Franc took in the number of vampires. "Twenty-three, more inside." He raised his nose and scented the air. "It isn't safe here."

Manny was the fair-haired of the three. His casual movements were so unlike the other two guards as he moved forward. "Sire, we've heard rumors—" He didn't finish his thought when the man Roark was dreading to speak with pushed through the line of lycanthropes. Of average height and weight, Martin held himself erect, with pride, but Roark could see concern rimmed Martin's eyes. Roark waived Manny back when he stepped forward to block Martin. A cool breeze ruffled his dark hair threaded with gray.

"Is it true? Is my son dead?" Martin's backbone was ramrod straight as if he knew the answer even as he awaited Roark's response.

There wasn't any other way to say what Roark dreaded to reveal. "I'm sorry."

Martin's hold on his composure slipped. His complexion bled. His vacant expression made him appear older than his fifty years. He stumbled, reaching aimlessly for something or someone to steady him against the emotion that visibly washed over him as he began to tremble. Roark waved Stephen to his side. The fact that Martin accepted the guard's assistance revealed his pain at learning of his son's death. Martin batted his eyelashes at tears threatening to fall.

An invisible fist squeezed Roark's heart. Sorrow narrowed his throat making it difficult to speak. When Martin shrugged out of Stephen's hold, Roark swallowed hard, dreading what he knew would be Martin's next question.

As Martin struggled to find his aplomb, a nervous tick played at his jaw. His body stiffened. Tears dried as his face hardened. His steely glare filled with accusation moved over the sentry of undead with distaste. "At the hands of a vampire?"

Roark hesitated only a moment wishing this could be handled anywhere but in the courtyard of Donne's mansion. The lycanthropes were outnumbered. If a fight broke out he couldn't promise the outcome.

"Yes, but—" He didn't finish his sentence before the pack began to rumble. Several moved restlessly aligning themselves to guard their backs. Calls for justice made the vampires present take a defensive stance. Someone hissed a sound of derision and contempt. Vampire? Lycanthrope? Hot glares flew between the undead and wolves. The slightest misstep and Roark knew his people would attack.

He held up his hands. Raising his voice, he yelled, "Hear me out." The noise level softened, but the undertone of unease still remained. His pack wanted Grady's death avenged.

Martin expression was a mixture of pain and fury. "Where's my boy?" Again, Stephen moved to Roark's side, but this time to intercept Martin if the need arose.

"Grady wasn't well. He stepped out of line," Roark insisted as he took the final steps to close the distance between them.

Moisture seeped into Martin's eyes once again. He trembled. Roark knew the man's beast was close to surfacing. *Dammit.* He could almost hear its mournful howl.

"I want the bloodsucker responsible for my boy's death. Who's at fault?" Again Martin scrutinized the undead, pausing to level his eyes on each one. The bitter scent of anger simmered off him, arousing the pack. Snarls and growls rose initiating several vampires to hiss in return. A handful of Roark's people allowed the change to sweep over them. Anxiety sprang from their quick strides as they began to pace back and forth. The situation was becoming more volatile.

One of the vampires closest to the house slinked away

disappearing behind its doors. Roark had no doubt he sought reinforcements. An all out war would erupt if Roark didn't do something.

"Grady attacked an innocent woman." His words brought gasps of surprise from the crowd as disbelief played across Martin's face. "When Donne attempted to intervene Grady turned on him." Roark knew if he could calm Martin the rest of the pack would follow. "Martin, you know Grady hasn't been well since the attack."

From the pack someone yelled, "Death to the bloodsucker," another joined in.

"Donne did what he had to. He was in his right to defend the innocent." Roark found himself in an awkward situation defending Donne, a vampire, over one of his own. His beast crept stealthily below his skin, agitated and restless, demanding to be set free. He had to make his people understand.

"Grady broke the treaty we have worked so hard to make with the undead. He was in vampire territory when he attacked the woman and then the vampires' leader." When that didn't work Roark announced, "He broke lycanthrope law." That got everyone's attention. "He converted the woman." The throng grew deathly quiet, only the wind whistling through the branches of several Ash and oak trees aligning the fence was evident.

Martin stumbled and this time Roark caught him. The agony on the man's face was difficult to bear as he looked up at Roark. "Lamia? The rumors are true. My son is dead and a legendary hybrid has been created."

Uh-oh. The pack knew about Tammy.

Martin closed his eyes. When they opened something close to fear brightened them. "Damn the boy. Has she been destroyed?"

"No." Roark released Martin. Just the thought of losing Tammy made every muscle and tendon in his body stiffen. "The woman is my mate," he admitted without shame. "That is the reason I have yet to return home." He squared his shoulders as the whispers began anew. It started as a hum that grew in strength and volume.

Martin shook his head in rapid movements. "That can't be. You've heard the tales, boy. She's dangerous. You're lucky to be alive. Although my lineage runs through her veins, she must be destroyed."

That was something Roark would never allow.

"Your mate!" Someone roared with laughter. Too absorbed with Martin's remark and the cloud of sorrow that surrounded him, Roark hadn't seen Layton approach, but his guards had as they rallied closer. Layton, Roark's cousin, had been a thorn in his paw since the wolf hit puberty. He was itching to take control of the pack.

The werewolf whirled his muscular body around to the crowd and announced. "Our leader has taken a vampire to his bed. Grady will find no justice here." He began to pace back and forth between Roark and the crowd. His movements were fast and agitated, an intentional move to incite the pack into action—and it worked. Several more of his people morphed into their wolf forms. The sound of bones popping, the musky scent of fur filled Roark's senses.

White-hot fury rushed through him. His beast raised its head and howled, even as he fought to remain focused. "Careful, Layton." He kept his tone low, but firm. The change begged to be released as it pushed against every nerve ending. Family meant everything to Roark, but if he was forced to fight, he would.

"Careful?" Layton snickered, the derisive sound grated

across Roark's skin like fingernails scraping a chalkboard. Layton leveled his glare on Roark. "Where's the bitch? I'll kill her myself." He paused, taunting Roark with the words. His tone dropped, as he announced, "It's time for you to step down, old man."

Old Man? Layton was five years younger than Roark's thirty-two in human years. Yet the fact remained, it was a blatant challenge. What was worse, Layton had threatened Tammy and that was something Roark could not let go unanswered.

The pack grew quiet, waiting to see what he would do. Layton had left him no choice. If a fight is what he wanted, a fight it would be.

Donne stepped from the house as a sentry of vampires folded around him. Their protective stance wasn't hard to recognize. No one was getting to their master without an all out war.

A familiar high-pitched female's voice rose. "Let me through." Tammy pushed through the guards and came to stand by Donne. She gripped his arm. "Don't let him do this," she pleaded.

Across the courtyard, Roark's and Tammy's gazes met, their beasts touched. He saw fear in her eyes and knew that she sensed his disquiet. The robe she wore parted as she jerked forward to come to him, but Donne's outstretched hand grasped her arm, stopping her.

Roark's eyes shifted to Donne. *"Get her out of here. It will not bode well for us if she is present. She is too soon converted to witness such violence."* He spoke on their mental path. No way would Tammy be able to restrain herself if a fight ensued. The mere movement of Roark's eyes gave away his concern for her. Layton jumped on Roark's moment of weakness.

"So that's the *bitch.*" He threw back his head and roared with laughter. "Let me at her," he taunted Roark. "How about it, old man? Do you want me to do what you were unable to—kill her?"

Roark's pulse leaped as Tammy tried once again to break Donne's hold and come to him. His beast flung itself against his skin to be released, needing to protect her. Slowly, Roark began to remove his shirt. "Are you sure you want this?"

Layton stripped his sweater over his head, ruffling his hair, the same color as Roark's. "Oh yeah." Layton's shoes and jeans were quickly removed. Roark followed suit, until both of them were naked, glaring at each other. A growl vibrated in the back of Roark's throat as he freed his hold on the beast allowing the change to begin.

Thick hair pushed from his pores, covering him in a silky coat of auburn fur. As his jaw popped and his muzzle stretched, he issued another warning. "I will not be merciful." His words were slurred and garbled with the alteration of his mouth elongating. The hackles along the ridge of his back rose as his body continued to shift. Neither made the change swiftly, it was more posturing, using each distorted feature merely for effect. At one time they both stood before each other caught between man and wolf. Their steps awkward as their feet changed into paws with long, sharp claws.

Layton snarled, baring his teeth. His eyes were bright with the heat of the upcoming battle. Roark could hear the wolf's heartbeat race and smell the foolish scent of victory the imbecile thought was already his.

They both completed the shift, landing on all fours at the same time. Roark crossed the space between them in one leap. Mid-air he heard Tammy screamed his name, but there was nothing he could do as his body slammed into Layton's, knocking him to the hard ground. Layton was lithe, twisting and jumping to his feet quickly.

Circling, using slow, guarded steps, they took each other's measure. Both snarled and issued warning growls, which Roark knew were worthless. Layton would not back down and neither would he.

The crowd closed in around them, staying far enough away so that they would not hamper the fight. Roark could smell their need for blood—blood that would inflame the vampires, but more importantly drive Tammy into a heated frenzy. Bloodlust was hard to control for the strongest of lycanthropes or vampires. Instinctively, he knew she had not returned to their room. He didn't have time to think of her further as Layton lunged for his throat.

Roark feinted to the right, twisting so his jaw closed around the back of the wolf's head. The taste of fur filled his mouth. He held Layton motionless, using his weight and strength to intimidate him and give the idiot the opportunity to reconsider his actions. When that didn't happen, he raised the wolf into the air and slung him to the side.

Jaws snapping and paws flailing, Layton tried to gain footing. He slammed to the ground, crying out. His claws scraped air and then the grassy area beneath him as he sprung to his feet. He shook his head as if disoriented. It took only seconds for Layton to regain his composure. He raised his hackles in an attempt to appear bigger—intimidate Roark, but it was useless. Panting heavily, Layton was high in fight drive when he charged.

Once again, Roark dodged the attack to his throat. Instead Layton's teeth sank into Roark's shoulder. Like a steel trap, Layton's jaws clamped down hard enough to draw blood. For a moment, Layton stilled. Saliva dripped from his mouth, his breath hot against Roark's fur. A menacing growl slid between the wolf's teeth, before he viciously shook his head side to side, an attempt to rip and tear Roark's flesh before he released him.

Tammy screamed. Through a fog he heard her cry his name again. From the corner of his eye he saw her fighting against Donne's embrace and another vampire assisting his leader. Roark ignored the pain—the smell of his own blood. He tried to erase the fact that another man touched Tammy. The wolf lunging toward him was all he needed.

Wolves rarely fought to the death. Their fights were mostly symbolic to establish the dominance hierarchy. But Layton's action spoke clearly. He intended to kill Roark.

With a sudden push to his hind feet, Roark leaped into the air at his foe. Layton's teeth lacerated him again before he shook himself free.

Both rearing up on their hind legs, they threw themselves at each other. Biting and growling, spittle flung through the air. Tuffs of fur floated upon the steady breeze.

And blood...

Their fur was matted with blood and saliva as their teeth tore into each other. Time after time, Roark felt Layton's teeth. Each time he returned the wolf's bite with one of his own.

Layton was becoming winded beneath Roark's strength as he again picked the wolf up and slammed him to the ground. His powerful jaws closed around Layton's throat. The young wolf stilled. He whimpered, knowing death was seconds away. Heart racing, his breathing labored, Roark's jaws pulsed. His heart beat like drums pounding in his ears. Slowly he exerted pressure and began to crush bone and muscle beneath his hold.

A gentle hand on his shoulder made him pause. Through a cloud of rage, he shook with the force it took to stop his kill in mid-stream.

"Don't, Roark," Tammy cried. The wind teased the hem of her robe as she knelt beside him. The scent of her heat seeped through the stench of battle permeating his nose. He knew the rest of the clan had scented her as they stirred moving closer. "Please release him." Her voice shook. "There's been too much blood spilled on my account."

Martin stood over her. Weariness made his body sag, aging him before Roark's eyes. "She's right, son. Your dominance has been established. There is no need to kill a strong male, especially when our race dwindles in numbers and he is family."

Roark tried to shake the blood-lust from his head. The sudden movement forced another whimper of pain from Layton. Roark shudder with the effort it took to not finished what had been put into motion. Kill Layton.

"Please," Tammy slurred. Canines pushed from her gums, pressing against her bottom lip. Her eyes went wild with the taste of her own blood. Hands fisted, her face twisted in pain as the first spasm struck. She needed him.

Taking his gaze off Tammy, Roark released Layton. Alert, Roark stood, ready to reestablish his hold if his cousin made the slightest wrong move, especially toward Tammy. The beaten wolf rolled over on his paws, crouching low. He tucked his tail between his legs and whined.

Roark had won.

The pack rushed him even as he allowed the change to sweep over him. Bones crackled and tendons stretched. His shoulder ached as his body twisted, shaping back into human form. He hadn't remained in wolf form long enough for all his wounds to heal and he felt every one of the lacerations as he looked around for Tammy. Excitement charged the air as it always did when there was a fight for dominance. Lycanthropes pushed and shoved to get next to Roark, which carried him further away instead of closer to her.

"I'm proud of you boy," Martin said patting him firmly on the back.

"Thank you, sir." When Roark looked around the crowd again their attention wasn't focused upon him anymore. In fact they were surrounding something or someone on the ground.

Chapter Ten

Tammy couldn't breathe as she scrambled away from Roark and the crowd. Battle lust had swept over her fast and furious with the scent of blood during the fight. It had excited her as well as scared the hell out of her. She had the uncontrollable urge to experience her teeth piercing and ripping the flesh as the wolf fought him. Yet she had found the strength to move away from Marcellus and come to Roark's side to beg for the stranger's life.

Wrong move. Her act of kindness had turned against her. Being so close, the smell of the wolf's imminent death, and the taste of her own blood upon her tongue had been her breaking point. The scene overloaded her senses and sent her mind spiraling. If she hadn't thrown herself to the ground, Tammy would have changed and joined Roark. Even now as she hugged her knees, rocking back and forth, involuntary spasms erupted, tightening around her stomach and squeezing until she felt her body being torn apart from the inside out. Mentally, she attempted to fight her beast. It struggled for dominance. Tears stung her eyes. Her skin crawled with the need to shift into her wolf form. When she felt her red satin robe slip from her shoulders, someone drew the material up covering them only to caress her bare skin in the process. The warmth of his flesh touching hers sent her hunger into action.

Baring her fangs, she tossed back her mane of hair, the wind catching the long strands so they haloed around her head before cascading down her back. A hiss slid through her quivering lips. The crowd gasped, stumbling back before they fell silent.

The rest was a nightmare.

Like a demon spawned from hell she moved with preternatural speed. One minute she was on the ground, the next she was wrapped around the man who had touched her. As her teeth sunk deep into his neck and she began to suck, he stopped struggling and groaned a resonated sound of pleasure giving in to the seductive power of her bite. He lay submissively in her arms, willing to take anything she offered.

The rich taste of his blood fed the hunger inside her. But she needed more—so much more. Her body was burning up with need. She tore at his clothing, hearing buttons pop and seams give way beneath her strength. Somewhere inside, Tammy knew this man couldn't quench her sexual need, but the desire to feel skin, anybody's, next to hers was overpowering.

"Tammy!" Someone yelled her name, but her mind was a haze. There were only two things she wanted—sex and blood—and she wanted it now.

Familiar hands grabbed her around the waist, but she held on to her victim with all her might. In turn, he fought to remain with her as a group of men tried to pry them apart. The sound of steam releasing had nothing on the menacing hiss bursting from between her teeth when they succeeded. Through a fog of bloodlust and desire she glared up to see Roark.

"Stop fighting me." Tammy wasn't sure if it was his firm demand or the none-too-gentle way he shook her that broke through her craze. In the next second, his arms folded around her and his voice softened. "Please."

Tammy choked on air rushing her starved lungs. It stung, ached, making her more aware of her body, especially her blood which felt like it ran cold and then hot through her veins. Chills raked her as she tried to pull herself together. Feeding and Roark's naked body pressed to hers quieted the bloodlust, but not entirely. She needed to feel his mouth on her breasts, his cock buried inside her, and she needed to take the robe off, it was suffocating.

Tammy's teeth chattered. "I-I thought I c-could handle it." But she hadn't. When the hunger became too much, she had attacked the closest person to her. If they hadn't stopped her from feeding, could she have taken control before it was too late?

"Damn Donne." Roark rocked her in his arms as his gaze searched the crowd. When his frown deepened, Tammy knew he had found Marcellus standing off to the side, holding onto the man she had attacked. "He shouldn't have let you witness this. You are too vulnerable to control the response to violence which is only natural to one of our kind."

She sucked in another breath. "Not his fault—mine." Shame made her look away from Roark. Was she really going to rape the man in front of all these people? Her body ached. The robe rasping across her nipples felt more like razor blades cutting into the peaks. Needle sharp pains shot through her womb. She clenched her jaws, but she needed to know. "I-is he all right?"

Roark brushed the remaining tears from her eyes. "Yes, sweetheart. In fact, he is fighting Martin and Donne to get closer to you. I believe he is enamored with you." He tried to make light of the situation, but she knew differently. There was a bitterness in the air. Fear. Anger. Disgust. The last one made the contents of her stomach roll.

A tall, robust man with shoulder-length dark hair stepped to Roark's side. In his outstretched hands he held Roark's crumpled shirt.

"Thank you, Stephen."

Stephen nodded and then positioned himself between Roark and the crowd, standing sentry while Roark moved her gently off his lap and pushed to his feet. Another man who looked identical to the one guarding them handed Roark his jeans. He took a moment to step into his pants and zip them, before he leaned down and tugged the robe securely around her shoulders. "Let's get you inside." He intertwined his fingers in hers, but she jerked away from him. "No. I need to apologize."

"Tammy, you're in no condition for social calls," Roark insisted, reaching for her again. This time she let him assist her to her feet.

"Please." Her legs felt like rubber. She swayed, leaning on him for support, but in truth it was the heat of his body she drew strength from. Feeding had lessened her hunger, but there was still the matter of her sexual needs gnawing inside her, breaking down what resistance she held desperately to. "What is his name?"

"Manny," Roark whispered in her ear. "Like Stephen and Franc, he is a member of my guard." Stephen moved to his right as Franc stepped beside Tammy.

When they approached, she heard Marcellus apologizing for the death of Martin's son. He was trying to explain the events of that fateful night, but the hurt in the old man's eyes said he wasn't ready or couldn't accept the vampire's atonement. Three lycanthropes now strained to hold on to Manny as he fought for release. Hair the color of hers, with eyes a deep emerald, Manny was a striking young man. His body looked as if hard work had carved every muscle outlined by his tight black T-shirt. Cotton blue jeans caressed his thighs.

Tammy didn't detect animosity as she approached. She wet her parched lips, tasting him once again to send another shiver down her back. Leaning closer into the shelter of Roark's form, she reached for what was left of her control. "I'm so sorry."

Manny stilled his struggles. He bowed his head. "My queen, it was my pleasure to serve you." When he raised his eyes meeting hers, his smile appeared genuine. He glanced to Roark and offered him the same gesture of respect, nodding. "Sire."

"Release him," Roark demanded as he guided Tammy forward into Marcellus's arms. Both the guards exchanged confused glances.

Marcellus cuddled her close, burying his nose into her hair. Tammy couldn't tell if the gasps of surprises were from vampires, werewolves, or both. No one looked particular happy at the moment, including the man who held her. "I'm sorry, Tamanen. I should have insisted you stay inside." She drank in his spicy scent and pushed closer to feel his warmth next to hers.

"Now you think of it," Roark bit out, before he extended Manny his hand. "Thank you."

Once again Manny bowed. "My attempt to guard our queen failed. Next time she is in need of me I will not let her down." Beneath his shaded eyes, Tammy saw a glimmer of light. Lust. The masculine scent filled the air with the potency of a drug, attracting the temptress lying stealthily beneath her skin. The siren slinked to the surface releasing a purr that flowed across Tammy's tongue. Marcellus tightened his hold around her and she smiled up at him. *"Embrassez-moi."* Tammy wanted him to kiss her so badly she could already taste it.

Roark's face hardened as he nailed Manny with a glare. "I

will take care of her needs."

"Of course, Sire." Manny stepped back, but Tammy could feel his desire reaching out to her, hear the swish of his blood beating strong and virile. In fact, amongst the crowd she scented several wolves and vampires reacting to the pheromones that naturally eased from her pores to entice them. Even Martin moved closer to her.

"Donne, get her inside, now," Roark barked the command.

As Marcellus ushered her through the throng, she heard Martin ask, "What's going on here, son? If she is truly your mate why have you entrusted her to a vampire—the same one that has taken my son's life?"

Roark ignored Martin's haunting question, because at that moment his body was sabotaged by a flash of red-hot jealousy. With lightning speed it surged up his neck, consuming his face and ears. Too many lustful males were in the vicinity of his female. Even as he fought the rage building inside him, several of his clan stalked Donne and Tammy. Thankfully, they were dissuaded by the wall of vampires that closed in around the couple. But that didn't stop them from raising their noses and scenting the air, taking in the perfume of desire that trailed Tammy. Roark's body was rock-hard with need brought on by the aroma. His beast sprang to the surface, every muscle taut as he watched Tammy disappear into the mansion.

The vampiress who had brought him and Tammy dinner approached. "Master Donne has requested that I see to the comfort of you and your people. If you will ask them to enter the great hall, I will have refreshments served." She didn't look very happy with her master's directive as she waited impatiently for Roark's response.

"Stephen, Franc, round everyone up and follow—" Roark

raised a brow in question.

"Deirdre," the vampiress responded dryly. There was aversion in her narrowed eyes.

"Follow Deirdre into the mansion," Roark instructed. "Martin, I will explain all when we are assembled." The weight of world felt like it rest on his shoulders, until he heard Tammy's silky voice filter through his mind. "Mon prince, *I have need of you.*" Immediately, his cock hardened to a painful throb. His beast leaped with excitement. That's when Roark realized he was lost. There was something about Tammy that made him happy. Every minute spent with her was a new adventure, one he never wanted to give up. Yet, instead of falling into her arms this very minute, he had his pack to attend to. To make things harder, the mind connection between her and Donne had been unintentionally left open. Or *was* it unintentional?

Roark held his breath, tried to control the barrage of feelings that assailed him when Tammy's raging need was released upon Donne. The vampire's heartbeat raced. The blood in his veins seemed to call to her. He knew Donne wanted to take her blood as he satisfied her sexual desires. Sweet laughter taunted Roark, but it was the whimper Tammy released that broke the dam and filled his balls with so much blood that they pulled tight against his body.

So this was hell, the thought pushed from his mind as Manny ushered him forward. Walking only made the ache in his testicles worsen. He heard the silky words Donne whispered in Tammy's ears as he seduced her.

"*Deeper*," she responded, to send flames of desire burning across Roark's skin.

"Well fuck," he groaned aloud, earning another startled glance from Manny. They entered the mansion, his steps wooden, as they followed Deirdre down a spacious hallway.

Manny leaned into him, whispering, "Are you all right?"

"Yeah. Fine." But Roark was anything but fine. His body was heating with each pump of Donne's hips between Tammy thighs. He tried to brush away the image of their limbs intertwined, their naked shapes lightly flushed with perspiration as they rocked to the ancient music of lovemaking. Try as he might, Roark's breathing became labored, his pulse thumping out the beat of their bodies coming together, over and over again.

"Is this wise, Sire?" Manny looked around the great hall which could double as an elegant ballroom. Three sparkling chandeliers hung from the high ceiling. Priceless artifice from years long past graced the walls. A plethora of round tables draped with red tablecloths made the white marble floor and walls seem even whiter in contrast.

As the cautious group of lycanthropes looked around, Roark and his guards marched to the front of the room. His people's anxiety of being boxed in, surrounded by their enemies, thickened the air with a bitter scent of resentment and it was directed at him.

"Please take a seat," Roark instructed, facing their inquisitive stares. Sexy mewls and moans filled his head, making it difficult to focus on the faces of his clan and what he had to say. The last thing he relished was telling his people he shared his mate with a vampire, when what he really wanted was to be next to Donne, pleasing Tammy, feeling her willing body welcome his throbbing shaft.

Focus, he chastised. There would be plenty of time to address the painful need firming between his legs.

When everyone was seated, a handful of vampires appeared, each carrying either a tray of wine and water, or a selection of meats, vegetables, or dessert. Sweet and succulent scents wafted through the room, making Roark's stomach growl. *When was the last time I ate?* The thought vanished when Tammy whimpered.

Roark felt the moment her sex tightened. Contractions rippled through her body like ocean waves, building in intensity. Her climax released and the floor felt like it moved beneath his feet. He swayed, feeling her inner muscles tightening around his cock, squeezing and driving him to the edge of madness. But then he realized that it was Donne's thoughts being fed him. It didn't make it any easier. Each stroke of Tammy's body made him grind his teeth and hold his breath. He prayed he didn't spill himself in front of the pack as Donne's orgasm ripped down the vampire's erection. Roark's toes felt like they curled.

"Damn it to hell," he grumbled, receiving more concerned looks from Manny, Stephen and Franc. Before he could gather his control, a feather-light touch stroked his bare chest. A shiver visibly shook him. Tammy's silky laughter followed another caress.

"*Great, Donne. She's caught on to your supersensory capabilities, or did you teach her that little trick?*" Roark felt a tug at his zipper. He jerked a hand down to cover himself, but his pants were undisturbed, only his mind heard the rasp of the metal against metal separating, felt the release of his erection. "*Donne, control her,*" Roark bit out mentally, even as his cock flinched forward, seeking her touch.

Donne chuckled at Roark's predicament.

Damn vampire.

Truthfully, Roark had always envied the undead's ability to cast illusions and seduce someone's mind as well as their body with just a thought.

"*The temptress cannot be controlled.*" Donne's French

accent became more pronounced. *"The siren wants you—we both do. Join us, Lanier."* The seductive invitation was like a net thrown over Roark, pulling him into their temptation. He fought to keep a straight face, to relax his body, hide the fact that he was close to climaxing. It wouldn't take much to throw him over the edge.

"Venez à moi, mon prince," she purred.

Stephen stepped closer to his side. "Roark?" His forehead furrowed. His gaze shot from thoughtful to anxious. "They await you." He placed a comforting hand on Roark's shoulder. "Are you sure you are well?"

"Yes." *No.* Conflicting emotions warred in Roark's head as a tingling sensation teased his lips. He could taste Tammy's sweetness against his tongue. His mouth watered, his fingers curling into fists fighting the urge to raise his arms reaching for the image of her sexy body that lingered behind his eyes. Tammy and Donne were fucking with his head.

"Not yet, but soon." Her sinful promise was a whisper through his mind.

"Stop." It was a plea, even though his mind cried, *"More."* Gentle fingers answered by smoothing up his arms, as stronger ones moved lower, forcing Roark into action. "Excuse me." His steps were swift, moving across the room. He had to get out of there before he did something he would regret. Roark's pulse leapt, then sped as the button on his jeans released. He held his head low, avoiding the interested stares that followed him out of the room.

When he burst through the door into the kitchen, he barely had time to duck into the darkened pantry as he felt his cock spring from its cotton confines. Shock swamped him when he discovered it was his own hands wrapped around his erection. But he knew it was Donne's hot breath he felt upon his sensitive skin.

"*Donne.*" Roark's warning was stolen by the feel of Tammy's mouth moving hungrily over his. His mind was paralyzed to stop either of them as they ruthlessly explored his body. A touch here. A bite, nibble, then kiss there. When a tongue flicked across the swollen head of his cock, Roark's breath left his lungs in a single gush. He stumbled back into the shelves, rattling cans and spilling over boxes of food that aligned them.

"*Relax. Let* us *pleasure you.*" Tammy's voice was a wicked spell weaving around him to hold him captivate.

The harder he fought his heightened arousal, the more excited he became. His body and mind were united working against him. The conflicting emotions were like fire and ice, so fucking hot—and he wanted more.

"*Give in to my desire,*" she hummed, setting him ablaze. "Mon prince, *stroke yourself.*" Roark knew he should resist her, but he was powerless. She controlled his hand, his fingers closing tighter around his shaft. With slow, measured pumps from the base to the tip, he thought of Tammy's lips closing around his cock. He sucked in a ragged breath. Blood pulsed in his testicles to an almost painful beat.

His mate refused to show him mercy. Her mental caress was electrifying, igniting sparks everywhere her palms roamed. The hairs on his arms were energized with currents flashing brightly in the darken room. She nipped at his neck awakening her mark. It throbbed beneath her tongue. Without a second thought, he dropped his head to one side, allowing her more access, offering her his blood.

While Tammy stole his resistance, Donne broke him to his touch. Roark's beast threw back his mane and roared as the vampire's tongue moved like firebolts across his flesh. Donne teased him with long drawn out licks along his shaft, followed by lazy swirls around the sensitive head.

Instead of issuing Donne another warning, Roark firmed his grip around his shaft. He increased the friction of his hand, up and down, working his thumb over the moist slit with each pass. His world nearly came apart when Tammy said, "*Marcellus, take him into your mouth.*" The witchy woman had wanted this from the beginning and Roark was too far gone to deny her anything.

Strong fingers pressed into Roark's ass. He couldn't have resisted Donne even if he had wanted to. Strength and power lie in Donne's touch. The urge to spear his fingers through Donne's hair, take what he wanted—force the vampire to his knees and to accept his cock was nearly overwhelming. But force wasn't needed. In the next second, Donne slid his hot mouth over Roark's cock.

A shiver rattled Roark to the bone. His hips violently thrust forward. He glanced down, expecting to see his hand pumping away; instead he gazed into eyes so dark and haunting that goose bumps rose across his heated skin. The image of his flesh sliding in and out between Donne's lips made his knees buckle.

Before Roark could catch his breath, Tammy pierced his neck, turning his world into a kaleidoscope of awareness. Colorful lights burst from behind his closed eyelids. Razor-sharp sensations ripped from his very soul shooting down his erection. It burned—it hurt so good. His release was earth-shattering as he bathed the back of Donne's throat. Hips jerking wildly, Roark fought to draw air into his lungs, to grasp some semblance of control, but it was useless.

The pounding of his heart was all Roark heard when he slumped against the shelves. When he opened his eyes he shook his head and released a heavy sigh. The once neat pantry lay in disarray. His heart was racing. Had it all been a play of minds? He could have sworn Donne was there before him. He looked about the room, seeing no evidence of his white, milky come on the floor.

"Fuck," he grumbled, cramming his fingers through his hair. Where was his control?

"*Control is elusive, my friend.*" It was the first time Donne had ever called Roark or any lycanthrope anything but an adversary. More importantly, it was the first time Roark had felt the same.

Chapter Eleven

Marcellus trembled uncontrollably as his climax surged through him. He held himself still pressed firmly between the vee of Tamanen's thighs. His cock pulsated, jerking each time her fingernails bit into his skin. She raked his back, each stroke a path of fire that inflamed him more as her inner muscles squeezed and milked him. He had never experienced such a high, an out-of-body encounter like he had with Lanier. The need to see the wolf as he climaxed while entrenched in the illusion Marcellus had provided was too powerful. He had vanished for only a second, returning to fall into Tamanen's arms, taking her blood and the warmth her body offered as he tumbled into ecstasy.

The moment was perfection—she was perfect.

"Exquisite," he managed to say as the heat in his veins began to subside. He brushed his tongue over the wound, closing it before he moved to settle beside her on the bed. The sheets were cool as they caressed him. A sigh brought his attention back to Tamanen. She tossed an arm above her head, her expression one of contentment. He couldn't help leaning forward and dragging his tongue across the tip of one of her nipples. She giggled, pulling her arm back down and threading her fingers through his hair to hold him near. He pulled the peak into his mouth and sucked.

"I don't know what it is about you," her eyes were dreamy staring down at him, "but you make me feel so good. I can't ever remember feeling so cherished. Well, except for my father." Sadness crept into the moment.

He released her, eased back bending an elbow on the bed to cup his head with a palm and rest upon it. "You miss him?"

A thin smile tugged her lips. "He was all I had."

Marcellus smoothed his hand across her abdomen pulling her closer to him. "Your mother?"

"She didn't want me—*us*," Tamanen added quickly, "Guess she wasn't meant for motherhood." She closed her eyes, released a breath before opening them again. It was clear the subject was painful so he didn't push it. Instead, he leaned in and kissed her. When they parted she asked, "When— How did you become—a vampire?"

"Too much liquor and not enough brains." His chuckle lacked amusement. The night still haunted him. He had been twenty-two and such a fool. "I met a woman during a soirée at the palace."

"Palace?"

"I was a guest of Louis, King Louis XVI." The ruler had called a meeting of the Estates-General. Marcellus recalled his participation as one of the nobles, brought together with commoners and clergy to write a new constitution for France. They had met in Versailles and were celebrating a successful day when he met Suzette. Beautiful. Charming. And deadly. "She was bewitching, her father eager for the match. But there was something different about him—Suzette." That was putting it lightly. The night had turned into a nightmare.

In a secluded part of the residence, Marcellus had stepped out of her arms and come face to face with a monster. Even now his heart fluttered with the thought of that moment in time.

Fangs and the red glow in her eyes had sent him fleeing. "Unable to comprehend what she was, I ran. I was young and foolish." Again he chuckled. He had run, but there was no place for him to hide. He would discover that later. Benoît had chosen him. Suzette was only a pawn in the Master's game. "The weather had turned foul. I didn't allow the thunderstorm to detour me as I stumbled toward my carriage and climbed aboard." He paused, remembering his fear. It had been a turbulent time for him—for France. "I was reckless. The rain so heavy I couldn't see but six feet ahead. Too close to the edge of a cliff, by horses lost their footing." He looked away from her. "Their cries mingled with mine as we tumbled over the side. For them it was death. Suzette and Benoît found me just as I was inhaling my last breath. The rest, is as they say, history."

Tamanen's touch as she caressed her palm across his cheek was soothing. No one had ever been able to dash the past as quickly as she did when she nuzzled his neck.

"I was bitter for many centuries, and then I found peace." He turned into her arms and drew her close. "I enjoy the night, the power our kind possess. Let me show you what our world has to offer. Let me make you happy, Tamanen."

Marcellus looked so sincere. Gone was the casual amusement he usually exhibited. Instead his expression was heartfelt. Truthfully, Tammy was spellbound by what the three of them had just accomplished. Mentally she and Marcellus had seduced Roark. Of course, there had been a moment when Marcellus had disappeared and then reappeared. That in itself had been mind blowing. She had seen him down on his knees before Roark. Felt the connection ping-pong back and forth. Her body still tingled from the sense of power she had experienced. Adrenaline had surged through her veins. Lightheaded, almost tipsy, she felt drunk on the aftereffects. Yet there was a sorrow that remained. Like her, Marcellus had lost a part of his life he would never get back.

As if he turned a page in his life and it was gone, his eyelids shuttered. Marcellus lay back across the bed, a sated expression curved his lips. It was a façade, his way of dealing with hurtful memories. Still, she sensed that he had found peace—even enjoyed his life. Would she learn to come to grips with what she was? Find the peace that Marcellus had? Even as the thoughts played through her mind, she already knew the answer. There was no turning back. Tammy would make the best of what she had become.

"Mmmm..." he moaned, stretching to give her a good look at his impressive physique. Lean, powerful muscles tightened and released as he crawled across the silk sheets toward her. She'd never seen anything so sensual or arousing. When their lips met, his kiss was gentle and sweet, not reflecting the hunger that glimmered in his eyes. There was so much about this man she didn't know. One thing she did know, he was insatiable. Amazingly, he was still in a semi-hard state, even after climaxing when he brought Roark to completion.

Tammy had never dreamt seeing two men together would be so friggin' hot. Two omnipotent leaders and they were all hers. Her life might have changed drastically, but there were parts of it that were beyond her wildest dreams. She went from lonely to not one but two men in her bed. With their help she could beat her rampant desires. Now she was eager to learn more about her situation.

Jerking back the covers, she rolled off the bed. Her footsteps were silent as she crossed the room and opened the closet door. Rows and rows of clothing hung from hangers. There were so many outfits, so elegant and they appeared to be all her size.

"What else can I do?" She ran her palm over a black gown. "Can I fly or disappear like I saw you do moments ago?"

Rich laugher met her excitement. "We can discuss your talents later. Right now Lanier is confronting his pack. It would be wise for you to join him. If you feel up to it," Marcellus added. She heard the bed moan beneath his weight as he rose.

"Oh God, you're right." She scanned her choices, passing over the floor-length gown that would show off every curve and choosing instead a moderate mohair sweater and slacks.

Marcellus strolled up behind her, removing the clothes from her hands to place them back on the rack. "The gown is more fitting for the occasion." He pressed his naked body against hers, feathering kisses up her neck. "The truth is, the world is at your fingers, my pet. Mmmm...you taste good."

Tammy turned in his arms, capturing his mouth. He was a masterful kisser, teasing and caressing her lips with his tongue before slipping inside to devour her. When they parted, she asked, "What do you mean?"

He brushed back her hair. "Our strength lies within our minds. You already know that your hearing and eyesight are acute. The world is at your fingertips. We control the elements."

Her brows tugged together. "How?"

Warm palms drifted down her arms. "You have but to ask and it is yours." He must have seen her confusion because the next thing he said was, "Close your eyes." She let her eyelids fall. "Think about the gown hanging in the closet. Imagine the silk sliding over your firm breasts, teasing your nipples, gliding over your hips, before caressing your legs."

Everything about Marcellus was sensuous. Tammy let his words flow over her and she could actually feel the cool, light brush of material tickling her skin, stroking and hugging every curve until it settled around her feet.

"No, Tamanen. Keep your eyes closed. What else would you wear with a gown like this?" he asked.

"Diamonds," she breathed on a sigh. "Lots of diamonds." She'd never been able to afford any extravagance other than the small diamond-chip earrings she wore on special occasions. In seconds she could have sworn she felt something slither around her neck. It was the strangest feeling as something circled her wrist, and finger. Her earlobes drew heavy as she thought of the dangly brilliance she would wear if given the chance.

"Open your eyes." Marcellus stood before her, a big grin on his handsome face.

The large solitaire sparkling on her finger was the first thing to catch her attention. It had to be an optical illusion. But the gown covering her body was real. With just a thought she was adorned in silk and jewels. Her heart stuttered and then swelled. She threw her arms around Marcellus's neck and hugged him tightly.

His laughter was warming. "Now I think we should join Lanier."

"Yes." In her excitement she had forgotten that Roark needed her. She released Marcellus and headed for the door.

"My pet?" She swung around to see a pair of black stilettos dangling from his finger. "Did you forget something?"

Tammy glanced down at her bare feet and wiggled her toes. What a sight she would have been dashing into the room barefoot. After a second thought, she remembered that half the lycanthropes were barefooted. She just might fit in after all.

Marcellus stood before her. His eyes were mesmerizing as he drifted to his knees. When he raised her foot and slipped on the heel she couldn't help noticing how close this moment was to Cinderella, but with a sexy twist. Marcellus stroked up her calf, slipping beneath the dress to caress her thigh. Her heart fluttered when he moved up further, but to her dismay he smoothed his palm back down her leg and slipped on her other shoe. After securing the straps, he rose, offering her his arm. Tammy had never felt so special as she did walking out of the bedroom with Marcellus by her side.

That special feeling didn't last long as she climbed the stairs, realizing she would be facing a group of people who wanted her dead. A sinking feeling swamped her, the nearer they came to the great hall. Instinctively, her senses went on alert. The rumblings behind the closed door said Roark's people weren't any happier with her than Marcellus's were.

"I don't know if I can do this," Tammy admitted, jerking to a stop. "What should I say?" She raised her eyes to Marcellus praying he had the answer.

He cupped her hand in his, bringing it to his lips. "You are the queen of all lycanthropes and vampires. You will find the right words to win them over."

The door opened without a touch and she knew that Marcellus had used his magic. With a little shove he pushed her into the room and shut the door behind her.

Being thrown to the wolves took on a whole new meaning as she stood paralyzed.

The crowd went deathly quiet except for their heartbeats, which Tammy heard pounding in her head. She tried to swallow, but the lump in her throat prohibited it. Her saving grace was when she locked gazes with Roark and he smiled. Male appreciation filled his eyes encouraging her to take one step, followed by another until she stood before him.

Roark kissed her softly on the lips, whispering, "You're beautiful." Unexpected heat scorched her cheeks. When he pulled her to his side she went willingly. He raised his head, his gaze scanning across the fold. "Let me introduce to you your queen."

From somewhere in the crowd someone yelled, "Lamia."

Roark went rigid. His face hardened with fury. The three guards she had met earlier moved in closer to protect them. Roark was about to speak when she held up a hand. She shrugged out of Roark's grasp and took a step beyond the protection he provided.

"I know what you think of me." This time she swallowed past the lump. "I have become what I am. I will not apologize for something I had no control over. But you must trust me when I say that it is not my wish to harm any of you. The fates have brought us, your leader and that of the vampires, together. I look at it as destiny that we will become one. Stop fighting each other and learn how to live amongst one another."

The man who fought Roark in the courtyard rose. He frowned as his chair skidded across the marble floor. "You tried to kill Manny." His words stung, but she couldn't deny his accusation. In the chaos of the evening his name had escaped her, but she was determined not to let him shake her.

"His name is Layton." She drew her attention to Martin, the father of the lycanthrope who had attacked her and was now dead because of it. Emotion squeezed her heart that Martin, even in his sorrow, would assist her in this small way. Again, the sense that there was a tie between them rose, but she pushed it aside to address the man who threatened her with a scornful glare.

She raised her chin, looking him squarely in the eyes. "It's true that I grapple with my urges, but isn't it also true that all female lycanthropes struggle during their heats, especially the young ones?" From the nods she knew it was true. Thank goodness she had remembered that tidbit of information Roark had revealed.

"But you are a bloodsucker," Layton snarled, his eyes flickering with menace.

Her beast and the temptress lying inside her joined together, she felt their power unite making her stronger—more confident. It was amazing. She tingled from head to toes. "Which means that I am the link between the two races," she announced, hoping that she portrayed pride and confidence as she squared her shoulders. "Vampires and lycanthropes have fought for too long. We hide from the human race attempting to live among them and keep our secrets safe. Would it not be easier if we worked together?"

There was silence for longer than Tammy liked. Her aplomb wavered. She was just about to fade back into Roark's shelter when he stepped forward.

"What Tammy says is true. We have struggled with peace between our people. If I can share my mate with the leader of the vampires, then you can share this world we live in with them as well."

Layton shook his head. Defiance simmered in his eyes. There were several who exchanged expressions of doubt, some of disgust, while others seemed to ponder the idea. She held onto the thread of hope that these people would come to accept her.

The door of the ballroom opened and Marcellus entered. He waved his people inside, and then strolled amongst the lycanthropes to come stand on Tammy's other side. The power he elicited filled the room. She shivered under the knowledge of his strength.

"Whether you accept it or not, Lanier and I are bound by the woman that stands between us. I swear my allegiance to her and in doing so to the leader of the lycanthropes." Marcellus's words brought a rumble from the vampires who lined the walls, but none of them stepped forward to express their objection, including Titan who pinned her with a withering glare.

The back of Roark's hand caressed her cheek. He raised her hand and kissed it softly. "I pledge my allegiance to my queen and in doing so to Marcellus Donne, the leader of the vampires."

A million butterflies were set loose in Tammy's stomach. She attempted to speak, but emotion squeezed her throat. Tears misted her eyes, but she fought them back. It should have been a moment of joyous celebration, but the undercurrent in the room was hard to miss. She smelled their bitter resentment. Knew that what Marcellus and Roark offered was a threat to their way of life—the centuries of hate that had fed them. Even still she couldn't help being moved by Marcellus's and Roark's words and the compassion in their eyes when they looked at her.

Roark's chest filled with pride. Tammy continued to surprise him. She stood before a roomful of people who feared and hated her and spoke of unity and friendship. Without hesitating, she countered every one of Layton's objections. But Roark knew his cousin wouldn't be swayed so easily. Even now as Tammy, Donne and he took their seats at a table, he noted Layton's scornful expression. Roark had no doubt that he hadn't heard the last from him.

Donne leaned back in his chair catching Roark's attention. "I think that went well." The mischievous smile he always wore disappeared. "Which one of our people do you feel will revolt first?" he asked in all sincerity.

Roark shrugged. The moment was a little awkward as he looked into the same eyes that only moments ago stared up at him as he was brought to orgasm. A tingling erupted in his nether region, forcing him to focus on Donne's question and not the gleam that sparked in those haunting eyes. "Neither group appears too happy." That was an understatement. "I still think that perhaps the mountains would be the best place for Tammy for now. Will you join us?" Why did his words have such a sexual connotation? Heat simmered up Roark's neck and swept like a brushfire across his face. *Fuck.*

Tammy glanced over her shoulder, looking from Donne to him. "*It was beautiful. Nothing more needs to be said,*" she stated telepathically, putting an end to the conversation at least for now. Without another word, she turned back around and continued her conversation with Martin.

Regret flickered across Martin's face. "I'm sorry for what my son has done."

Tammy reached across the table and covered his hand with hers. The smile she gifted him with was genuine. "I'll admit that I'm not happy with the change, but Roark has explained to me that your son was not well." Roark could sense the pheromones she released to comfort Martin. Several of the other males, lycanthrope and vampire alike, perceived them too. They moved restlessly in their seat or where they stood. Their eyes were on Tammy, but she didn't act as if she realized it.

"*Yes. I am aware,*" she admitted without looking at Donne or him. Tammy kept her gaze on Martin. "*I must use everything in my arsenal to win over your people. Martin is hurting. He grieves for his loss. His shame at what his son has done to me is breaking my heart.*"

Martin was quiet for longer then was comfortable. "The legend—"

"—is a myth," Roark provided. "I don't think our people knew enough about what to expect when werewolf and vampire crossed the line."

"Maybe so, son, but the events of this evening don't bode well for your case." Martin's expression intensified. "You are my daughter, my blood runs in your veins, but I will not support the ruination of our clan."

Roark's chin dipped, his eyelashes shadowing the rising fury. The rumble in his throat turned quickly into a threatening growl, drawing stares from people nearby. Donne moved closer to Tammy, ready to protect if necessary. Again power radiated off the vampire, which triggered everyone else's attention.

The room fell silent.

Tammy removed her hand from Martin's, pressing her back against her chair. She reached out for each of Donne's and Roark's hands. Her palms were clammy. Roark felt her pulse jump, but her expression didn't change. "You have no reason to believe me. Only time will prove me trustworthy. All I ask for is a chance to learn your ways, become one of you." She spoke confidently, even though Roark felt her hand tremble. "Will you give me that chance?" she asked Martin directly. Before he could answer, she placed her palms on the table and pushed to her feet. Her eyes went icy as she looked around the room. Her heart was beating loudly in Roark's ears. "Will you give me the chance to prove myself worthy of your trust?"

Donne and Roark rose to stand beside her. Manny, Stephen and Franc followed. Surprise rippled through Roark as Martin got to his feet. He was the last man Roark had expected to support her, not without proof that the legend wasn't true.

He moved around the table to take her into his arms. "Yes." His voice shook. "Yes," he announced loud enough so everyone could hear. Emotion showed in his eyes and Tammy's as well. Several lycanthropes rose, while a handful of vampires stepped forward. The majority hung back. Disappointment played across Tammy's face.

Donne leaned into her. "Tamanen, you can't expect to win them all tonight. It will take time. Lanier and I will help."

The frustration on Tammy's face made her appear tired, her skin pale as she released Martin and turned into Roark's embrace. Her body was strung tighter then a piano string

"I think she's had enough excitement for one night. Put her to bed, Roark." Martin pivoted to address Donne. "I'm assuming that she can't be exposed to daylight?"

Donne nodded.

"I'll oversee the protection of your home, Roark," Martin offered.

"Perhaps the caves would be safer," Stephen recommended.

There were a series of mountain ranges with tunnels and caves that many of lycanthropes frequented. Some even chose to live there instead of the small town just northwest of Heber that Roark had settled. Timberland was a secluded area surrounded by state land on three sides, a private lake on the fourth. Four-wheel drives were necessary just to reach the backwoods. Only a few forest rangers ever passed through and that's how Roark liked it.

"Thank you, Martin and Stephen. We'll stay here tonight." Roark glanced over at Donne, who nodded his agreement.

Manny quickly stood. "Would you like me to remain behind and drive you?" The eagerness in his gaze as it landed on Tammy made Roark uneasy. Of course, Tammy was hard to resist, especially dressed the way she was.

Roark pulled her closer wrapping his arm around her shoulder. She glanced up at him, confusion in her eyes. He smiled trying to reassure her that all was okay. "No. Just leave me a vehicle." He gave her a little squeeze. "Come on, baby, let me put you to bed."

Donne reached out and placed his hand on Roark's shoulder. "If any of your people wish to stay over, I'll ensure accommodations are made for them."

"Thank you, but as you know we have several homes around the valley that will suffice." Roark might like to live in the backwoods, but he was a business man. They had several financial ventures that made it necessary to frequent the city on more occasions then he would like. As Roark and Tammy moved to the door, Stephen, Manny, and Franc fell into place behind them.

Stephen positioned himself next to Roark. "I'd feel better if you allowed us to stay, and escort you and the queen home tomorrow."

"I appreciate your concern, but I need you to get the feel of the pack. Martin's support has helped our cause, but Layton and some of the others still concern me." Without speaking further, they strolled through the hall and stopped before the bookshelf where the hidden entrance to the chambers, which lay below. "Ensure that the events of the evening are accurately relayed to those of our people not in attendance. Double check the arrangements Martin supervises. Your queen's safety should be your first priority."

"Your safety should be at the foremost," Franc corrected quietly, but firmly.

Roark's grumble of displeasure received an unexpected whack from Tammy's right palm against his chest. His eyes, as well as the others in attendance, widened in surprise.

"Don't growl at him. He's right." Tammy raised a brow, daring him to oppose her. It seemed his mate still had some fight in her. Stephen coughed behind his hand, looking at his brother, while Manny didn't even try to hide his chuckle.

"Baby, you are undermining my authority." Roark slid the

surly words from the corner of his mouth. In his mind's-eye he heard Donne laughing. *"Damn vampire. I could use a little help here."*

"Lanier, we might as well admit who wears the pants in our triad family. Good night, my pet. I have business to attend to before I can join you."

Roark didn't like the sound of that. *"Is everything okay?"*

"Just a few people needing further clarification as to what our relationship means to the masses. Nothing I can't handle. Sleep well, you two."

"Donne?" But Donne had closed down their connection. Roark didn't like that fact either.

Stephen must have sensed his unease. "I still think it would be wise for one of use to stay with you."

Roark admired the three men who had dedicated their lives to him. He hoped one day they would find mates of their own. Tammy looked up at him with such warmth he couldn't help taking her mouth in a tender kiss. She was so pliable. He nudged her nose with his and pressed his lips to hers once more.

Again, Stephen coughed behind his hand. "Roark?"

Roark's eyes never left Tammy's. "I'll ask Donne to arrange a room for you."

"No need to bother him." There was a hint of laughter in Stephen's tone. "All I need is a chair outside your bedroom."

"If that's the case, make it two chairs," Manny added gleefully.

Tammy blushed the prettiest pink, burying her face into Roark's shoulder. He couldn't help the amusement that touched his mouth. "Ha-ha. Donne has already posted guards outside the room."

"Well, then it sounds like a great opportunity to get to know my new comrades better." Stephen folded his arms over his barrel-chest striking a formidable pose. "Besides, they can't guard you during the day and I can."

"Actually I discovered that they can move about during the day as long as they are shielded from the sun." Couple that with their magic and the fact no one knew they had this capability, they could be a dangerous foe indeed.

"Even more reason that one of us remain behind," Franc stated, moving beside Stephen to mirror his brother.

It was clear that Roark wasn't going to win this battle. "All right, you win. But I need the others to prepare the pack for our arrival tomorrow night. Make it a celebration."

Tammy snapped her head up. "No—" The anxiety in her expression was hard to miss. "I mean… It isn't appropriate. Martin will be taking his son home for burial. He needs time to grieve, time for his pain to heal. I'm afraid I'll be a reminder to him of what he's lost."

Roark cupped her face in his palms. "Baby, you have already helped to ease his sorrow. Martin has accepted you as his daughter, his only living relative. You carry his son's blood, therefore his. Our children will be his grandchildren."

Something close to fear brightened her eyes. She swallowed hard, but remained silent. He was just about to ask what was wrong, when Franc interrupted. "We have a long drive. Manny and I should leave now." He made a slight bow. "Welcome to the pack, my queen."

"Thank you," Tammy murmured, forcing a smile.

Manny reached for her hand, holding it to his chest. "It will be my pleasure to serve you." He released her, making a bow toward Roark as he moved quickly to catch up with Franc. Stephen stood back, watching the scene unfold with interest.

"Let's go, Stephen." Roark turned toward the bookshelf filled with ancient writings. He pushed and then pulled on one of the shelves as he had seen Donne do and the shelf sprang open, revealing the hidden passageway.

Stephen glanced down the sparsely lit staircase. His brows rose. "Who would have thought? I'll go first." He moved past them cautiously, looking around with each step. Roark guided Tammy in front of him and they began to descend.

"Shit." Stephen glanced over his shoulder at Tammy. "Excuse me, my queen." He quickly took in the maze of hallways at the bottom of the stairs and hesitated. Shadows bounced off the walls under the flickering candles that lined them. "This doesn't look good. Damp. Cold. And a little spooky."

"Oh, you big coward." Tammy pushed by him and started down one of the hallways.

"Uhhh...Roark, your mate did *not* just call me a coward, did she?"

Roark barely held back his laughter. In all the time he had known Stephen, he doubted anyone had ever called him a coward and lived. Yet, Tammy felt so comfortable around people that she tended to say just what she liked. For some reason that pleased him, he had never wanted a submissive mate, but one that could rule beside him.

Roark moved past Stephen to catch up with Tammy. "Hey, if I have to take her sass so do you," he tossed over his shoulder

Stephen's footsteps echoed down the hall. "Yeah, but I'm not bound to her."

Tammy had a wonderful sense of direction as she led them down one corridor and then another, stopping in front of their bedroom door. Down the hall a ways stood two of Donne's guards. It concerned Roark that the previous guards from last night, Anton and Henri, were absent. They were Donne's most trusted sentry. The two vampires he had never met nodded to Roark, releasing a slow hiss when Stephen came into view.

Stephen wiggled his fingers in their direction and their dour expressions deepened. "Looks like fun." He turned the doorknob and opened it to allow Tammy and Roark to move inside.

Tammy glanced back at Stephen. "If you get scared, you can climb in bed with us."

"The hell he can." Roark slammed the door shut. Stephen's laughter was drowned out by Tammy's. Roark pulled her roughly to him. "What am I going to do with you?"

"Make love to me, Roark." She tilted her chin up to receive his kiss.

Chapter Twelve

The air was thick enough to slice as Marcellus entered the training yard behind his mansion. A slight breeze stroked his hair as several of his sentries walked beside him. They had risen in ranks of his trust over time. Some of them, like Anton and Henri who walked closest to him, had shared the same Maker, Benoît.

For them the tie was broken when one night the powerful vampire had been ambushed—outnumbered by his adversaries. It wasn't easy to kill an immortal, but with enough blood loss anything was possible. After his Maker had perished, Marcellus had taken over his reign. He had held onto the power throughout the centuries. Tonight would be no different.

Titan loomed in the shadows of a barren oak tree. The leaves had fallen earlier in the season. Its branches like fingers reaching toward the sky. Three of Titan's cronies, new arrivals, stood around him while several dozen other vampires filtered into yard.

Marcellus dreaded the confrontation. He would rather be lying beside Tamanen and Lanier. He sent them both comforting thoughts even though his were anything but cheery, remembering to close the mind path between them. Tonight someone would die and he didn't want to bother Tamanen or Lanier with the details.

Titan stepped forward, the wind rustling through his hair. Moonlight shadowed his features. Even still, Marcellus saw him look about the crowd and a cocky grin slid across Titan's face. Marcellus could sense the vampire's confidence grow with the assurance the throng followed him, but he only fooled himself. Vampires were no different than werewolves when it came to a struggle for power. The possibility of a fight drew them like flies to honey.

Marcellus's people had pledged their oath to serve him. Only a fool would challenge him.

Titan spoke loudly as he announced, "You no longer have our people's best interest in mind." Once again he gazed around the group assembled. "The Lamia has tainted our leader. He is trapped in her web."

Marcellus couldn't contradict that he was trapped in Tamanen's web, but he still ruled. His people meant everything to him. He had devoted his life to them. He was known as a fair sovereign. His empire had grown on his reputation. His people wanted for nothing. He guarded and fought for those under his protection.

"You must relinquish your leadership. The Lamia must be destroyed." Titan's words were like a match to a fuse. It ignited a flame inside Marcellus, but he kept his composure calm as he leaned against a wall that surrounded the yard.

Marcellus yawned behind his fury. "Titan, I tire of your babbling. No one is caught in a web, except you—a web of deceit." There were some chuckles from the crowd when he stopped speaking. As he pushed from the wall, his voice lowered. "You have offended me." The few people who murmured fell silent when he moved from the wall so quickly his form was a mere blur. Titan stumbled back as Marcellus came so close they were almost nose to nose. Through clenched teeth, he growled, "Threaten my mate again and you will die." This time he released his anger letting it fill the air so that it vibrated around him.

Titan nodded. "Forgive me, Master." He took a step backward.

Had Marcellus won without a fight?

His thought was dashed when two of the vampires who had flanked Titan attacked. Marcellus barely eluded their grasps by springing into the air, hovering above them. They floundered for a second, looking around and then up when the third vampire's feet left the ground. He lunged forward, hitting and bouncing off an invisible barrier Marcellus erected around him.

Marcellus wasn't so lucky with Titan.

The vampire had slipped through the barrier before it was intact, body slamming Marcellus to the grassy surface. As they struck the ground hard, air squeezed from his lungs. Before he could take a breath, Titan caught him with a talon that cut through his side like a razor. The burn was excruciating, causing him to drop his guard for only a moment. All the time needed for his enemies to attack.

Marcellus was quick, rolling and jumping out of the way, slicing the throat of one of his assailants with a sharp talon as he made a turn and ducked the hand of another. The vampire's shriek was bloodcurdling as his life essence squirted from between his fingers wrapped around his neck. He fought uselessly to staunch the flow. For a mere second everyone stopped and watched the vampire sway and then fall. His body jerked several times before laying motionless.

When Marcellus's enemies lunged again he found Anton and Henri at his side. Even though the odds weren't to his liking, he knew that if he were to win the respect of his people this was a battle he had to fight alone.

"Stand down," he yelled as he waved a hand, sending Titan through the air. He crashed against a tree, limbs breaking and falling, but Titan was back on his feet before Marcellus could bat an eye. Both of his guards obeyed, but not before they drove their talons deep into their opponents, wounding them. They shared a grin before stepping aside.

Once again, Marcellus felt a burn to his side. His teeth crashed together as he bore down and tried to erase the pain. He barely dodged a killing blow to his throat as Titan's talon almost made contact. The sharp movement sent soul-wrenching agony throughout him.

The crowd remained quietly watching, but he knew what bloodlust did to them. Tonight they would have a whirlwind of sex and feeding. He wouldn't be so lucky.

Catching one man by the neck he twisted, snapping bone. The compound fracture tore through skin—jagged bones covered in blood that flowed like a river from the injury. Head dangling to the side, the vampire tried to raise it, but it was no use. His eyes glazed, he wandered aimlessly before falling to his knees. Two sickening gurgles percolated from the wound in his throat as blood oozed from his mouth, and then he fell forward.

The odds were better now, two to one, but Marcellus was beginning to feel the chill from his injuries. He'd lost too much blood. The only satisfaction he felt was his two remaining foes weren't moving very fast. They breathed heavily as they dealt with their own injuries and loss.

Something from the corner of his eye caught Marcellus's attention. One of the vampires had pulled Deirdre into his embrace. Sasha started to run to her assistance, but Henri held her off.

The vampire's claws pulsated against Deirdre's breasts, too close to her heart. "I'll kill her," he threatened. Blood streaked her white gown from his hands moving across her, but her face showed no fear.

"My life is worth yours," she said, making something tighten in Marcellus chest. "Finish this."

A hiss pushed from the vampire's lips now curled into a snarl. His fangs pressed against his bottom lip until he slowly began to open his mouth. "Bitch," he grunted as he angled his head and started his descent to bite down.

Marcellus had had enough. With a roar of fury, he called to his strength, unleashing hell.

He moved like a streak of lightning in the sky, snapping a branch off the tree and sending it soaring through the air. It struck true, impaling itself in the vampire's mouth, knocking him backward as it penetrated through the back of his head. Deirdre stumbled forward, free. There was no sound as the wounded vampire's eyes rolled back into his head.

Before Marcellus could celebrate his victory, Titan attacked from behind. His hand pushed through bone and muscle straight for Marcellus's heart. As the vampire with the branch through his head fell, Marcellus felt the cold fingers of death wrapped around his pulsating organ. His sight dimmed as he reached behind him. Titan's head now in his grasp, he pressed his thumbs into the vampire's eye sockets, pushing harder and harder.

The result was a horrifying shriek, but it worked. Titan released his hold to allow Marcellus to suck in a much needed breath, but the damaged had been done. He would die tonight if he didn't end this now. With what strength remained, Marcellus twisted around, his hands reaching for Titan to pull him to him. Without delay, he buried his fangs deep into the vampire's throat.

Bones crunched and veins severed, releasing a gush of

blood into Marcellus's mouth. He drank his fill until Titan lay limp in his arms, and then he continued until no life remained. Exhausted and weary, he let go of Titan and the man fell with a thud.

It was Deirdre and Sasha who were at his side as he missed a step and almost tripped over Titan's leg. Dizziness washed over him and he fell forward to be caught by Anton.

"He must go to ground." Sasha's voice faded in and out.

"Tamanen," Marcellus said. He must have it bad for her if all he could think about was his mate as life seeped away. But Sasha was right—he needed to go to ground. "Tell her—" He couldn't finish his sentence. Anton and Henri both swung an arm around him and in the manner of their people they vanished. The next thing he remembered was his toes dragging along the dirt floor in the basement.

"Elements of the earth open your arms for one of your own." He heard Deirdre's chant as she parted the soil. Anton and Henri lowered him into the grave. "Take him into your care and heal him with your wisdom." As she finished, Marcellus felt the coolness of the dirt fold around him. His nostrils filled with the dusty scent. Before his eyelids slid closed he wondered if Tamanen would miss him or was she wrapped in Lanier's arms?

Tammy had no idea how sensual being undressed by a man could be. Roark peeled one strap off her shoulder, kissing the very spot he uncovered, before repeating the process on the next one. Hand resting on her hip, he moved to stand behind her. With a brush of his fingertips, he pulled her hair back and out of the way.

"You were wonderful tonight." His breath caressed her neck, sending shivers up her spine. She lolled her head to the side, loving the way he feathered kisses along her skin.

The whisper of the gown's zipper falling was followed by a finger that caressed down her backbone, stopping at the small of her back. His seductive touch made her breasts grow firm, her nipples draw into taut nubs. Even the loosening of her gown as it exposed her back ignited her arousal. When his finger trailed lower, a flood of desire anointed her thighs. Something inside her belly fluttered and then moved south.

Tammy attempted to turn around, but he held her stationary with a strong grip on her waist. "Roark, I need you."

Ignoring her, he dropped a kiss upon her bare shoulder. "Patience, baby." The grate in his voice was as sexy as his touch.

"Patience—" She gasped as his tongue touched her skin. Slowly, he licked his way down her backbone. With each swirl and stroke the silky gown slid further down her body, until it pooled around her ankles and she stood in nothing but her stilettos and jewelry.

"Roark." His name came out a whimper, a small cry of need.

"Damn. You have a beautiful ass made for lovin'. But it's your long, slender legs that give me this hard-on." Tammy didn't need to see him to know he was aroused. It was in his tone, his touch, his masculine scent filling her lungs. As if to emphasize the point, he pressed his body against hers. His chest was bare, warm against her back. His lower half was covered in stiff cotton, but it wasn't his jeans that made her wiggle her ass. The firm bulge wedged between her cheeks was what she wanted to feel.

The sudden pinch of a contraction vanished her perseverance. Tammy willed his pants gone—and it worked. For a brief second his bare legs were pressed to hers. His rigid cock nestled between her cheeks. With a startled gasp, he yanked back his hands as if she suddenly had turned into a ball of flames. That's exactly how her body felt, hot and combustible. Another cramp assaulted her. *Dammit.* She hated this part. When he didn't immediately touch her, she tensed. Had she done something wrong?

"Well, that's certainly a useful trick." There was an air of amusement in his tone that made her release the breath she held. When he spooned her back once again, it was flesh to flesh. Adjusting his hips, he pushed his erection between her thighs.

"Yes," she moaned, sliding her wet folds along his shaft to ease the building need tightening and releasing her sex. That's exactly what she wanted to feel. It would be even better if he bent her over and drove deep inside her pussy.

Roark must have read her mind. With penguin steps, he inched her closer to the bed. "Bend over and grab the bedpost." She did as he asked, looking over her shoulder to meet hungry eyes. "I've dreamed of taking you this way—from behind." His nostrils flared as he scented her. His cock jerked, growing firmer before her eyes. "Your scent— It drives me wild." Trembling hands grasped her hips. Chest rising and falling with each breath, he positioned himself and thrust forward.

There was something compelling about Roark—strong, yet almost vulnerable. If she didn't know better she'd say he had real feelings for her.

Tammy cried out as he parted her folds and drove inside her. The gentle pace he began, rocking back and forth, turned her pain into pleasure. With each stroke he placed tinder to her fire. When he reached forward, grasping her breasts in each hand and squeezing, she cried, "Roark." The tingling that splintered through her breasts intensified as he rolled her nipples between his fingers, pulling and pinching. At the same time, he continued to glide in and out of her body. Each stroke teased her inner muscles, clenching desperately to keep him nestled inside her.

"Baby, do you like it slow and easy?" He released her breasts to firmly grasp her hips. Thrusting forward, he ground their bodies together, touching a sensitive spot that took her breath away.

"Ohhh my..." Tammy was at loss for words. The depth and fullness of his takeover consumed her completely. She shivered with ecstasy, thinking it just didn't get any better than this. He held them suspended in that special place before angling his hips so she could feel the pulse of his erection against the walls of her sex.

"Or do you like it hard and fast?" he growled, suddenly plunging into her over and over, until her breaths turned to short pants.

There was no tenderness in the pace Roark fucked her. The sound of flesh slapping flesh, the scents of their juices mingling, the unrestrained way he took what he wanted released the animal in both of them. He snarled, a grating timbre calling to her beast. She answered with a surly growl that made him bend forward and nip her shoulder.

Bone crunched as her canines pushed through her gums. The taste of blood on her tongue made her rear back, slamming her body into his. She needed to taste him, feel his blood flow down her throat.

A rumble vibrated in his throat as he withdrew his cock, taking himself in hand. Tammy felt him tremble against her back as he used her own juices to anoint her anus. Needing to get her mind off his beating pulse, the swish of his blood calling to her, she felt pressure at her entrance and pushed into his touch. Fire lanced her opening. She screamed, lights flashing behind her eyelids as he slid past the tight rings and buried deep inside her.

"Fuck." He shook uncontrollably as he fought to hold still, give her time to adjust. "Baby, I'm sorry."

She was anything but sorry. The pain helped her gain control of her thirst. "D-don't s-stop." She bared her fangs, releasing a steady hiss as she writhed beneath him. He answered her demand with a thrust, one after another. Not slow, but fast. Hard.

"Tight," he breathed. "So fucking tight." His hand caressed over her hip, across her abdomen to find the pulse between her thighs. When he touched the bud nestled there, she went off like a siren, throwing back her head. Her scream could have awakened the dead. It did the guards beyond their door.

Stephen and the two vampires stationed outside burst into the room, the door slamming and then bouncing off the wall back at them. Like statues they stood there, eyes wide and their mouths slack-jawed.

Tammy was too lost in the climax that ripped through her like a tornado to care about them. Roark groaned, "Shit," as he came hard and fast. Not a very romantic comment, but somewhat apropos for the moment. The last thing she remembered before she collapsed on the bed was hearing the door quietly shut and Roark stepping away from her.

As she lay there trying to catch her breath, Tammy felt a warm washcloth against her skin. Roark touched her like she was porcelain and any minute might break as he cared for her, ensured her comfort. Tears welled in her eyes, racing down her cheeks. No one had ever made her feel so cherished.

"I'm so sorry." Roark speared his fingers through his hair. He looked upset. "God, I didn't mean to hurt you."

Rolling upon her back, she wiped at the tears but they just kept flowing. "You didn't hurt me." The pleasure he gave her was short of miraculous.

"Then, what? Oh..." He glanced toward the door. His expression hardened. "Forget them. They're trained to be discreet."

An uneasy burst of air squeezed from her lungs. "I wish I could." Lord, what they must think of her.

Roark gathered her in his arms. "I don't know how to fix this." He sounded so forlorn, which only made her tears fall even faster. "Tammy, please don't cry. I'll think of something."

Tammy cradled his cheek in her palm and inhaled a ragged breath. "Thank you."

"What?" Shock drained the sorrow from his eyes to replace it with confusion.

"Thank you for caring about me," she explained. "Helping me through this adjustment. Not giving up on me."

He released a breath she took as relief followed by a burst of laughter. "I thought— Well— I'm just glad I didn't hurt you." He looked a little sheepish. "I've never lost control like that before."

"It was wonderful." She buried her face into the curve of his neck, realizing it was the wrong move when the place she had marked him began to pulse. Her mouth watered as she moved her tongue over it in a swirling pattern, tasting salt and his male essence. She was just about to bite down when she stopped mid-way. Easing out of his embrace, she drifted away from him, getting to her feet.

"What's wrong?" he asked, moving off the bed and coming toward her as she stepped backwards.

"Hungry." She licked her parched lips tasting him. The

sound of Roark's heart beating grew louder in her head. The temptress inside Tammy slinked beneath her skin. She willed her to stay put, but Tammy could have sworn the vixen laughed at her. *I will control you.*

Roark tore a sheet off the bed, wrapping it around her, guiding her to sit down. Quickly, he moved to the door and beckoned Stephen inside. The guard didn't say a word, but his eyes sparkled just the same.

"I need you to stop her from feeding if I don't," Roark said, moving to Tammy's side. Stephen flashed him a look of concern.

Tammy crawled across the bed away from them. "Roark, leave me or get Marcellus." The temptress inside looked through her eyes at Roark and then Stephen releasing a seductive purr. She pinched her eyelids together. "Get out."

"Baby, you can control your hunger," Roark reassured. "Come to me. Let me help you."

Tammy began to shake. Saliva gathering in her mouth as hunger gnawed on her backbone. She had to fight the need. *"Juste une petite morsure." Just a little bite.* The words slipped out of her mouth. Like a magnet she was drawn to Roark's side. The sheet slipped down her shoulders, catching Stephen's eyes, and she smiled seductively. Moving to her knees, she leaned into Roark to thread her fingers through his hair and tilt his head to the side. She breathed in his wild scent, caressing her tongue over his skin to feel the vein beneath her touch swell invitingly. Slowly she opened her mouth, canines dropping as she leaned in, pierced his flesh, and began to suck.

Roark groaned. His sound of pleasure exploded in her ears. Rich blood flowed down her throat, quenching her thirst and awakening her body. Continuing to feed, she moved closer, feeling his heat as she straddled his hips. He was hard, ready. With a gentle glide she smoothed her moist folds over him.

"Release him, my queen." Stephen's voice barely penetrated the haze her mind was becoming. Tammy felt a tug on her shoulders and she hissed around the flesh in her mouth. "Stop now." He firmed his voice. His fingers did the same as they buried into her arms.

Tammy swung out, striking him across the face to send him hurling off the bed and landing on the floor with a thud. In the next minute, she found herself pinned to the bed, Stephen's knee in the middle of her chest, squeezing the air from her lungs. She tried to move, fight him, but it was useless. Her mouth gaped. *Air.* She needed air.

"I'm all right. Let her go, Stephen."

When the big ox moved off her, Tammy curled into a ball, sucking in one breath after another. Someone draped the sheet back over her. Fingertips massaged her back. Her chest ached, throat stung, but her breaths were finally flowing evenly.

She'd done it again—lost control.

Shame was becoming her companion. As she raised her head and looked into Roark's eyes, no condemnation stared back at her, only affection.

"You all right?" he asked.

"Yeah," she coughed. "As soon as the Hulk released me."

"Hulk?" Stephen repeated. "You mean that big, green guy?" Before she could answer, he said, "I think I've been insulted."

"Insulted?" She huffed. Damn man didn't have to be so rough. "Next time you try that I'll rip your arm off and feed it to you." She added a growl to her voice for good measure.

Stephen only grinned. "Sounds like your mate has a temper."

"Temper," Tammy barked. "I'll show you temper." As she started to push to her feet, Roark hauled her back into his lap.

"Let me at him." She squirmed in his embrace, until he captured her mouth and the whimper she released.

"Looks like you've got everything under control." Stephen chuckled. The click of the door shutting behind him was all she heard before Roark laid her gently upon the bed and moved atop her.

୫୬

Dammit. Roark was falling hard for Tammy. It was difficult to watch her snuggle up to Donne and kiss him passionately as they said their good-byes. The vampire gazed into her eyes with such passion that Roark's loins tightened. He knew how hypnotic those eyes were. Holy shit! What was he saying? The incident in the pantry was only a mind game—a fantasy—nothing more.

Fuck. Who was he kidding? Roark couldn't help eavesdropping. He heard every seductive word Donne spoke to Tammy. Last night had been hot, even more exciting having a man with such power on his knees before him. From the corner of Donne's eyes he flashed Roark a glance that sent his heart to racing.

This was ridiculous.

Roark shook his head, pushing the thought out of his mind. Instead, he attempted to focus on the news Stephen had shared with him upon their rising this Thursday evening.

Donne hadn't joined Tammy and Roark last night. Apparently, Titan and several of his followers had demanded Donne relinquish his leadership. Like Roark, Donne took insubordination seriously, dealing with it swiftly as Roark had with Layton. Rumor had it that Titan and three of his buddies were no longer a problem. Dead. One of Donne's guards had confided in Stephen that his master had gone to ground to heal from the battle.

An unexpected spark of anger flared inside Roark. Donne shouldn't have fought the vampires alone. The unexpected emotion that swamped him made his pulse stammer.

"Thank you, my friend. Our queen had need of you." Donne's deep voice seeped into Roark's troubled thoughts.

Donne's injuries had to have been severe if he required the healing powers of the earth. From what Roark knew of vampires, they did not sleep in caskets, nor did all of them burrow beneath the ground. Some preferred to sleep in beds like anyone else, except when their injuries were life threatening. If there was a chance of survival the rich minerals in the soil and the elements of nature would heal them.

"You should have called on me," Roark grumbled.

Donne glanced over Tammy's shoulder. *"A mere scratch."*

"I doubt that." Roark should have been there to protect him. Donne's warmth surrounded him as if Donne had put his arms around him. Oddly, the vampire's closeness soothed the anxiety that only moments ago held him in its grasp. Roark crammed his hands into the black leather jacket Donne had supplied along with the rest of his clothing.

"I will join you as soon as I am confident my people are at ease with my decisions." Donne pulled the edges of Tammy's sheepskin coat closed, fastened the buttons and stole one more kiss before he released her. The coat and the rest of her clothing, sweater, jeans, and hiking boots were only an instrument to make her appear human.

Donne slung an arm around her shoulders and escorted her to the Jeep. When he raised her in his arms, she laughed. She looked happy for the first time since her conversion. Well that was until Stephen took her out of Donne's embrace and plopped her down on the backseat.

"Ox," she grumbled, rubbing her butt before moving away from him.

"Brat," Stephen returned the backhanded compliment over his shoulder. Roark could see his guard fight the twitch in the corner of his mouth as he moved around the vehicle and scooted behind the wheel. With a tug, Stephen pulled the collar of his shirt up. He was dressed in the same shirt and slacks he wore last night.

Tammy raised her middle finger, flipping Stephen off. This time he flashed a wolfish smile as he caught her gesture in the rearview mirror.

A scornful expression pulled Donne's brows together. He shook his head discouragingly. "Not quite how I pictured my queen to act." The mirth in his voice exposed his ruse, when he said, "How about you, Lanier?"

Roark moved to the passenger side, grasped the roll-bar and climbed into the vehicle. "It does seem that Stephen brings out the worse in her." There was a strange relationship developing between Tammy and Stephen, but there was something about it that didn't bother Roark. He couldn't quite say why, it just felt more like a brother and sister's playful bickering—a friendly camaraderie. Besides, unlike his other guards, Stephen and Franc had been his closest confidants since they were children. He trusted them to guard his back as well as his heart.

"Me?" Stephen feigned innocence. "I'm just doing my job, boss. She's the one causing trouble. Do you want the top up?" he asked, before adding, "The wind might mess the little princess's hair up."

"Bite me," Tammy snapped, glaring into the rearview mirror at Stephen, before she puffed her hair up with her palms and

Tammy buried her face into the crook of Roark's neck. The masculine scent of his skin urged her to sample him. She kissed him, her tongue caressing his salty flesh.

"Mmmm…" she hummed. "You taste so good."

He turned in her arms and she captured his mouth. As she stroked his bottom lip with her tongue, he growled, spearing his fingers through her hair to take control. What started as a seductive exploration turned hungry, urgent when he firmed the kiss. Just knowing he wanted her as much as she wanted him hardened her nipples. A flutter erupted low in her belly. There was something different about Roark's kiss. It was more primitive—the other half of who he was. She knew immediately that he was at home—at ease in this place that was unburdened by civilization.

"I want to run with you," he murmured against her mouth. "Show you the night like it's meant to be experienced." His eyes were disarming.

Tammy wanted Roark naked, his body pressed to hers, limbs intertwined, his cock buried inside her. The image made her fangs burst through her gums. The taste of blood on her tongue, the scent caressing her nose, was all she needed to entice her to stroke the throbbing vein in his neck.

Stephen cleared his throat, breaking the spell that had bewitched her. He jerked his head backward, his dark mane brushing his shoulders. "Ice chest in the back."

"What?" Her voice held an edge of irritation that she couldn't hide. Even still, she glanced behind to see there was indeed a blue and white cooler just within her reach.

"Donne packed supplies for you. I suggest you partake of one of the packets inside instead of Roark."

Blood wasn't the only thing that was on her mind as the temptress inside her emerged to slide her heated gaze over

looked away.

"Isn't that your thing?" Stephen teased, before he turned the key over. The engine began to hum, the oily scent of gas rose.

Roark twisted in his seat to look from Stephen to Tammy. "Look here, you two. I refuse to listen to you squabble the entire way." He tried to hide his grin, but he knew Tammy saw right through it.

She wrinkled her nose. "Maybe you should muzzle the mutt. Better yet, put a leash on him and he can run beside us." Biting her bottom lip, she tried to hide her giggle, but couldn't. Her joyous laughter was intoxicating. He had never heard anything so lively, so beautiful. The melodic sound wound around his heart and squeezed. If he lived a life time he would do whatever it took to hear her laugh again and again.

Donne threw his hands in the air. "Lord have mercy. What happened to the sweet girl we all know and love?" His arms plopped down to his side brushing his slacks.

Tammy raised her chin. Her voice sassy when she quipped, "She had Mr. Tons of Fun sit on her last night."

"Only after you did your imitation of Count Dracula," Stephen countered.

Donne threw back his head and roared. He slapped Roark on the back. "Can't say that I envy you." They shook hands, Donne's warm against Roark's. When their eyes met, Donne's laughter died. "Keep her safe." There was more in his expression, but Roark couldn't read it. "I'll try to join you as soon as I can."

Roark attempted to tap Donne's mind, but Stephen shifted the Jeep into gear. A sudden release of the clutch, the vehicle lurched forward pausing briefly, before he gassed it and took off. Roark knew the rough start was for Tammy's benefit as the jerky motion flung her back then slid her forward. She caught the back of the seat before she landed on the floorboard. A tight squeal was followed by a derogatory comment that escaped Roark, but it resulted in Stephen's grin deepening.

"Dumb shit." She struck the back of Stephen's head lightly with her palm, causing him to flinch and laugh out loud.

Roark wondered if this new side of Tammy revealed that she was becoming more comfortable with her situation. Her acceptance meant everything to him.

For the first time since he arrived in Phoenix, Roark leaned back in his seat and began to relax. He even took the opportunity to take in the beauty of Donne's mansion. Blue Christmas lights hung from trees and netted bushes, presenting a cold, but dreamy effect. Every eave and window of the manor was traced in lights. Even the light posts aligning the driveway cast a blue hue. It truly was a spectacular sight.

As they drove beyond the gates and down a deserted road, the city lights glowed like a halo. Roark had always preferred the wilderness to the chaos the valley represented. Acres of lush grasses, pine trees and nature were what most lycanthropes craved—he was no different. The weight on his shoulders rose with the knowledge he was headed home.

Chapter Thirteen

At the first patch of snow dotting the highway, excite bubbled up inside Tammy. She loved the snow, especial Christmastime. Not to mention, the mountain air free of made the night crystal clear and it smelled heavenly. As breathed in the scent of pine, she looked to the cloudless Stars so bright they glistened in the velvety blanket above. moon was a picturesque view of craters and landforms so its glow cast a spell around her.

Happy, Tammy leaned forward and wrapped her a around Roark's neck and hugged. Things seemed so diffe from this side of humanity. From the small seedling sprou in the soil, to the night owl that screeched before landing tree branch high above, everything was alive. New sights sounds sprung up all around her making her giddy experience them all.

Perhaps being a member of the undead made all thi living so precious or maybe it was the beast inside her t brought nature to the forefront. Whatever it was, Tammy free for the first time in her life. Free from the invisible cha society held around her. Free to explore worlds she thou only existed beyond the television screen. *The world is at y fingertips,* were Marcellus's earlier words.

Roark's impressive physique. He was a beautiful man. She loved the way his hair was mussed by the wind, appearing wild and unrestrained. She was dying to feel him beneath her palms, between her legs.

"My queen." Stephen's tone was clip. "Ice chest. Now."

Tammy snarled, her beast responding to the guard's aggression. The animal inside pushed against her skin, prickling her flesh. The muscles in her neck and shoulders tightened. The thing that pissed her off the most was that Stephen was right. Two sets of headlights rushing up behind them only validated the fact they needed to keep going. Pulling off the road would attract attention. Not to mention if anything went wrong—

She held the beast and temptress restrained as she unsnapped the hinge to open the cooler. A block of ice sat in the middle surrounded by numerous white plastic containers of blood. Her hands trembled as she reached for one. The minute her fangs pierced the sack and the rich liquid flowed down her throat, her eyes closed on a sigh. With long pulls, she sucked every last drop from the bag. That was good, but not as good as Roark's or Marcellus's essence and definitely not as good as drinking embraced in the midst of an orgasm.

Hunger appeased, her body still hummed with the need to be fulfilled. She squirmed against the seat, needing to quiet the burn of desire heating her body. Fingers of sensation played at her sex, teasing and taunting her to seek what she needed— Roark.

He must have sensed her unease as he reached back and squeezed her hand. "Hold on, baby. Just a little further. As soon as we're through Heber we'll be free to run."

She raised a brow in question. Roark was crazy if he expected her to run alongside the Jeep to keep the edge of her desire at bay.

He must have heard her thoughts, because a burst of laughter met her confusion. "Not exactly." Lifting her hand to his mouth, his lips were warm against her skin. "There's nothing more exhilarating than a night run in our wolf forms." His voice became raspy, as he continued. "I can't wait to run beside you. Exercise our muscles and race until our lungs sting from exhaustion."

That wasn't the only thing that excited him. Tammy smelled his arousal, as well as Stephen's. The masculine scents were like a love potion, an aphrodisiac which awakened the temptress and caused Stephen to hit the gas.

Tammy stretched her lithe body across the seat, arching her back, her eyelids growing heavy. *"Venez à moi, mon prince."* Her French accent was perfect as she pronounced every syllable to beckon Roark to her. For good measure she released the strong, penetrating perfume of her body that would entice him. From the rearview mirror, she saw Stephen take in every one of her seductive movements. His knuckles turned white as he gripped the steering wheel.

"Holy shit, Roark. How do you deny her?" Stephen was breathing hard. She could hear the swish of his blood race through his veins and pump through his heart. He was aroused and that pleased her.

But the subject of her assault hadn't moved, hadn't crossed the distance between them. Roark remained seated, watching her intently. Slowly she began to unfasten her sheepskin coat to shrug out of it before she moved a booted foot off the floorboard and placed it on the seat, slowly inching her legs apart. She tossed back her head allowing the wind to carry her hair on the breeze. With a swipe of her tongue, she smoothed it across her bottom lip to lure him.

Roark's voice was coarse when he answered Stephen's question. "It isn't easy. I'm one lucky man. Now if you don't mind, go faster." Then he did the unthinkable. He turned around and ignored her.

With a huff, Tammy planted her feet on the floorboard. She leaned forward and nipped at Roark's ear. When she slid a hand inside his jacket to caress his chest, he captured her wrist holding on tight.

"Don't," he breathed. "Baby, I'm holding on by a thread here."

"Let go and give in to my desire," she whispered against his ear, nuzzling it, and then tugged the lobe between her teeth.

"Behave, you wicked wench." His laughter was strained. "We don't have much further."

"But I need you now," she whimpered, the temptress refusing to relent. "Let me strip you naked, ease the tension in your body with my touch, my tongue, my mouth."

"My respect for you has risen ten-fold, Roark." Stephen shifted his hips, drawing her attention to the bulge in his slacks that matched the one in Roark's jeans.

"Pull over, Stephen." She purred, "Puleez..."

"Keep going," Roark retorted, increasing the hold he had on her wrist.

"I need to feel your cock inside me," she moaned, not caring if Stephen heard.

"Woman, if you keep talking like that I can't be responsible for my actions." Stephen released a pent-up growl. She could feel his beast close to the surface.

"Keep your hands on the wheel—your eyes on the road," Roark grumbled as the lights of Heber appeared in the distance. "And you, you little minx." He pinned her with a glare as he gave her hand several firm shakes. "Keep your mouth *shut.*"

Tammy felt a smile beam across her face. "But—"

"Shhh... Quiet now or I'll turn you over my knee and spank your ass."

"I just might like that," she cooed.

"Not what I have in mind for you. Stop tempting Stephen," he snarled, baring his teeth. He wasn't teasing. In fact, he appeared angry.

They shared a tense moment as they entered Heber. Silently, they drove down the main street. Even nestled in the pines, Christmas was evident in lawn ornaments and decorated Christmas trees shining brightly from the windows of the homes and the businesses they passed.

When they were several miles beyond civilization, Roark said, "Pull over at the next exit." The strain in his voice concerned Tammy, but not enough to stop her from burying her nose into his hair and inhaling his fragrance.

As the next exit came into sight, Stephen gently steered the Jeep over until it came to stop, the engine still running. The passenger side door moaned as Roark flung it open, gravel popping beneath his boots. In seconds he was standing outside the vehicle and pulling her over the side into his arms. She released a startled cry as her feet hit the snow-ridden ground and he pressed his nose to hers.

His eyes were liquid gold, so intense she felt their burn. "I ought to pull your jeans down to your knees and spank the pretty ass until it's red-hot."

His words heightened her arousal. She tried to get closer to his heat, her beast screaming for his, but he held her inches away.

"We are animals, Tammy." As if to prove it, his canines

dropped. She smelled the blood that tinted them, until he licked them clean. There was a slur to his words as he continued. "Do not taunt the males of our pack because they will answer your call. When I get my hands on the offending party the results will be deadly." His warm breath washed over her. "You are mine— never forget that." A shiver assailed her as he firmed his hold on her. "I share you with Donne only because fate has declared it to be." He was trembling when he released her. "Now strip." It wasn't a request, but a demand that infuriated and thrilled her at the same time.

Tammy thought to defy him, but a gleam in his eyes, something wild and untamed, made even her temptress take a step backward and sulk in the background. Her fingers fumbled with the buttons of her shirt. Evidently, she didn't move fast enough because his hands jutted out with lightning speed, gathering her shirt and tearing. The ripping of material, the popping of buttons and the cool night air as it hit her chest made her mind whirl. Her heart was pounding against her breastbone, when he extended a single finger, the nail elongating to a sharp claw. With one swipe he cut through her bra, baring her breasts. Immediately, her nipples drew into taut, aching nubs.

"Roark, do you think this is wise?" Stephen's question jerked Roark's head around. A rumble filled his throat. "All am saying is that—" A snarl and a hiss hushed Stephen.

Although being manhandled by Roark was hot, Tammy knew the moment was volatile. It was in the predatory way he stalked her as he moved around her, and in the angry glances he shot toward Stephen. Using her vampire gifts, she removed the rest of her clothes, including Roark's. Stephen didn't dare a look, instead he kept his gaze forward, his beast pacing and itching to emerge as hers was.

"Leave us," Roark issued the command, his cock rock-hard,

arching against his abdomen. Stephen didn't hesitate as he shifted the vehicle in gear. The back tires spun, spitting gravel and black snow from beneath them as the Jeep jumped the curb and hit the asphalt. The red taillights were fading when Roark murmured, "Come here."

When she was within his grasp, he yanked her to him, chest to chest, hips to hips. She felt his arousal hard against her belly. Her nipples were sensitive against the rasp of his chest hairs, the spot between her thighs moist and aching. His fingernails bit into her flesh. There was no tenderness in his touch or his kiss as his mouth descended upon hers. He didn't ask for admittance, he stabbed his tongue between her lips taking what he wanted. Their tongues dueled. A fang pierced her bottom lip and he captured her cry.

The next was a whirlwind of sensation. Knees and palms pressed against a soft bed of pine needles and snow, he thrust forward and parted her folds, burying deep. She cried out, almost losing her balance at the exquisite feel of him moving in and out, hard and fast. His throaty groans caressed her ears and stoked her desire, drowning out the sounds of a startled deer quickly moving away. It was only Roark and her under a blanket of stars.

Currents surged through her body as the muscles inside her pussy contracted around him. His reaction was to pick up the pace, fuck her with an intensity that bordered on the edge of pain and pleasure.

And she loved it.

It was a powerful awareness, a stimuli, to feel him tremble, knowing he rode the edge of control. "Yes," she whimpered, needing—wanting to be there with him when his aplomb shattered, allowing his vulnerability to bleed through.

Looking over her shoulder, she watched him toss back his

Manny stood behind him.

"That mountain lion could have killed her," Roark barked.

"*But he didn't and she's safe. What do you say we get her home?*" Martin moved beside her as the other three wolves surrounded them.

Roark grumbled something she was unable to decipher as he bounded forward into the woodland. She had the good sense to follow. It was the second time tonight that he had become displeased with her. She certainly didn't want there to be a third opportunity.

Roark kept a steady pace and she struggled to keep up. Snow covered her legs clear up to her belly, weighing her down. How many miles they ran she didn't know, but her lungs stung and she was panting when the trees parted and they broke into an opening. Before her lay a cozy village with streets of cobblestone that paved the way. No asphalt or its oily smell hampered the air. Instead the smoky scent of pine curled from the chimneys of almost every home. Tucked away from civilization it was a breath of Christmas in the mountains. Colorful lights adorned most cabins. A large, decorated Christmas tree stood in the middle of town.

Pebbles popped beneath Tammy's paws as she padded across the road. She was tired, but more than that she wanted to nip Roark's ass. The big bully held no sympathy for her. She didn't know anything about his world. Everything was new and a little scary. Even as her stomach growled and the first signs of her heat awoke, she knew it would be a cold day in hell before she let him touch her tonight.

As the entourage of wolves led her toward the largest of the log cabins, three stone chimneys jutting from the roof, she felt a little weepy. Even still, she couldn't help take in the beauty of the two-story home. Trapped in two worlds, neither of them was

mane, his mouth parted to release a howl toward the sky. His grip firmed. His cock jerked several times, and then he thrust his hips, holding their bodies together as a warm jet of come bathed the walls of her sex.

Tammy's orgasm stole over her like a thief in the night. Her length stretched as taut as a bow. When the first spasms struck she fought the inevitable—needed to make the moment last forever. One right after another rolled through her. She couldn't breathe holding on to the iron grip of passion that pulled her into ecstasy. She wasn't strong enough to fight it. As she released her hold, let her body go, she screamed. The potent feeling of soaring into the heavens took her higher and higher.

When the last contraction released and she began to descend, her arms gave and she crumpled to the ground, taking Roark with her. But he wasn't in an amorous mood—a nip to her shoulder proved that as he rose.

Was he still angry with her?

Tammy rolled to her side just in time to see the change overtake Roark. Bones crackled, muscles and tendons popped, grinding. Auburn hair seeped from his pores to produce a silky pelt of fur. She pushed into a sitting position. His handsome features blurred, his mouth elongating into a muzzle. A twist and a turn, he morphed completely, landing on all fours before her.

Immediately, Roark's ears stood erect. A tilt of his head, he sniffed the air and she knew he searched for danger. When it appeared he was satisfied, he narrowed his gaze on her. Not a sound could be heard as he approached. While pine needles snapped beneath her with every move, she was amazed that she didn't feel the biting cold. When he was near enough to touch she buried her hands, and then her nose into his coat. He smelled like the earth itself, fresh and wild.

"You're beautiful," she said with awe in her voice. "Roark, I've never seen anything so fascinating."

"*Join me.*" He touched her mind with his.

"How?" she asked. Each time the change had held her in its grasp she had been out-of-control. It hadn't been a moment of decision, but an ugly, scary time in her life.

"*Let your body relax. Think of each muscle becoming fluid.*"

Tammy was filled with excitement as she moved to her knees and sat down on her haunches. She closed her eyes, rolling her head side to side to ease the tension in her neck. Muscles softened, a prickling sensation spread across her skin as if her very flesh was shrinking, drawing into her body. At the same time there was an indescribable strength that filled her limbs, pulling and tugging on them as they reshaped into strong legs, paws, and claws. Her nose twitched and her eyes opened to a new world.

Roark waved his tail. "*You're gorgeous. My blonde bitch.*" There was no derogatory clip to his tone, just pride. He dug his back feet, one after another, into the earth sending dirt and pine needles behind him.

She yipped, the sharp sound high-pitched and definitely female. A leap to her feet, she was off in a flash. It was amazing the freedom she felt. Power abounded each stride as she jumped over fallen trees and darted around large boulders that stood in her way. She didn't know where she was going—didn't care. Nor did she know how far or long she'd run. Her carefree attitude was suddenly curbed when Roark landed in front of her, snarling.

"*Party-pooper,*" she grumbled. He plopped his large head on Tammy's back forcing her fast upon the ground. She started to struggle beneath his hold, but he snapped at her holding her neck firmly between his pulsating jaws. "*What the hell—*" she

whimpered just as she caught a whiff of something pungent and offensive.

Tammy tuned in her animal senses and almost peed right where she squatted. The blood in her veins froze. Standing on a cliff a distance away from them was a mountain lion. The path she had been headed down would have taken her right beneath the cat that had sunk to its belly, positioning itself to pounce on an unsuspecting victim—namely her.

Slowly Roark released her. His steps were silent as the grave as he led her away from the cat. Her heart was racing. Her steps mimicked Roark's path in the snow as they ran, for how long she had no idea.

When they were a safe distance away, his ears went rigid "*You must always scour the land for enemies. They ar everywhere.*"

Tammy felt like a child being scolded and she didn't like "*I'm sorry, but—*"

"*Sorry won't cut it. What if I hadn't been here? What if* His body stiffened as he bared his teeth and released a d growl. A stirring in the underbrush caught Tammy's attenti When four large wolves stepped beyond the hedge she alm lost her lunch. Her stomach pitched and she couldn't moving closer to Roark, ignoring his anger for the momen seek his shelter.

One of the wolves was the flaxen color of her fur, while other three were as dark as the night, except one of t appeared older with streaks of silver through its coat. particular wolf stepped closer undisturbed by the incre vigor in Roark's growl.

"*Ease up on her, son.*" Tammy recognized Martin's and now that her pulse was beginning to slow she recog his scent too. If she wasn't mistaken, Stephen, Franc,

willing to accept her. A push from her hind legs, she leaped on the wraparound porch on the bottom level of the house after Roark.

A young woman dressed in a blue plush robe opened the large oak door as if it were nothing to allow six wolves into her home. She stepped aside while they tracked mud and snow on the polished wood flooring. The large room opened up to a picturesque window that faced the mountains. Tammy knew it would be a gorgeous view in the light of day, but she would never experience that again.

Why at this moment had she finally realized what all she would be missing? Wallowing in self-pity, she wasn't paying much attention to what was going on around her until all five men shifted into their human forms.

Yeow! There wasn't one thing lacking in form or substance on each man. They moved casually about the room as if unaware of their state of undress. The temptress in Tammy was very aware of them. She slinked just below her skin.

The petite dark-haired woman gathered a pile of towels and began to hand each of the men one. Instead, of covering themselves, they briskly ran the towel over their heads drying their hair and then their bodies. Only as a second thought did they wrap the cover around their hips.

"Tammy?" Roark raised a brow.

Well excuse her for not knowing the protocol. If the lord and master of this place wanted her to materialize in all her glory before all these men, who was she to disagree. More than a little cranky, Tammy let her hold on the wolf slip. It tickled as the hair on her skin disappeared. It was a little disconcerting to hear her bones snap, her muscles creak as the wolf disappeared. Stark-ass naked, she stood before everyone.

Roark's eyes widened.

What had he expected? She answered his surprise by placing her palms on her hips. A fiery glare dared him to say something—just one word—and she'd turn into the blonde bitch he'd called her earlier. Near tears, Tammy turned to the woman and asked, "Where is my room?"

"Lonnie, give her your robe," Roark demanded. As Lonnie began to wiggle out of her wrapper, Tammy raised her hand halting her.

"Keep your robe, Lonnie. Just tell me where my bedroom is."

Lonnie's gaze darted toward Roark and then back to Tammy. She made a small curtsy. "The sire's rooms are on the second floor, second door on the left."

"Not *his* room, mine?" Tammy clarified with enough heat behind her words to wither a flower.

An expression of confusion furrowed Lonnie's brows. Her mouth opened and then snapped shut.

"Give her your robe." Roark's firm tone made it perfectly clear what he wanted and further more expected from Tammy. It appeared the most important thing at the moment was to cover her from the curious stares she received from the other men.

Martin moved forward, casting his eyes off her to direct his attention to Roark. "I had the room adjacent yours protected from light as well."

"That won't be necessary," Roark replied sharply. "My room is hers. She sleeps with me."

Tammy released a huff of annoyance that brought both Martin's and Roark's stares back to her. "In your dreams, buddy," she mumbled.

Beneath the robe Lonnie tried so desperately to shrug out

of she wore the cutest pair of flannel pajamas, white with red lips all over them. When she managed to disrobe, she approached Tammy, placing the wrap into Tammy's hands. She took it only to relieve the worried expression on Lonnie's face, even as Tammy pierced Roark with a heated glare. Slowly she held the robe high into the air away from her body, letting the material slip through her fingers to pool at her feet. Squaring her shoulders, she pivoted and headed for the stairs. She didn't glance back, but she heard Stephen clear his throat and Manny chuckle, followed by a growl that had to be Roark's.

At the top of the stairs she didn't hesitate. She passed by the second door on the left without a thought. No one was going to tell her what she could and couldn't do. Roark might as well discover this about her right now.

Chapter Fourteen

Baffled didn't even begin to describe how Roark felt as he watched Tammy's naked ass sway up the stairs and disappear around the corner. To make it worse, five other sets of eyes watched too—four of them very intrigued males.

What the hell had come over Tammy?

She went from seducing him in the Jeep, to making mad passionate love beneath the stars, to bounding through the forest with abandonment, to seconds away from ripping his head off with a single look. He had seen her agitated, yes—but not outright defiant.

"Welcome to blessed matrimony," Franc mocked dryly. His gaze was still fixated on the top of the stairs. Although he appeared unaffected by Tammy's bold departure, the tent in the towel around his hips said differently. On further scrutiny damned if every man in the room wasn't aroused by her show of opposition, or was it her curves and that sweet ass that had them mesmerized?

A snicker from Martin drew everyone's eyes toward him. "She reminds me a little of Beth." His redheaded wife had been a spitfire. That was where Grady's uncanny sense of humor had come from. A mine cave-in had taken her life five years ago. Martin had never found another.

A moment of sadness swamped Roark. He would miss Grady.

"I think perhaps you miscalculated the docility of our queen's nature." Stephen's words made Roark slide a frown in his direction.

"You think?" Roark didn't even try to mask the irritation in his voice. With each rising he discovered something new about Tammy. She never ceased to amaze him, but this side of her he hadn't been prepared for.

"Perhaps you were a little too hard on her in the Jeep and forest. She's unfamiliar with our ways—the dangers we face each day." Evidently, Stephen didn't know when to keep his mouth shut, because he continued. "Maybe a gentler hand—"

"When I want your counsel I'll ask for it," Roark bit between clenched teeth. "Good-night." They remained rooted where they stood until he repeated, "Good-night." Each of the men bowed and turned toward the door. "Stephen, the ice chest?"

"Lonnie has taken care of it," his guard and friend responded before taking his leave behind the rest of the men. When the door clicked shut, Roark glanced back up the stairs. What exactly was he supposed to do?

"I've placed several packets within your chamber's mini-bar. The rest I placed in the refrigerator. If you'd like I'll take a drink up to her," Lonnie offered. "Perhaps it will calm her."

That sounded like a reasonable plan, better than the one he was pondering, bounding up the stairs and asking Tammy outright what the problem was. "Thank you."

Lonnie curtsied, which should have been odd from a woman dressed in flannel. Like her mother, she had chosen to stick to the old ways and protocols. It made no difference to Roark if someone curtsied or bowed or even called him by his name instead of a more formal title. Since her mother retired three years ago, Lonnie resided in his home and took care of his household needs. Without a sound, she turned and disappeared into the kitchen.

Roark walked toward the blazing fireplace that covered half the west wall and stared into the flickering flames. Stephen was right. Roark had handled Tammy poorly. She had done only what was natural to her. He had to remember that she was not only lycanthrope, but vampire—a combination of both with human thoughts and ways. She would make mistakes. It was up to him to counsel and guide her with patience, not jealousy.

Yet Roark had seen red when he witnessed how aroused Stephen had been to her flirty words, even though he knew it was a lycanthrope's nature to service their females during their time of need. If he had been away on business and Tammy came into heat, Stephen or any one of his guards who was entrusted with her care would have seen to her comfort. Logic didn't play in his thoughts tonight. The only man he could stand to touch Tammy was Donne. For some odd reason he actually missed the irritating vampire.

Roark listened to Lonnie's footsteps as she climbed the stairs. The scent of the blood she carried to Tammy filled his nostrils. Quietly, he said a prayer that Lonnie was correct, that if his mate's hunger was satisfied so would her temper. He waited until he heard Lonnie descend the stairs, and then he turned to face the music.

As he climbed one stair and then the other, he realized in the turmoil of their arrival he had forgotten to ask Franc about the spirits of their people. At least Lonnie did not appear frightened by Tammy's presence. She even sought to make her queen more relaxed and welcomed.

Crying met his ears, when Roark topped the stairs. He moved quickly toward the sobbing behind the bedroom door adjacent to his. Mentally, he reached out and heard her sadness, the grieving she felt for a mortal life lost. When she felt his intrusion, she immediately broke the mind link between them. She was getting stronger—her abilities were growing. Even still, that didn't stop him from feeling her pain. Not only did her body ache, but her heart as well.

A twist of the doorknob, he found it locked. There was a brief moment of agitation that she or anyone would think to bar him from any room in his own house.

What was he thinking? He rapped gently upon the door. "Tammy?'

There was no answer.

He leaned against the door. "Baby, let me in."

She sniffled, indelicately blowing her nose. "No. Go away."

"Ahhh...baby, don't be like this." With lightning speed the door sprung open and he fell into the room, hitting the floor with a thud. He glanced up into icy blue eyes.

"Don't be like this?" Her strained tone coupled with the heat in her eyes was all he needed to see to know he was in big trouble.

She was adorned in a pair of pajamas much like Lonnie's, flannel, but solid black, matching her mood. There were little red pitch forks on them and for a moment he wondered if they were symbolic. Her hair was mussed around her shoulders, still wet from the trek through the snow. The flare of anger in her eyes made him think she wanted to give him a swift kick for good measure.

Slowly he moved to his feet, putting a safe amount of distance between them.

"Exactly, how am I supposed be, my lord?" Sarcasm dripped from her mouth. Before he could answer, she said, "You growl and bark at me for things I don't even know are wrong." Her chin quivered, but she quickly gained back the steel in her voice. "You know what my nature is. I try to restrain the hunger, the temptress, but—" She turned her back on him. "Just go away."

Cautiously, he moved up behind her, noting the empty glass that sat on her nightstand. The comforter on the big king-size bed was pulled back. She had been getting ready for bed, without him. The knowledge stung his pride. Tammy was his mate. Her place was beside him in his bed. His movements were almost hesitant as he slipped his arms around her.

She tensed, flailing her arms outward to break his hold, but he had anticipated her reaction pinning her arms to her side as he pressed his chest to her back. The rapid beat of her heart echoing against him couldn't bode well for him.

"I'm sorry," he whispered. She smelled heavenly, soft and feminine even if her temper reveled otherwise. Her anger was an aphrodisiac when it should have been just the opposite. Blood rushed his groin. His cock jerked against the towel pressed to her ass. She flinched and once again tried to break free of his hold, but she wasn't going anywhere. "This is new to me too," he tried to rationalize with her. "I've never had a mate, never been faced with the jealousy I felt when I sensed Stephen's desire. He wanted you. It infuriated me."

She harrumphed, jerking once more to escape him. He scented her arousal and knew her pussy would be hot, moist— just how he liked her. Yet the rigidity in her body said she wasn't giving in. Not even when he felt a contraction squeeze her abdomen.

"When I saw the mountain lion, thought of the danger it posed, I lost it," he admitted. The thought of losing her made his blood run cold. He hadn't been gentle with her forcing her to the ground. His comments afterward where fed by his fear. Martin had been right. "I can't lose you, baby."

Tammy turned in his arms. "Damn you, Roark." She thumped his chest. "I'm a city girl. By all means I'm still human. I think like one. Act like one. You can't expect me in the mere matter of days to forget all that is normal to me. I didn't ask for this." She sucked in a shuddering breath. "God, I feel so alone." Tammy slumped against him.

Roark brushed back her hair. "You're not alone. I'm here, Donne too."

Her burst of laughter held irony. "No one is going to accept me. We're just kidding ourselves."

He kissed her forehead. "You're wrong. Martin, my guards and even Lonnie have already accepted you."

She buried her face against his shoulder. "I just wish I'd fall asleep and wake up to find this all to be a bad dream."

Her words cut straight to his heart like a knife. If he could turn back time, would he? How selfish was it to want her by his side even when she longed for her old life? Why the hell was he even thinking this way? What had happened could not be reversed. Like it or not she was stuck with him for eternity. A swipe of his arm beneath the bend of her knees and he whisked her into his arms. She held on to his neck as he walked out of the room into the hallway. Using one hand, he twisted the doorknob and gave it a shove with his foot. Familiar scents assailed him. He was home.

How did everything become such a mess? Tammy felt drained from the evening's events as Roark laid her down upon his bed. The highs and lows she rode were too much for her too bear. She needed some kind of stability in her life. Someplace where she wouldn't have to look over her shoulder and wonder who wanted her dead. Tammy had thought Roark's village was the answer. As she gazed into his eyes, she wondered if she was just fooling herself.

Somewhere between her conversion and now, Tammy had developed real feelings for him, which only complicated things. When he was near it was hard to breathe. Her body needed him as much as air to survive. Other than today, he had always been gentle and understanding. If being around his people would cause him such jealousy there was no hope for them here. The fact that he was the lycanthrope leader only added to their dilemma. He couldn't just run away with her. He had obligations, responsibilities to his people. So where did that leave her?

A single finger smoothed over her forehead. "You're thinking too hard." He leaned in and brushed a kiss across her lips. "One day at a time."

Was that the answer? She didn't have time to ponder the thought when he tugged on the elastic band of her pajama bottoms and pulled them down her legs. He raised her shoulders up far enough so that he could work her shirt over her head. In seconds she lay naked upon the crushed velvet of his chocolate-brown comforter. It was soft gliding against her skin.

"Roark—" He placed a finger against her lips.

"Let me make love to you." He pulled the towel around his hips loose and tossed it aside.

Sleek, powerful muscles moved beneath his skin. His erection jutted from the curls between his thighs as he climbed on the bed and eased beside her. In circular patterns, he traced the mound of one of her breasts working his way to the nipple that puckered in anticipation of his touch.

"I love how responsive your body is to my caress." Trapping

her gaze with his, Roark leaned forward and flicked his tongue across her nipple. A gasp left her mouth when he pulled the nub between his teeth applying enough pressure to send tingles exploding through her breast. Immediately, the fire coursed down toward the pulse of her sex. A flood of desire anointed her thighs. She squirmed beneath him trying to appease the throb.

"Don't tease me, Roark. I need you," she whimpered, wrapping her arms around his neck and pulling him to her. She wanted him now, needed him to vanquish the insecurities that plagued her.

As Tammy spread her legs, welcoming him into her cradle, he eased between them but didn't enter her. Instead, he pressed his lips to hers. His kiss was gentle, everything their previous loving was not. Slow and meticulous, he traced her mouth with his tongue, nipping occasionally. His gaze was fixed on hers, so hot it simmered.

"Mine," he breathed against her mouth. His touch, the intensity in his eyes left no doubt in her mind. She was his.

Tammy raised her hips, invitingly. "Take me, Roark. Make me yours all over again." There was a desperate plea in her voice, but she couldn't help it. She wanted to be this man's woman, wanted to fit into his life, be his mate.

A million questions flooded her thoughts, as she threw up a mind block. Could she have his children? Did vampiress carry babies? Could she be the woman he needed? Would he dismiss her if she couldn't reproduce? And, what about Marcellus? She cared for him.

His voice was sandpapery when he said, "Baby, stop thinking."

Stop. Stop. Stop. Her mind cried. *Take what you have now. Don't think about tomorrow.* Roark didn't leave her a choice when he angled his hips and thrust.

185

Tammy arched her back, her mouth parting, as his cock slid between her folds and filled her completely. "Roark. Oh God, yes." It was like hot iron meeting cool water, steamy and oh, so nice. Her inner muscles gripped him.

"Tight, baby. So fuckin' tight," he groaned, breaking eye contact for the first time as his eyelids slid closed.

Slow, measured strokes, he began to work in and out. Drawing far enough from her shelter that he left her feeling empty, starving for more. The moment was poignant. Each thrust meant to drive her crazy—and it was working. With each perfect stroke, he tuned her body like an instrument, drawing it so tight that if he plucked the right chord she would do anything he wanted.

The walls of her sex felt like a rubber band, shortening and thickening, growing ultra-sensitive with each rock of their bodies. Tammy was lost in a maze of sensation, not knowing which path would lead her to fulfillment and which one would make the ride go on forever. One particular thrust had her perched on the cliff, ready to soar into oblivion, and then Roark moved from atop her leaving her panting and confused.

He didn't say a word—didn't have to. All he did was roll to his back and present himself like a feast on a platter. Tammy wanted to pleasure him. The temptress inside her knew exactly what he wanted.

"*Mon prince.*" Her long fingernails scored his nipples and he flinched beneath her touch. A half-smile curved his mouth. The heaviness of his eyelids as he gazed down at her heated her blood. He was so sexy, so handsome. She was so lucky.

Muscles bunched beneath her palms as she stroked a feather-light path across his chest and down his solid abdomen. He sucked in a breath. "Come on, baby. Do it," Roark coaxed. Tammy wasn't through playing with him, but let him think what he wanted.

Leisurely, she moved down his body, parting his legs to glide between them. The grin on his face deepened. She could feel his anticipation when he caressed his hands up her arms and pulled her forward. She went willingly, inching closer to his eager cock, which jerked, once, twice when she released a warm breath across it.

Roark raised his hips and moaned. His grip tightened, pulling her closer to force her all the way.

She turned her head just in time to have his member graze her cheek. "Nuh-uh. It's my turn."

In truth, Tammy didn't know how long she could hold out. His scent was driving her insane. Low in her belly, one after another spasm was raising havoc. Just the thought of having him in her mouth made her horny as hell. She wanted him to look at her as he had Donne, with so much lust that she'd burst into flames. Just thinking of the two men together intensified the contractions.

His brows tugged together. "Baby?"

"I'm fine," she assured him.

"I feel you." Roark tried to pull her atop him, but she resisted him.

"You'll feel more of me when I wrap my lips around this." She folded her fingers around his erection, caressed her palm up and down.

He narrowed his gaze on her. "Damn, that feels good." Pumping his hips, he slid through her fingers until a pearly drop of come squeezed from the slit. "Take me now," he growled.

Tammy flattened her tongue, dragging it over his salty essence. He hissed, sucking a breath through clenched teeth. Around and around, she teased the sensitive crown, watching his eyes dilate, loving the almost painful expressions that played across his face. Muscles and tendons bulged beneath his control or lack of.

"Fuck me, baby." His breath caught and a tremor shook him. "Mouth. Now."

She took him between her lips, deeper still until she felt him at the back of her throat. The desperate sounds he made were as if she was killing him. Tammy wanted him to lose control, to let go. Closing her mouth around him, she sucked hard, skimming up his length. His fingertips buried into her shoulders as she made a downward spiral, stroking him with her tongue all the way. She let her teeth graze him gently, before pressing her tongue against the opening at the head.

Roark moved so quickly she didn't realize what was happening, until she sat astride him, his cock buried inside her. "Can't. Waste. It." The groan that pushed from his diaphragm was coarse. His release was sudden and unexpected as its warmth filled her. Spilling his seed inside her set off a series of spasms, Tammy only had to adjust her hips, find the right spot, and she joined him.

Palms flat on his chest, she threw back her head and let the orgasm wash over her. Her skin felt alive, tingling and throbbing. Every inch of her body was engulfed in the thrill of the man beneath her. The one who made her soul soar, her body burn, her heart ache. He was her life, her vein of existence. She was still enraptured by the moment, when he tugged her down.

His mouth moved hungrily over hers. "Love you," he moaned between the frenzy of his actions, licking, nipping, sucking. For a moment, Tammy thought she heard wrong. "So much," he added, before sealing their lips.

A knot formed in her throat. His hands were everywhere,

e an answer she raised her head. "Roark?" His eyes were
. His breathing was shallow.

he damn man was fast asleep, snoring softly.

sweeping across her skin, holding her tight
then caressing and stroking to set her body a
instance, she found herself flat on her back, l
like a blanket.

"Gotta have all of you," he murmured,
beneath her knees and spreading her thig
desire made his eyes glow like gold beneath
breathed in the sight of her. A resonating gro
throat. A single thrust, he entered her agair
she cried out with pleasure.

Like before, things elevated quickly. He'c
move when her pussy bore down on him. H
back his head sending his mane to flow arou
Skimming his palms up her calves, he circlec
his fingers drawing her impossibly wider
choreographed, when his hips shot forward th
in unison.

Two becoming one.

Together they plummeted into heaven; the
their souls intertwined.

Heart pounding, breathing erratic, he shift
side and plopped down beside her the bed
process. "Okay, that's never happened before."
up in his arms and smiled so sweetly at her. "
to me." He kissed her forehead, before falling sil

Tammy's body still hummed. For once th
beast had lain dormant and neither had he
which had to be contributed to her feeding ju
came to her. She moved placing her head on h
smoothing across the light auburn down, as sh
steady beat beneath her ear.

"Roark, do you think the heat is over?" V

Chapter Fifteen

The missile cut through the night heading for its victim with such accuracy that when it struck, it exploded on impact. Stephen howled as the cold wet ball of snow plastered his eyes shut. He spat, blinked several times, snowflakes falling from his eyelashes as he searched the horizon for his assailant.

Tammy jerked Roark behind the tree that hid her. Her body shook with quiet giggles. "He deserved it," she whispered.

"Are you ready for his retribution?" Roark brushed the hair from her face to gaze on her beauty. Last night he had admitted his love for her. Did she feel the same? Could she possibly in the short period of time? What about Donne? How did he fit into this triangle?

Laughter danced in her eyes as she peeked around the tree once more. "He wouldn't dare. I'm his queen," she said with confidence.

Roark liked the sound of that. He couldn't help dragging her into his arms and kissing her soundly. She was pliable, soft and feminine, beneath his caress.

Her expression turned seductive. "Do that again." Her voice glided over his skin like silk across glass. He answered her request with another penetrating kiss.

"Ah-ha!" Stephen startled Tammy right out of Roark's arms. She skirted around him using Roark as a shield against the man who still had remnants of her assault hanging from his brows.

"What do you mean, ah-ha, and what the devil happened to you?" she feigned innocence. Her eyes twinkled as she fought the grin that twitched at the corner of her mouth. Stephen bent to scoop up a handful of snow. "Roark?" His name was a high-pitch cry on Tammy's lips. "Tell him it wasn't me."

Roark remained silent, curiously watching the interplay between them. Loving the fact that she felt safe, guarded by his presence.

"Then who, my queen?" Stephen asked. Compacting the snow with his hands, he gazed around once more.

Just then Franc strolled into the opening. Tammy jutted a finger in his direction. "Him. It was Franc." Stephen let go of the snowball and it smacked his unsuspecting brother square in chest.

"*Umph.*" Confused, Franc looked from the splattering of white on his chest to Stephen. "You crazy sonofabitch. We're too old for these games." Even still he retrieved enough snow that Roark worried if his friend's aim strayed they would be struck instead. He moved Tammy further behind the tree, out of the line of fire.

In just seconds all out war broke out between his guards. Roark's little minx stood back and watched, pride glowing on her pink cheeks. She laughed, cramming her hands into the fur-lined pockets of her coat. Dressed in white, from head to toe, she looked like an angel in skintight ski leggings. Yet Roark knew the truth. There was a little bit of witch inside her.

Ducking behind the tree once more, she dodged a stray bullet. What had begun as a snow fight, turned into a wrestling match when Franc dove at Stephen's legs knocking him to the ground. Franc was older by three minutes, but in all the time

Roark knew them, he couldn't say which of the brothers was stronger or faster. Their feuds as children had always ended in a tie. This one was no different. The question was which would give in first. They were huffing and puffing tangled in each other's arms, mumbling.

The merriment on Tammy's face faded. She reached out and grasped Roark's arm. "I didn't expect this. Make them stop. Please."

Roark knew they would never hurt each other. It was what brothers did. Grown or not. Tammy wouldn't know that being an only child and a girl at that. "You are their queen. You make them stop." He received a frown for his retort.

"Fine." She straightened her backbone, raised her chin like he was getting accustom to seeing her do when she took control. Cautiously, she stepped beyond the safety of the tree and moved toward Stephen and Franc. "Stop it, you two." When they didn't immediately release each other she stepped closer. "Right now," she stated firmly. "This is not becoming of the king's guards." She sounded like a mother hen chastising her chicks.

"Now," Stephen yelled as his hand snaked out and caught Tammy by the ankle. She released a high-pitched cry of surprise, throwing her arms into the air, flailing, before landing along side of them. Franc was quick with the handful of snow he had secreted away and smashed it right into her face.

Her wide-eyed expression was priceless. But the brothers weren't through with her. They pelted her with one snowball after another before she could crawl to her feet. She swayed, brushing away the flakes from her face. She looked like a snowman—woman, ready for Christmas.

"R-R-Roark." She sputtered clearing the ice from her mouth, but he was caught in a fit of laughter. His mate had received her just deserts. "Ohhh..." She scowled. "You think this is funny?" He couldn't answer her for the tears in his eyes.

When she bent low, he knew exactly what she intended. "Don't do it, Tammy." Before she could release the ball, two other ones smacked his jacket, knocking him off balance. He stumbled and fell the rest of the way when his mate rammed him. Roark reached out, taking her with him. Together they tumbled to the ground, Tammy face first.

For a moment, she didn't move and Roark feared the fall had hurt her. It began only slightly, a timid movement, then her shoulders began to shake, a stream of laughter followed. Covered in snow she rolled upon her back. "I don't remember when I've had so much fun." She looked up at him and Roark thought he'd melt. "Thank you." He was about to pull her to him, when Franc and Stephen approached. They stood over them, chuckling.

"Trouble. I tell you she's trouble," Stephen said staring down at Tammy. She kicked a leg out, but he avoided it by jumping aside.

"Were they like this the whole trip?" Franc asked, shaking his head.

"The whole way," Roark confirmed.

Franc extended Roark his hand. "Must have been painful for you. Looks like I got the easy job of facing the pack."

Roark hadn't forgotten about that particular detail. He just hadn't had the opportunity to speak with his guards after he and Tammy rose this evening. As he spoke to Franc, Stephen assisted Tammy to her feet. His guard raised his hand as if to brush the snow from her clothing, and then he stepped back, allowing Roark to take over. "You need to get out of those wet clothes."

As Roark and Tammy walked hand in hand back to the

cabin, Franc talked. "The pack is hesitant, but willing to accept the queen. Martin is her biggest supporter. If he can look past the death of his son, most of the pack can as well." Snow crunched beneath their feet. "In all honesty, I'm a little surprised." His gazed darted toward Tammy. "No disrespect, my queen."

"Tammy," she said.

Franc nodded.

"As you are aware, Martin has a lot of pull in the pack. It has been a long time since we have had a queen. Everyone is curious about the queen— Uh, Tammy." Franc stumbled over her name as if he was having a problem between the formalities he felt were due her. "Yes, there is some fear—the legend has been conveyed over and over. The undead perspective is what troubles them the most. Of course, it didn't hurt that Manny has professed her beauty and made her into a fairy princess amongst our people."

Tammy blushed. The worry that had dulled her eyes when Franc began speaking seemed to lift with each of his words. Yet Roark knew Franc. There was something in his delivery, a piece missing he wasn't sharing. For Tammy's sake, Roark would wait until he and Franc were alone to uncover it.

As they entered from the back porch of his cabin, Roark stomped the snow from his boots. The rest did the same. A finger beneath Tammy's chin, he kissed her nose. "Go upstairs and change."

Tammy frowned. "There's something Franc did not say?"

"You're being paranoid. We have guests or I'd join you, that's all," he lied. When she hesitated, he thought she saw through him. He breathed a sigh of relief when she marched from the kitchen. They each took a seat around the large pine table. The scent of stew simmering on the stovetop made his stomach growl. Lonnie had been busy. When Roark was sure Tammy was out of earshot, he turned to Franc and raised a brow.

"Your cousin has been busy." Franc scraped the legs of his chair across the floor as he scooted it closer to the table. "He has gathered a small following. Layton has worked throughout the night to convince the pack, especially the women, that their men will fall under the Black Widow's spell."

Roark's eyes widened. "Black Widow?"

"That's what Layton is calling her. He repeated what happened to Manny. I'm afraid the admiration Manny has shown for our queen has backfired."

"Well shit." Roark rubbed his hand over his damp hair. As he studied the swirling grain in the table, he pondered the situation. If he'd learned anything it was to never underestimate women. They could be more deadly than a male wolf if their children or mates were threatened. Stephen cleared his throat, bringing Roark's head up. "There's more?"

"A town meeting tonight." Stephen glanced toward the microwave glowing eight forty-five "It starts in fifteen minutes."

Roark pushed from the table and stood. "Let me change clothes, talk to Tammy, and then we'll go." He stopped at the door leading into the front room. "One of you must stay with her. Stephen?"

"Of course. I'll just run over to my place and change."

"Okay, be back in ten." Roark heard the back door slam as he headed for the stairs taking them two at a time. At the top he paused. What the hell was he going to say to her? Drawing closer to their bedroom door, he could scent her perfume—and orchids? He pushed the door open hearing water splash. He followed the sound into the bathroom. There amongst a million bubbles lay his mate. A tranquil expression softened her face as she soaked in the large Jacuzzi tub.

Without opening her eyes, she said, "*Joignez-moi?*" She exhaled softly. "Join me?" Her hair was pinned atop her head. She was a vision of seduction.

Roark wanted nothing more, but it wasn't in the cards. "Baby, there's a town meeting shortly. I'll be back as soon as I can. Stephen will be down stairs if you need him." Okay, that wasn't too bad.

Slowly her eyes opened. She eased into a sitting position. Bubbles hid her delectable breasts from his sight. "I'm going with you."

"It's better if you don't." He kicked off his shoes and started to strip out of his coat, jeans and sweater. "Truth is Layton, my cousin, has stirred up several of the folk. I just want to put their minds to ease. Relax, baby, I'll be back as soon as I can." He disappeared into the walk-in closet off the bathroom and grabbed some clean clothes. When he returned to the bathroom she was still sitting in the tub.

Tammy swallowed hard. "You don't want me go?"

He jerked on his pants, leaning against the counter to roll a sock on one foot, before switching feet and donning the other sock. "It's not that. I don't want you hurt by his comments. Layton can be cruel." Roark stood and pulled a sweater over his head.

"You don't think I know what they're saying?" Her broken laughter made him stop midway of pulling on his boot. "Do you think your people are any kinder than Marcellus's? I'm a freak in their eyes. Wouldn't it be better if they saw firsthand the demon that I am?" She stood. Soap slithered down her body.

He slid his foot all the way into his boot and then went to her and cupped her cheeks. "Please. Wait for me. I won't be long." A knock on the bedroom door put him into action. He grabbed his other shoe and headed for the door. When he opened it and stepped into the hallway Stephen met him.

"Franc and Manny are waiting downstairs. Creighton and Bryant are with them." Two more of Roark's guards. "I hear it'll be a full house. Good luck." Stephen shook Roark's hand.

Roark pulled the bedroom door closed before tugging on his boot. "No matter what happens keep her safe. Get her to Donne immediately if— Just get her to Donne." Stephen gave him a friendly pat on the back and they both turned toward the stairs.

Roark was not looking forward to the night ahead.

Chapter Sixteen

"This is bullshit." Tammy paced the length of the bedroom again. Her ankle boots clicked across the wooden floor. She started toward the door to join Roark and then pulled to a halt. His guard dog would stop her. "He'd have to catch me first." Well, that was smart. Even if she made it past Stephen she had no idea where to go. She had yet to take in the town. In fact, this evening Roark pretty much hid her from the very people that were supposed to call her their queen.

Tammy glanced at the clock above the fireplace for the hundredth time. Ten o'clock. Roark had been gone for an hour. Even the garland draping the mantel didn't cheer her up. She tugged nervously at the cowl neckline of her oversized red sweater.

The sudden ring of the telephone startled her and she pressed a palm to her chest. As the ringing continued, she moved toward the telephone and picked up the receiver. "Hello."

"My pet, how's it going?"

As if all bone mass in her legs deteriorated, Tammy plopped down on the bed. "Marcellus?" She clutched the receiver. "Oh, Marcellus, I wish you were here." It was the truth. She missed him horribly.

"What's the matter?" His anxiety bled through the line.

Her chin quivered and she fought to hold it together. "Roark is at a town meeting."

"That can't be good. Where are you?"

"In Roark's cabin."

"Alone?"

"No. Stephen is downstairs."

"Tamanen, I know this is tough on you, but Lanier knows what he's doing. If he thought it best for you to remain behind, there is a reason. Trust him."

"I do, but—"

"But what, my pet?"

"I hate this."

"I know. Sit tight. I hope to join you tomorrow night."

The click on other end of the telephone was deafening. Tammy set the telephone back in its cradle and rose from the bed. Maybe she could convince Stephen to take her to Roark. Reaching for the door, she heard a crash and then another. She swung open the door and raced toward the stairs coming to a screeching halt at the first step. The scent of blood filled her nose and awakened her hunger. She had fed upon rising, but there was something more that gnawed at her gut. Tammy didn't need to see to know that violence had made a visit. It hung heavy in the air.

"Stephen," Tammy cried, as she flew down the stairs. He lay unconscious on the floor beside the couch. Blood oozed from a gash to the back of his head pooling around him. She kneeled beside him and pressed two fingers to the pulse in his neck. It beat, but sluggish. She needed to get help.

Without thinking, she sprung to her feet and raced for the door, stopping dead in her tracks when she saw Lonnie. The woman who had taken care of her and made her feel welcome lay in a puddle of blood. Her neck ripped open, her body covered in cuts and scrapes. Nauseated, Tammy knelt to feel for a pulse—one that didn't exist.

Tammy gagged, cupping her mouth, even as the blood and violence called to her like it had when Roark fought the wolf. She pushed to her feet, slipping in the blood, falling only to rise and stagger forward. Her beast raged inside, itching to be set free. It raised its head, sniffed the air. She recognized a scent. The unusual aroma ran through her memory banks, but she didn't come up with a face to go with it. Or maybe she just didn't know enough to understand what she scented, because she would have sworn she detected a vampire amongst the lycanthrope.

Trying to figure out who was to blame was wasting time. There was no hope for Lonnie, but she could save Stephen—had to.

Tammy jerked the door open, nearly pulling it from its hinges with her preternatural strength and ran out into the street. Snow was lightly falling as she trudged through its depths. Tears blurred the Christmas lights on each of the homes she passed. She didn't know where she was going, until she heard the sounds of people shouting. In the distance, lights from a large building in the center of town glowed brightly. As she drew closer, Tammy could hear arguing. The words weren't clear as her mind became hazy. She couldn't shake the scent of blood that intensified her thirst. She needed to feed, but not before she saved Stephen.

Someone screamed, but she ignored them, focusing on the door—on getting to Roark. Just as she reached for the doorknob, the door flung open and Tammy stumbled and fell to her hands and knees. It was then she realized her hands were covered in blood. When she looked up she stared into condemning eyes. There were all around her.

"Tammy." She heard Roark's voice as he pushed his way through the crowd. "What happened?" He pulled her into his arms and began to smooth his hands over her.

"Not me. Stephen. He's hurt." She licked her lips tasting blood and her vision blurred. Spasms clenched her belly. She barely got the words out, "Lonnie's dead," before another spasm twisted her abdomen. "Help me," she whispered holding on to him. "I don't know how much longer I can control it."

"Black widow," someone yelled from the back. "She's killed again." The low rumble of the crowd built into a roar.

"No." Tammy grasped the sides of Roark's jacket. "I didn't do it." Oh God. She hadn't even thought that this would be blamed on her, which made her a complete idiot. Of course, they would believe she was guilty.

"Franc, take Manny and check on Stephen. Creighton, determine who is missing amongst us." The tall, lanky man with sable hair began to look around the room as Roark issued orders one after the other and then turned to her. "Tell me what happened." His expression was cold as he pinned her with a glare.

"I didn't do it," Tammy repeated frantically. "Please make them believe me." She shuddered as hunger gnawed at her belly.

"I know, baby. Just tell me what happened." All color drained from his face. "It's bad. I can feel it." He pulled her arms from around him, stood, and leaned down to pick her up. "Try to hold on."

Held in Roark's embrace was both heaven and hell. The swish of his blood flowing freely through his veins caused her to snuggle up to his neck. But the penetrating eyes that followed them made her cling tighter to her control. Her mouth salivated. Twice she almost gave in as he moved through the snow that began to fall harder all around them.

His boots were loud against the porch as he made his way through the already opened door of his home. There were several people Tammy didn't know standing around Lonnie. A woman who was the spitting image of the dead girl, only twenty years her senior, was crying softly. When Lonnie's mother raised her tear-stained face to Tammy everything inside her died. She didn't need to hear the words to see the accusation in those red-rimmed eyes.

For once Tammy wished she could just disappear, and she did—vanish—right before everyone's eyes. The next thing Tammy knew she was standing knee-deep in snow at the back of Roark's cabin. She heard him scream her name as the change swept over her. She shook off her clothing and ran.

In her wolf form, Tammy bounded over fallen trees and other obstacles, the desire to turn back around and go to Roark strong. The need to set him free was even stronger. No one would believe that she hadn't attacked Stephen and killed Lonnie. Roark was the leader of the lycanthrope pack. Like the vampires, the wolves would never accept her. They saw her as the ultimate Black Widow. Death rode beside her.

The wind kicked up and bit cruelly at her ears as she headed south, down the mountain. Reality was slow in coming as she covered one mile and then another. Hunger and now desire wreak havoc inside her.

Seeking Marcellus would only start another set of problems. If the pack didn't catch her in Phoenix, Marcellus's people would see to her demise.

Tammy had nowhere to run—nowhere to hide.

The knowledge felt like an anchor around her neck. Her footsteps leaden, she trudged through the deep snow. Her eyes stung. Ice crusted her fur. The snow was falling faster, thicker.

The only saving grace was that her footprints and scent would be carried away. There would be no chance of either Roark or Marcellus finding her—if she lived the night. Soon it would be morning. The vampire within would perish, ending the monster she had become.

A whimper pushed from her muzzle with the thought of her death. Yet Tammy knew she couldn't live like this. She knew Roark and Marcellus would never let her go, even if it meant their life at her hands or by someone else's because of her.

A sharp cramp tore her feet from beneath her and she stumbled to the ground. She shook with its intensity. For a moment she thought of lying there, waiting for the light of day. She was tired and her paws hurt almost as much as her heart. Her chest heaved. She couldn't find the energy to rise until she heard the howl of a lone wolf in the distance.

Roark. He was calling her.

Regret for what she would never experience or have nearly suffocated her. A family—someone to love her.

Tammy thought of Roark and Marcellus and found the strength to push to her feet, now bruised and bleeding in the snow as she began to run. Time truly wasn't her friend. She had no idea where she was going, only that she had to keep miles between Roark and her, allow the sun to crest the Four Peak Mountains that were just a shadow through the dying snowstorm.

A stone sliced the bottom of her paw and she yelped in pain. Tuned to survival mode, she opened her muzzle to howl, barely catching herself. She couldn't let Roark find her. Desperately, she continued onward.

Several times Roark howled—calling to her. Each time spasms clenched her belly. The fur on her back ruffled in fast waves. Hunger clawed at her stomach. She needed to feed—she needed rest—she needed Roark.

For miles she sprinted, pushing herself. The burst of energy died a quick death as she became engulfed in the screams of her body. Her legs melted from beneath her. The whimper that surfaced turned into a cry as her human form replaced that of the wolf.

Curled in a ball, she rocked from side to side, stones and sticks beneath the snow stabbing her. A blazing fireball burned in her stomach releasing a flood of moisture between her naked thighs. Nipples taut with need ached, shooting more flames toward her belly.

"Roark." Breathless she called his name. In her tormented state she could smell his earthy scent replace that of pine permeating her nose, feel his warm arms cradling her.

"You foolish woman," Roark scolded, as the last of his fur dissolved, leaving him naked and vulnerable to the elements. "Why the hell did you run away?"

"Roark." Even as she snuggled closer to him, Tammy knew she had to leave him. The spasms were coming faster, more violent, as she twisted and jerked out of his arms. "Leave me. Now," she groaned. Heat whipped through her like wildfire, hot and out of control. His rapid pulse did nothing more than feed her hunger.

"I'll never leave you." Voice low and strained, he sounded so sincere. "We need to hurry. The sun will be rising soon. There's a cave several miles back."

No. Tammy scrambled onto her hands and knees to avoid his outstretched hand. If she fed from him now she would kill him. Besides, it was almost dawn, all she needed was thirty more minutes. Already the glow of the rising sun was cresting the mountains.

Frantically, she kicked at him. He dodged her feet, but that didn't stop him from trying to reach her. "Get away. Please, Roark. Run," she screamed. But it was already too late.

A contraction clamped down hard and vicious. Her gasp turned into a purr. Her body undulated, letting the pain wash over her. His closeness—his smell—drove her over the edge of sanity.

Tammy rolled to her back and arched as the temptress presented herself. She ran her hands down her hungry flesh, palmed the weight of her heavy breasts, as she pinched their peaks between her fingers.

Fangs pushed through her gums. She stroked them seductively with her tongue as her eyelids fell half-mast. "*J'ai besoin de vous,*" she cooed, repeating mentally, "*I need you.*"

Without pause, he went to lie beside her, and she turned onto her side to face him. His arms closed around her. "I know, baby. But first we need to leave here."

"No," she insisted, curling her fingers around his semi-hard cock. It twitched against her palm, lengthening. She stroked him, up and down. Satisfaction touched her mouth, before he captured her in an urgent kiss.

He tasted of male, of heat and hunger. She couldn't get enough. Her body writhed against his, as she sucked his bottom lip between hers and bit. The sweet flavor of blood made her fingernails dig into his back pulling him closer.

He tore his lips from hers. "Tammy. We have to go." A hint of unease whispered in his voice.

But she couldn't stop—not now.

She guided his cock between her splayed thighs and impaled herself on his hardness.

"*Oui...*" Immediate gratification rushed through her like a cool breeze. The knots in her stomach released. Her hips thrust against his seeking more.

In a quick move, he rolled her onto her back. "We have to hurry." His eyes were dark with desire. His nostrils flared. He slammed his hips into her cradle, over and over. Fast and deep, he penetrated her. Even as anxiety furrowed his brows, he murmured, "Wet. So tight."

Her climax came swift and without mercy. She arched, bucking beneath him. He growled, pinning her to the ground by her shoulders as he quickened the pace. Pleasure and pain blurred as it tore at her insides. He swallowed her scream with a kiss that matched the savageness of his body driving between her legs. Roark came violently and in the process his canines pierced her tongue, blood filled her mouth. She trembled at the exquisite taste flowing down her throat. Her mouth watered. She needed to taste him.

The smell of his skin so close clouded her senses. Tammy didn't realize she had pierced his flesh until his essence trickled down her throat. His heart beat out a staccato against her chest. Still she continued to drink. Her fingernails scored his back, sinking into his flesh to mark him.

"Tammy." His voice was strangely hollow against the thudding of her heart. "Tammy," he repeated weakly.

Awareness struck.

She froze.

There was a faint flutter to his heart, not the strong rapid beat that existed only a moment ago. Her tongue swiped over her bite, closing the wound, as she wiggled out from beneath him and pulled him into her arms.

Cradling him in her lap, she cried, "Roark. Oh God, I'm so sorry." As she sobbed, she glimpse the rays of dawn shimmering over the mountain tops. Tammy didn't care that in a moment, she would breathe her last breath. All she could think about was saving Roark.

With the sharp end of her canine she tore open her wrist and pressed it to his lips. "Drink."

Nothing.

She pushed with her mind to get him to follow her command—needing him to live. A cry of relief surfaced when she felt a tickle against her wrist. With each swallow the suction grew stronger.

Her belly tightened. How much was enough? When she felt faint, she extracted her hand and closed the wound on her wrist with a stroke of her tongue.

"Tammy?" His voice lacked vitality, but he was alive. She pressed her lips to his forehead.

Night had faded. Tammy glanced down at Roark desperate to speak before it was too late. "I have something to say. I don't know if I'll say it right—"

"The sun— Tammy, no..." He tried to rise, but his strength waned and he fell back into her lap.

Emotion stole her breath, but she found her voice. "I love you." The words rushed out. "I don't know when it happened," she gulped in air, filling her lungs too fast, "or why so soon. But I love you. Don't ever forget that."

His fingers curled around her arms as if he wouldn't let her go. With what was left of his strength he pulled her to him and held her tightly.

The light of day immersed them. Seconds ticked by. Nothing happened. There was no bursting into flames. Absolutely nothing, except for the uneasy masculine chuckle that rose and grew in volume.

Talk about an embarrassing moment. Tammy had just spilled her guts to the man and he was laughing.

"Ahhh...baby. Judging by the pout on your face, you almost look disappointed in not becoming a human torch."

She pulled away, whacking him on the chest. "It isn't funny. I was scared shitless."

A mischievous grin curved his lips. "So you love me?"

Crap! She did admit that. "I—" Yes. She felt a deep connection to him, but also Marcellus. The week had been a whirlwind of life shattering change. Logic told her it just wasn't possible to love two men, especially in such a short period. "I thought I was dying."

His brows dipped. "Then you don't love me?"

Tammy sighed, feeling as if she held the weight of the world on her shoulders. "Roark, I'm so confused." How could she be in love with him and Marcellus too?

"Don't be." His face softened and he cupped her cheek. "Inherently, mates bond together. I knew I loved you the minute my beast touched yours. It's nature taking control of our needs that our human side is too stubborn to admit."

She frowned. "But in this case nature really fucked up. I could have killed you."

"But you didn't. Instead you saved me." Roark brushed his lips lightly across hers. He was shivering so hard that their teeth clinked together. She brushed her palms briskly over his skin. He was so cold. Oddly, she wasn't as fazed by the biting wind as he was. Thankfully, it had quit snowing. A new blanket of white covered the horizon as far as she could see.

Tucking her hands beneath his arms, Tammy helped him to his feet. "We need to get you somewhere out of the cold." Wait. If she could dissolve his clothing could she—

Thinking warm thoughts, she imagined them clothed. A gust of wind stirred the snow, picking it up to surround them.

The air shimmered. Wide-eyed, his shock was apparent, matching her own. In seconds, they were both covered head to toe in gloves, sweaters, fur-lined parkas, ski pants and snow boots.

"Nice, but—" He tried to smile, but it didn't reach his wary eyes. "Our wolf forms are more appropriate for the return trip, plus it will restore our energy."

"Return?" Tammy's voice pitched sharply. Her heart started to palpitate. "I can't go back." What was he thinking?

He reached for her, but she dodged his grasp. "Baby, you have to go back. Prove your innocence."

"How? No one is going to believe me."

"Something wasn't right about the scene. You disappeared before I could get to the bottom of it. By the way, how long have you known you could vanish like that?"

"Believe me. I was as surprised as you were."

"Why did you run?" There was so much hurt in his eyes, she immediately felt ashamed. But what choice did she have?

"No one would have believed me."

"I did." Roark opened his arms and she flew into them.

"How did I get so lucky to find you?"

"It was destiny. Now get us out of these clothes and let's go home."

Chapter Seventeen

A search party met up with Tammy and Roark as they entered the boundaries of his land. Franc, Manny, Bryant, and Creighton were joined with several more of Roark's guards, each wearing an expression of disapproval. Roark had heard their howls—their calls, but he had thought it better to not announce their arrival. He needed time to strategize. Even with the long trek home, not a single idea had come to him.

The sun shining high above them glistened off the snow. The blinding reflection hurt his wind-burned eyes. His coat was crusted with snow. His legs ached. He was tired in both body and mind. Glancing at Tammy, he knew she felt no better. She moved slowly, her head bowed, her muzzle agape. She panted against the frosty air. He could smell her anxiety as his guards folded around them.

"*So?*" Roark asked, using the telepathic link between them.

"*Stephen said the blow came from behind,*" Franc supplied. "*He thought Lonnie was at the town meeting, that he and the queen were alone. He was still unconscious when I found him.*"

"*There were no signs of struggle?*" Roark asked.

"*None,*" Creighton, the long lanky sable wolf said. "*Which is odd in itself.*" He chanced a quick look in Tammy's direction. Roark knew the rest of his guards were curious about their queen, especially one accused of the death of one of their own.

"Lonnie died quickly. Her death staged to look like an attack."

Bryant, the only white wolf in the group, moved up beside him. *"Do you believe her?"* Roark's guard didn't even flinch when Tammy's ears lay flat against her head. She bared her teeth at him and snarled.

"Yes." Roark didn't hesitate. He tried to restrain his anger but a rumble vibrated in his throat. Bryant lowered his head and backed away. *"Not only do I believe her, but the fact that Stephen had not been ravished is evidence that she is not at fault. New to her conversion, she wouldn't have been able to cause such violence and control it enough to only wound Stephen."* Additionally, a wolf's first kill was savage and unmerciful. Mutilating and devouring the kill would have been a normal reaction. His people knew this.

"So what's your plan?" Franc asked.

Roark drew his ears erect. He raised his head. *"To walk down the center of town."*

"Bold. But do you think it wise?" Franc slowed his pace as if to give Roark an opportunity to rethink his decision.

A gentle breeze ruffled the hair down Tammy's back. *"Listen to Franc. Perhaps we should enter from the back of your home."*

Roark met her startled gaze. *"We have nothing to hide."*

"But she ran," Bryant interjected, playing the devil's advocate. The wolf was young, but he balanced the group by critically examining the facts and raising objections. Sometimes he was a little trying, but Roark knew he meant well.

Creighton, who loped ahead of them to conduct reconnaissance, was quiet strength. He followed orders and felt strongly about the old ways. He preferred to remain behind when trips to the city were required. The chocolate-brown wolf pulled to a halt atop the hill. He held his head high, alert, as he scanned the countryside.

Roark drew his attention back to Bryant's comment. *"Running isn't always a sign of guilt, but fear. What choice did your queen have? Our people have not embraced her, neither have Donne's. If you were in her shoes what would you have done?"*

"Run," Bryant relented.

As they topped the mountain joining Creighton, Tammy jerked to an abrupt stop *"Roark?"* Her voice quivered. *"What if you can't get them to believe me?"* She didn't wait for his answer, before she continued. *"I am what I am. I will fight with everything in my power to survive."*

If she expected his disapproval, she was wrong. *"I would expect no more or less from you. You are my queen. Strong—alpha. You were meant to rule beside me. Now raise your chin and let's go."*

Tammy did just that. She held her head high as they trotted down the hill and straight into town. Several people strolling down the street stopped in their tracks. From homes and store fronts doors opened and more people spilled out into the street. It wasn't long before it looked like the entire town converged upon them.

The mood of the crowd was eerily calm, like the quiet before the storm. No one stirred as Roark and his entourage continued to pad down the cobblestone street. The only movement was the shifting of eyes as condemnatory gazes followed them.

Head held high, Tammy strolled regally by his side, but he sensed her tension growing, knew she dreaded even feared the confrontation with their people. He moved closer brushing her side, lending her strength. She leaned into him, presenting him with a half-smile.

As they made their way further into town toward the large Town Hall building, the masses folded around them. Just before they reached the large Christmas tree decorated in silver ornaments and white lights, Layton emerged from the throng. "We demand justice."

"*Justice*?" One minute Roark stood before them a wolf—the next a man. His aplomb wavered slightly when a whisper of wind swept up his legs, caressing his body to clothe him from neck to toes in a thick flannel shirt, jeans, boots and a parka. There was a single gasp from all present as their stares fell on Tammy, knowing exactly where the magic had hailed from. As each of his guards released their hold on the wolf, she gifted them with clothing similar to his. If the moment hadn't been so grave, he would have laughed at their shocked expressions.

Tammy was the last to take human form. In a great show of strength and power, a flurry of snow rose, shielding her from all eyes. Pride squeezed his chest as she made the change smoothly, so that he didn't hear a single muscle or tendon pop. When the snow fell to the ground again, Tammy stood donned in black—leather boots and a skintight bodysuit that showed off every curve and mound of her sensual body. Amazingly, he could almost see a curtain fall to mask her true feelings behind a wall of indifference. Power shimmered around her like heat waves rising from asphalt on a blistering summer day. The unmistakable show of sovereignty made the people in the front take a step backward.

Tammy's position was clear—she would not cower beneath their animosity.

Roark pinned his stern sight on Layton. "Find me the murderer and you will receive your justice."

"She stands beside you," Layton snarled, watching both Roark and Tammy cautiously.

In a blur of speed, Tammy went from standing beside Roark to behind Layton, her arm wrapped around his throat.

as pregnant—carried not one, but two of Roark's
'or the first time her beast felt appeased, her
seeking out Roark as he stood before his people and
ended her.

ts of Marcellus crept into her mind and Roark's
d. How would Marcellus feel about her pregnancy?
rive a wedge between them? He had to accept it,
e had dreamed of a family—wanted a stable, normal

he hell was she saying? This was as far from normal
ld get. The fairytale—the happily-ever-after—was not
was living. She cast her gaze across the horde of
clearly resented her existence. Frowns and barely
natred were on their faces. This world didn't exist in
mpires and werewolves didn't exist. Not to mention,
anted her out of Roark's life to the point of murder.
were no different than Marcellus's.

y placed a palm on her flat belly. Two lives grew
—sons. The knowledge made her heart swell. The soft
the child next to her drew Tammy out of her
s. She once again eased to her knees.

s wrong, Sue Ellen?" she asked, brushing back a
ril.

s sensitive to the pack's outburst." Numerous people
ng at the same time. The noise level rose with their
e Ellen feels their emotions. It's too much at times,"
red the explanation. "It's time for us to leave." She
l her fingers in her daughter's. Mother and daughter
nuch alike. Would Tammy's boys look like Roark?

lled eyes gazed up at Tammy. "Will you come with

d, Tammy started to reach for an excuse when Laura

Surprise turned to fear as Layton grabbed her arm and attempted to break her hold. But his strength ebbed beneath hers. When her incapacitating grasp tightened, his mouth and eyes widened.

"Do not fight me." Tammy's words were a whisper of menace that forced Layton's hands to his side. Her hold lessened and he sucked in a strangled breath of relief. Yet she wasn't finished. Releasing a hiss, she pressed her lips to the vein throbbing in his throat. A cry met her touch. She answered it with a slow caress of her tongue from his neck to his ear. "If I wanted to kill you," she paused, "you'd be dead."

In a blink of an eye, she stood by Roark's side once again. Layton's knees buckled. He fought to keep his footing.

Legs parted, Tammy's nostrils flared as if she dared Layton to speak. Roark could sense her strength, the power of her beast and temptress standing together, presenting them as one. It was an omnipotent moment. She had never been so sexy or dangerous. Electricity crackled and popped in her hair as it fell around her shoulders like a crown of light, even in the daylight.

Several members of the pack faded toward the back of the crowd. Others stood slack-jawed. It was a child, Sue Ellen Chambers, who slipped from her mother's grasp and approached.

"Sue Ellen!" Laura Chambers screamed, but it was too late. Her daughter already stood before Tammy.

A tilt backward of her head, long dark ringlets fell down the child's back as she narrowed her curious stare on Tammy. "Terry says you will kill me in my sleep."

A hush fell over the crowd.

"And who is this Terry?" Tammy asked dryly.

Sue Ellen jutted a finger toward her ten-year-old brother who skirted behind his mother. A bushel of black hair appeared as the boy chanced a peek toward his sister. Their mother took a step forward, but Roark motioned her back.

Tammy knelt to come eye to eye with Sue Ellen. "What do you think?"

Sue Ellen shook her head as she reached out to touch Tammy's hair. There was a crackle and a spark upon contact. The child burst into a fits of giggles that died slowly. "I felt you. Knew you were coming."

Tammy's forehead furrowed. She shot a questioning glance to Roark.

"Sue Ellen is a special child. At six she has already shown exemplary psychic powers. She knows things others do not," Roark explained, ruffling the child's hair.

"Well, Sue Ellen, it is a pleasure to meet you." Tammy pushed to her feet. She extended the girl her hand, but was taken aback by the child's sudden embrace as she hugged Tammy around the waist.

"Oh, Momma." The child gasped, glancing over her shoulder. "Come here and listen." She drew her attention back to Tammy. The child's eyes were as large as saucers, her grin from ear to ear. "There's two," she breathed.

"Two?" Tammy and Roark asked in unison.

Laura stepped forward, her son following cautiously behind her. The woman dipped her head to Roark as her daughter leaned forward, pinning her ear to Tammy's abdomen. "Babies, my queen. Sue Ellen is saying you are with child—twins."

Neither Roark nor Tammy spoke. They just stared at one another. Like a bird his heart took wings and soared. Tammy carried his children. Elated, he jerked her into his embrace and kissed her soundly.

"Oh God. Who's the father?" Roark knew by the shock on

---

her face that she hadn't meant to shar

"I am," he answered on their men *procreate. They're my children."*

Time stood still. No one existed until Sue Ellen released a contrite sigh

Roark felt his pulse stutter as the happiness right from beneath him. "Yo

"No." Sue Ellen twisted her mout they're boys and not girls." Her cre Roark and Tammy burst into laught celebrating their precious moment, esp

"N-no," he stammered. "She mur to the crowd, his voice rising in de meant Layton's chance of leading t away. "How do we know that Grady hand?"

"Enough," Roark roared. "You tr accusations, cousin. I gave you lenier not be so generous the next time.' constituents. "Your queen is inno evidence and you will find it so. Lo Your knowledge of our women's heat c is proof enough. What is of most ir person or persons responsible for our he knew—someone wanted to frame Ta

Tammy was on a rollercoaster of up one side and down the next. She composure when confronting Roark': slipped, took a nosedive, when Sue F fear. Within a heartbeat, the very br stolen.

She children temptre fiercely

Tho words fa Would i because life forev

Wha as one the life people concealE normal. someonE His peop

Tam inside h crying wonderir

"Wh fallen te

"Shε were tall anger. "§ Laura o intertwir looked sε

Tear us?"

Star

genuinely smiled and nodded her head to send her short bob of black hair bouncing. "Yes, we would love you to visit with us. Let the men deal with this unpleasant subject."

"*Mom!*" Terry screeched. Panic tightened his features.

"Hush." Laura pushed her son behind her. "He's been listening too much to the older boys, my queen."

Tammy's eyes began to burn. Dammit. This woman's kindness would not make her cry nor would she allow the child's fear to steal this moment away from her. Before she could refuse Laura's invitation, Roark said, "Thank you, Laura. I would appreciate it."

"Roark?" Tammy couldn't leave him at a time like this.

"There's nothing you can do here. The facts speak for themselves. Go. Enjoy yourself." Roark brought her hand to his mouth and kissed it. He turned to Franc. "Guard her with your life."

Franc ran his knuckles over Terry's head. "Come on, boy. Looks like we're stuck watching the females." Funny thing was Franc didn't appear disappointed as he glanced toward Laura and she blushed.

Several women joined them as they made their way through the throng. Tammy tried to ignore the condemning glares flashed her way, but it was difficult. Her beast and temptress became agitated, crawling beneath her skin, until Sue Ellen took her hand and smiled so sweetly up at her.

As they entered a small cabin, the three women who had joined them began to move in all directions, peeling off their jackets as they separated. It was clear they felt comfortable in Laura's home as one went toward the refrigerator, another to a cabinet, while a plump, grey-haired woman who had introduced herself as Betty headed toward a drawer. Dishes and silverware clinked.

Several minutes later they sat around the kitchen table with steaming cups of hot chocolate before them. The rich smell caressed Tammy's nose. The scent of cinnamon and pine burning in the hearth mingled. All around her were signs of Christmas. From the homey stockings hanging before the fire to the tree decorated in strings of popcorn and homemade ornaments.

"Where are you from, my queen?" asked Betty as she pushed a plate of gingerbread cookies in front of Tammy. There was a brief pause around the table, until Tammy reached for a cookie and took a bite. She guessed it was normal that they would wonder whether she ate or if blood was her main course of existence.

"Please call me Tammy." She sipped her cocoa feeling its warmth slid down her throat. "I'm originally from Boise, Idaho. I moved to Phoenix three months ago after my father passed away last spring."

Betty placed her hand over Tammy's and squeezed. "I'm sorry, dear."

"Thank you." On the way over, Sue Ellen had whispered in Tammy's ear that Miss Betty was their elementary school teacher. "So you teach?"

"Oh my, yes. Have for forty years." From the corner where Franc and Terry sat came a snicker. "Behave, Mr. Chambers, or you will be staying late come Monday."

Terry groaned and Franc chuckled.

How domestic it all seemed. Just a group of werewolves and one Lamia—hybrid—sitting around the table chatting as if outside there wasn't a lynch mob foaming at the mouth to end Tammy's life. She glanced at the door and wondered when Roark would arrive. Damn. She wished Marcellus was here.

Jennifer, a tall slender woman with red hair and devilish

pretty eyes spoke up. "We don't all think like Layton. We are curious, even more so now that you carry our leader's children."

"It's unbelievable," Tammy said more to herself than anyone present. "I wasn't sure I could conceive since I'm—" What? Undead? Immortal?

They leaned forward on her every word.

"Well, let's just say this is as new to me as it is for you. I don't even have the legends or rumors to go on. Each day is literally a surprise for me."

Until now Cathy had remained quiet, her big brown eyes pinned on Tammy. "You're so beautiful." The awe in her voice made heat rush up Tammy's neck and spread across her cheeks.

"Thank you." Tammy gauged Cathy to be about nineteen. She had the youthful look about her.

"Is it true that Manny is under your spell?"

"Cathy!" Laura chirped.

"It's okay." Tammy had to get use to people looking at her as an oddity. "A vampire's bite is seductive, but not a spell. I'm just fortunate that Manny believes that I'm not the monster most of your people think I am."

Sue Ellen crawled off her chair and onto Tammy's lap. She snaked her arms around Tammy's neck. "You're not a monster." The innocence in the child's eyes touched Tammy, especially when she shot a glance toward her brother. "See, Terry. She is a fairy princess—a queen."

"Yeah. Yeah—" Franc placed a hand over Terry's mouth before he could continue.

The conversation flowed casually for the next two hours. Tammy discovered that Laura was a widow—a hunting accident. It was also obvious that there was attraction between her and Franc as they shared secret glances. Cathy was heading to college in Tucson. Jennifer was playing her cards wild and free. She didn't want a man that would tie her down, especially a lycanthrope. In her words they were "overbearing and just a regular pain in the ass".

When the first hunger pain struck, Tammy almost cried out. Her heat cycle might be gone, but her thirst wasn't. The beating of hearts, the swish of blood was a symphony in her head. Her mouth watered. Her stomach even growled. Cathy shot her an inquisitive glance. This couldn't be happening now.

No. No. No. Tammy was shocked when the temptress faded in the dark. The first real sense of self-control made her inwardly smile. Perhaps there was hope for her after all.

A sharp knock on the door and they all turned their heads. No one appeared worried except for Franc who sprung to his feet and crossed the room with preternatural speed. "Who is it?"

"It's me." Roark's voice caressed Tammy's ears. She shivered with the need to see him, be near. Franc opened the door and Roark entered. His eyes were weary, his smile a little weak. "Ready to go home, baby?"

Home? If only she could find a home amongst these people. Tammy knew she could be happy here. She placed Sue Ellen on her feet and scooted the chair out to rise. This was just the type of place she would want to raise her children. Clean and spacious. Untouched by the hustle and bustle of the city.

"Thank you, Laura."

Tammy was pleasantly shocked when Laura hugged her. "Thank you for visiting. We'll see you tomorrow at Grady's and Lonnie's funerals?"

As each of the other women present gave her additional hugs, Tammy stammered on Laura's question. "Uh..." If everyone thought she was guilty of their deaths, she was the last person they'd want to see there. Tammy glanced at Roark for confirmation. He nodded. "Yes, we'll be there."

After saying their goodbyes, she, Roark and Franc left. The scent of burning pine filled the air along with a variety of other smells. Someone was barbequing. A small restaurant down the street had the most delicious Italian scent seeping from its chimney.

There was a sense of peace in the surrounding forest that felt almost deceiving. She watched a bushy-tailed squirrel race up the bark of a tree. The animal scampered from branch to branch without a care in the world. Would she ever feel that way? Would her children? She felt tired. Of course, not sleeping since the previous day wasn't helping.

"*Yes. In time, life will be as it should for us and our children.*" Roark touched her mind, snaking his arm around her shoulders to pull her closer. "Franc, I haven't seen Stephen since our return?" His breath met the chilly air and crystallized as he spoke.

"He had a massive headache. He took wolf form to heal," Franc explained, snow crunching beneath his boots. "If I know Stephen, he is leading the investigation. He was pretty pissed when he woke."

"We need to find the culprit, soon. Too much has happened. The pack acknowledges that Lonnie's death was staged. But the why has them on edge."

"Either way they blame me. I'm the why." Tammy glanced at him, but he looked away as if he could hide the truth. She fell silent. Why belabor the point—it was what it was.

No one spoke the remainder of the trip. It was a little eerie stepping inside the cabin. She couldn't help looking toward the spot where Lonnie had lain dead. Funny, how a little soap and water could wash away the evidence, but the image was burned into her memory. She blinked finding the picture still there.

Tammy hadn't realized she had stopped until Roark said, "Come on, honey. You need a bath and a nap."

She needed a helluva lot more than a bath and a nap—she needed a miracle.

Chapter Eighteen

How long Tammy slept she had no idea. She stretched, opening her eyes to darkness and silence. Patting the bed next to her, she realized she was alone. A moment of panic gripped her, but she pushed it away along with the covers tucked around her. When her naked body touched the chilled air, she shivered. The tremor vanished as quickly as it had arrived. The automatic thermostat inside her was convenient. Even still she thought of a robe and in seconds she was wrapped in a blue creation of her mind. The matching slippers were an afterthought as she stood.

The fire had died in the hearth, only a thin strip of light shown beneath the door leading to the hallway. Her slippers made a wispy sound across the floor. When she opened the door, the light caused her eyes to sting and water. She rubbed them as she made her way to the top of the stairs. Muffled voices met her ears and several masculine scents pushed her exhaustion aside. Marcellus was here. His spicy aftershave was difficult to miss among Roark's cologne. Energy abounded in her steps as she flew down the stairs.

Their eyes met hers as she entered the room. Both men stood, but it was Marcellus who approached to wrap her in his embrace. "My pet."

Tammy had missed his sexy French accent, the feel of his hands on her skin, the taste of his lips as they touched hers. When they parted, his eyes burned with desire, awakening her temptress and her hunger. It seemed like forever since she had both men in her bed. Just the thought of being sandwiched between them made her lean into his warmth.

He cupped her face. "Lanier informs me the heat is gone." Had Roark told him she was pregnant? Tammy tensed, waiting to gauge Marcellus's reaction. "We are to be a family," he said and then smiled.

Relief spilled from her lungs in a single gush. She threw her arms around his neck and hugged him.

"Ahhh...Tamanen." He drew her away from him. "You thought I would be unhappy?" Tammy swallowed hard. "I am elated. You and Lanier have gifted me with an experience I never thought possible. I'll be a father." His voice was thick as his gaze met Roark's. "Thank you." There was a moment that stretched between both men. They cared for each other. The knowledge touched her to the depths of her soul. They could make this work—this threesome and soon to be five.

Marcellus cleared his throat. "Now tell me how you are." He sat down on the couch before pulling her into his lap. She snuggled close, feeling his hard erection press against her ass. He wagged his brows and that mischievous grin slid across his face. "I've missed you."

Her heart thudded against her chest. "I've missed you too."

His hand slipped beneath her robe, smoothing up her leg, stopping with the urgent pounding on the door. It flung open before the three of them could get to their feet.

Wide-eyed and out of breath, Bryant said, "All hell is breaking loose down at town hall." He didn't wait for anyone to respond, he just turned and ran.

Marcellus moved her quickly off his lap and she landed sprawled upon the couch. "Stay here." It was a demand as he and Roark moved toward the door.

"But—"

"I'll send Franc or Stephen back. Lock the doors and don't let anyone other than them inside," Roark tossed over his shoulder as he pulled the door closed behind him.

Tammy could still feel Roark and Marcellus's anxiety. Something was wrong. She got to her feet and started pacing. With each step the air thickened and her unease grew. The next series of knocks on the door made her nearly jump out of her skin.

She ran to the door, fingers folding around the doorknob, and then she paused. A deep breath told her Bryant had returned. She flung the door open and he stepped inside.

"My queen, Roark asked me to escort you to the hall. If you will dress, I'll take you to him."

Tammy didn't think twice, calling her magic forth. Her robe and slippers morphed into boots, jeans, and a comfy sweater.

"That's amazing," Bryant said as he pushed the door wide and let her pass.

"What's happening?" she asked.

"Donne brought a constituent of vampires with him. Werewolves don't play well with the undead—that is until you came along." There was a hint of bitterness in his voice. She spun on a heel to face him when something hard struck her against the head. Lights burst behind her eyelids as nausea crashed into her. Her knees buckled and everything went dark.

"Why the hell can't our people get along?" Roark mumbled as he and Donne pushed through the crowd. Franc and

Stephen were both holding Layton as he struggled for release. His cousin's face was twisted in a mass of hatred. The vampire who curled a come-and-get-me finger taunting him was just as angry.

Anton and Henri moved to Donne's side, Deirdre watching his back as he entered behind Roark. "Stand down, Darta," Donne commanded, waving Anton and Henri to move behind Darta. The tall dark man ignored his leader until Donne released a menacing hiss that not only jerked Darta's attention to him, but everyone else's in the room.

Roark remembered that Darta was one of the men Tammy had nearly killed when she was first converted. Since the altercation included his cousin, Roark knew this couldn't be good.

"Donne's people are guests in our town. As such, they will be treated with respect," Roark announced with enough strength behind his words to leave no question as to what he expected. "Stephen, please return to my home and tell your queen that all is well. Stay with her until I return." Stephen released Layton, but Franc's hold remained.

"Let me go," Layton snarled.

Franc looked to Roark for direction. He shook his head. "Not before you explain what this is all about."

"Are you kidding?" Layton grumbled. "We're overridden with bloodsuckers. Look what mating with one of them has brought about. We're not safe even in our own homes."

"Safety is only an illusion we allowed you to possess, dog." Darta's lips parted and he bared his teeth.

"Enough, Darta." Donne moved forward to stand beside Roark. "Lanier and I understand that what Fate has bestowed upon us many of you are not pleased with." That could be the understatement of the year, Roark thought, but remained quiet as Donne continued. "Even if we had a choice in this matter, neither of us would have chosen differently. It is time that we quit fighting each other. Learn to live in harmony."

"But she is breeding with that wolf's mutts." Donne moved so quickly it was a blur. He held a single hand around Darta's throat. Slowly he raised the man off his feet so the tip of his toes barely touched the floor.

"Speak of my family like that again and I will kill you." The menace in Donne's tone sent a shiver up Roark's back. There was no doubt Donne meant every word.

A heaviness developed in Roark's chest. It squeezed even harder when Stephen burst into the room announcing, "She's gone."

Marcellus's knees almost buckled as he released Darta and the man fell to the floor. Marcellus had suffered being apart from Tamanen this last couple of days. Cranky and short-tempered, his nights had become a trial of arguing with his people and trying to reassure them that his mate meant them no harm. The loneliness and need to hold her had been unbearable. He was like an addict—his fix—Tamanen.

Now she was gone.

He turned to Lanier and saw the same despair that squeezed his chest reflected upon the wolf's face. "We have to find her." They said loneliness made the heart grow fonder. In his case, it had led to the discovery that he loved her. How it happened he didn't know. When it occurred? The first time he laid eyes on her.

"We will," Lanier said as he moved hastily from the room. A handful of his guards followed, as well as Marcellus and his several of his sentries.

His gaze darted around taking in the open space. He was

229

unfamiliar with this territory. Unusual scents bombarded him, confusing him or was it just the thought that he would never see Tamanen again?

Damn. He had never felt so helpless.

With preternatural speed they made their way back to Lanier's empty cabin. The door was shut as they stepped onto the porch. Deirdre and Lanier were the first to enter the cabin. As the rest of them entered, several guards split in all directions, some heading up the stairs, other toward the kitchen. Lanier called out her name, the quietness ripped through Marcellus like a knife. Inside the scent of violence from the night before lingered, but there was nothing new to guide them as they made their way back outside.

The moon draped the landscape with blue shadows. For a moment, he longed for the city, lights, noises, and scents. But most of all, he needed Tamanen in his arms. The woman had awakened his heart. She was the link between Lanier and him. Without her— He didn't want to think of the answer.

Immediately, several of Lanier's people took wolf form. They sniffed the air, while the rest of them scoured the country side for footprints or any sign of which direction she might have been taken. Old Man Winter was not their friend. Each second that past, the wind increased in volume stirring up the snow so that it ruffled the ground and covered any evidence that might be left behind. It also appeared to confuse the wolves as they once again raised their noses to the sky.

Marcellus's own people glanced at him as if awaiting his command. For all the power he possessed he had no idea which direction to start their search. He reached out to Tamanen on their mind path, but either she was too far away, unconscious, or—

Dammit. Marcellus refused to think the worse. They had to

find her and soon. "Spread out. Search everywhere."

The lonesome howl of a wolf jerked Lanier's gaze toward the trees. "Franc has found something."

Lightning speed carried them to the tree line where Franc in wolf form sat beside a slight hollowing in the snow. From the spot drag indications were evident, but too soon the marks disappeared beyond the trees.

Thank God. At least they now knew where to begin their search. Marcellus couldn't remember the last time he had prayed or asked the divine Master above for help. But as they trekked through the trees, over one hill and then other, he prayed for assistance in finding Tamanen—prayed that they would find her before it was too late.

℘

A dusty scent penetrated Tammy's nostrils as the curtain of consciousness rose and her stomach pitched. Her head felt as if it was spinning on an axis. The vertigo didn't stop when she forced her eyes to open—it got worse. Her surroundings whirled, she felt her legs give. A sudden yank and the muscles in her arms tightened, pain splintering in her wrists. Déjà vu hit her hard. She was shackled by her neck, wrists and ankles, but this time in a damp cave. The rocky surface scraped up her back as she found her footing. She muffled her cry of pain, clenching her jaws together.

Angry voices and echoing footsteps faded above the pounding of her heart. She tried to clear her head, hear what they were saying, but it was useless. Bryant and whoever else had abducted her were gone. The only sound was the distant hollow dripping of water.

Tammy wasn't a fool. There was no leaving this place alive

unless a miracle happened. What she needed was to calm down and think. Yet the more she attempted to control her racing pulse, the faster it pumped clouding her thoughts. Fear for her unborn children sent ice through her veins and she found the energy to pull against her bindings, but they didn't budge.

"*Roark? Marcellus?*" She reached for them mentally. When no response came, a cry squeezed from her lips. How long had she been unconscious? Distance broke the connection between them, which meant she had to be far away from the town.

God help her.

When the earth shook and bits of rock fell brutally against her skin, scraping and digging into her, a scream pushed from the top of her lungs. Although it seemed a long time, the shaking actually lasted only a fraction of a minute, and then it started anew. The floor lurch beneath her feet, seemingly to wave and buck. She barely stayed afoot as the ground and walls surrounding her shook violently. From within the bowels of the earth a low moan began. The rumble that followed became a deafening roar as the walls and ceiling imploded suddenly and forcibly.

In a handful of seconds, she was torn from the wall and knocked forward several feet by a blast of air that flung her like a rag doll. Above, below, and all around her an unending series of sonic booms caused her to scramble, trying to get back on her feet, but it was impossible to stand. The floor of the cave turned into an ocean of waves rolling and churning, except it wasn't water but soil and rock.

Hell had been unleashed upon her.

Tammy struggled to breathe with the crescendo of air pressure and atmospheric vibrations. The loudest sound mankind had ever made nearly burst her eardrums. She curled her arms around her head and prayed her death would come swiftly. Once more the earth rose up and shattered spraying debris in all directions pelting her with rubble and pinning her to the ground.

Then her world fell silent.

The roar was devastating as the blast threw Roark, Donne, and the rest of the scouting party to the ground. Roark had never heard or experienced anything like the sudden force of wind, dirt and rock that pummeled them. Arms sheltering his head, he prayed the explosion had nothing to do with Tammy, although he knew it was a lie.

As they crawled cautiously to their feet, Franc said, "That was no earthquake."

Roark looked toward the underground caverns and even in the dark of night saw the cloud of dust that filled the sky. Blood froze in his veins. For a moment, he couldn't breathe. His legs wouldn't move. The thought of Tammy buried beneath the mountain was more than he could stand. His body began to tremble. His world became blurry through misty eyes. When he found Bryant he would tear him apart, one limb at a time. His trusted guard had almost gotten away with his betrayal. After hours of searching and finding no trail, masked beneath the smells of a variety of animal's droppings he had recognized Bryant's as well as Tammy's scent.

The question remained—why? And was Roark too late to save Tammy?

Stephen wrapped an arm around Roark's shoulders to steady him. "We'll find her."

Roark attempted to suck in air that felt too heavy to ingest. The dusty atmosphere choked Tammy's perfume from his nostrils. He was losing her bit by bit. Swaying, he shrugged out of Stephen's grasp. Despair made him throw back his head and howl. The cry ripped from his diaphragm, taking with it his energy as he crumbled to his knees. He couldn't live without her. Even now his beast wept for hers.

Donne's face was drawn and pale as he knelt beside Roark. "Our mate is a survivor. Don't give up on her." Spoken with confidence, but the vampire's composure wasn't much better than Roark's. Donne's hand trembled as he placed it on Roark's back. Together they rose and headed for the mountain.

How much time passed Roark didn't know, but morning would arrive soon. As they exited yet another cavern, Anton and Henri glanced at the mountain range to the east. Their unease was obvious as they stirred nervously. They had joined the search party when the explosions began.

Every cave opening they had searched came to a dead end, causing them to waste more time as they retraced their steps. There were so many places Tammy could be. The task seemed insurmountable, but Roark would not give up until he found her.

Dead or alive.

Chapter Nineteen

Blinded by a wall of dust, Tammy tried to move and almost fainted. If the pain in her chest didn't confirm she had broken several ribs, the agonizing pain that ravished her with each breath did. She held motionless, willing herself to take only small breaths. Yet the undertone of discomfort remained. In the minutes that passed she thought of the children she carried.

When lying there and dying was no longer an option, she began to slowly dig out of the mountain of rock pressing atop her. Each movement sent daggers of fire through her ribcage. Every rock she moved brought ten more like it down upon her. It seemed hopeless, but she wouldn't give up. She had too much to live for.

It felt like an eternity, but little by little she saw progress. Finally Tammy could move her legs and she carefully rolled over only to cringe in pain. Slowly she pulled her legs and arms beneath her and tried to rise. Pain and nausea slammed into her out of nowhere. She fought the darkness that threatened to close in on her. When she could breathe again she resorted to crawling on her hands and knees. Rocks and debris sliced into her skin. The scent of her own blood made her incisors push through bone and gums.

She was hungry and tired and hurt.

When her beast cried out in rage, she allowed it to take control and let the change sweep over her. She lay on her side, half-covered in her shirt and jeans, feeling her bones knit together. Her feet slipped out of the ankle and wrist manacles, but the one around her neck remained. Half-crazed laughter spilled from her dry lips. If she'd only thought of this earlier.

Tammy knew if she was to survive she needed to pace herself and allow the change to heal and rejuvenate her. It was difficult, but she lay perfectly still, when what she wanted was to run to safety—to Roark and Marcellus. When she couldn't stand it any longer, Tammy carefully pushed to all fours. The bearable ache that throbbed in her chest, she chose to ignore. Instead, she padded across the rocky surface heading for where, she had no idea.

One path led her to a mountain of stone. She attempted to dig past it, but in the end felt the need to reserve her strength, resorting to backtracking and heading down a different passageway. The chain dragging behind her caught on a pile of rocks and jerked her off her feet. She yelped, striking the ground hard enough to take her breath away. After that she picked the chain up in her mouth to carry it.

A rumbling in the earth made her quicken her pace. As she ran, stones, large and small, fell from the ceiling, some striking her to make her yip in pain and drop the chain. Others rocks barely missed her; one particularly large boulder struck her in the flank and she skidded across the unforgiving floor of the cave.

When she came to a stop, she lay panting. A pain in her leg revealed a jagged tear bleeding profusely. She had to stop the flow. Tammy licked the open wound, staunching the blood and quenching her thirst at the same time. A sob gathered in her throat as she pushed to her feet and limped forward.

It seemed like forever that she walked, head held low. When she came to yet another dead end, she crumpled before the mountain of stone. "*Roark*" she cried out in desperation.

"Tammy!" Roark's muffled voice freed her tears as she jumped to her feet and placed her front paws on the barrier that stood between them.

"*Tamanen, are you all right?*" Marcellus touched her mind, making her heart stutter.

"*Yes,*" she sniffled. "*Get me out of here.*"

"*We're trying, baby. Hold on.*" She heard Roark throw orders to Stephen and Franc to start digging beside him.

The scraping sounds were halted when Marcellus said, "*That isn't necessary. Step aside. Come to me, my pet.*" His words melted her existence. The manacle that was around her neck fell to the ground. In the beat of a second, she stood wrapped in his embrace.

"Why didn't you think of that sooner," Roark grumbled, pulling her out of Marcellus's arms and into his own. His grip was tight. He held her as if he'd never let her go.

Of course, neither had Tammy thought of just popping herself out of her dilemma.

A sheepish expression spread across Marcellus's face. "Must I admit that I was too upset to think?" He appeared in full control as he cleansed her body, stroking and caressing her with just a thought before donning her in warm clothing. "Let's get out of here."

The shimmer in the eastern sky announced morning was fast approaching. They moved swiftly through the forest until Tammy's lungs burned and her legs ached, especially the one that she had injured. It was healing, but not fast enough. When the lights of the town appeared in the horizon she stumbled and fell. Before Roark or Marcellus could reach her, a black woman

Tammy remembered seeing at Marcellus's stepped beyond the trees. She moved so quickly that before Tammy knew it she was encased in her grip. Sharp claws pressed against Tammy's throat. She grasped the arms that held her.

"Deirdre." The shock in Marcellus's voice was obvious. "Release your queen." He took a step forward.

"Stop. I will kill her." To emphasize Deirdre's point, her talon broke skin. A warmth slithered down Tammy's neck. She was still breathing hard, but now it wasn't from exertion but fear. This time Tammy tried to pop out of the woman's grasp, but her magic failed.

So this was who Bryant had been arguing with in the caves before the explosion. A vampire had been his accomplice.

"Why?" Marcellus's asked.

"To save you from yourself." There were tears in Deirdre's voice. "She is poison in your veins. I can't let you die at her hands." Her tears fell on Tammy's wrists. Deirdre trembled. Each tremor drove her nails deeper into Tammy's skin.

"The light will be upon us shortly. We will all die." Marcellus tried to reason with her.

"Not you, Master. Seek your shelter so that you will live."

His laughter held irony. "That's not how this will end."

"Go, Marcellus. Take your people now." Tammy touched his mind.

"I will not leave you."

"The sun won't harm me."

"It's true," Roark confirmed without looking at Marcellus and letting Deirdre know they communicated. *"My cabin holds shelter for you. Upstairs, third door on the left is a guest room. Second door on the left is our room. Please, go now before it's too late."*

"Please, Master. Go." Deirdre's tone held compassion and love for Marcellus.

He hesitated and Tammy's heart skipped a beat. The glow of day was rising quickly. "Follow me," he said, turning and fleeing for the cabin nestled below.

Tammy would have breathed a sigh of relief if Deirdre's hold wasn't so tight. "You love him?" Her voice was strangled.

"Yes," Deirdre replied, easing her hold as the sun began to rise.

"It was you who killed Lonnie?" Roark asked.

"Regretfully, yes." Deirdre's voice hummed in Tammy's ear. "The dog said the Lamia would be blamed, that her life would not be spared. Can you not see she has poisoned you as well?"

Roark took a step closer, Stephen and Franc followed. "Where's Bryant now? And how did you mask your scent."

Deirdre firmed her hold. "The dog died for failing me a second time. I hid the same way the dog did among stronger scents in your cabin." She tightened her grip on Tammy. "But you knew, didn't you?"

"Yes." The word was strangled. Tammy had thought a vampire had been present at Lonnie's death, but she hadn't been confident in her abilities.

Deirdre continued, "Since I began the search with you it was easy to camouflage each scene we approached." She squinted into the sunrise. "Leave us—the time is near."

The noxious stench of burning hair stung Tammy's nose, but it was the skin beneath her touch blistering and oozing that made her stomach roll and flip-flop.

Deirdre cried out in pain, releasing Tammy. Roark closed the distance between them and took her into his embrace as the vampire crumpled upon the ground, screeching and clawing at her skin. Tammy had never heard such a horrid sound as the last of life gurgled in Deirdre's throat, and then she burst into a ball of flames.

"Don't look, baby." Roark pressed Tammy's face against his shoulder. Eyes closed, she tried to erase the scents and sights of dying, but they would be forever more etched into her memory. "Let's go home," he said, leading her away.

As they reached the bottom of the hill, Sue Ellen and Laura ran to their side. Several more townspeople joined them. There were hugs and warm wishes. Not everyone was pleased with her return, but at least this was a beginning, and a new beginning is what she needed.

Tammy swallowed hard. "Can Sue Ellen tell if my babies are unharmed?" So much had happen, she feared the worse.

"She can." Laura ushered the child to Tammy. "Check the children."

Sue Ellen raised Tammy's jacket and shirt so that she could press her ear to Tammy's stomach. She listened for a moment, pulled away and smiled. "They sleep."

Happiness raced down Tammy's cheeks. Roark dabbed at her tears and then kissed her, before he said, "Let's go home."

Roark breathed his first sigh of relief when he opened the door to his cabin and let Tammy pass through. Even with Bryant and Deirdre gone, he had asked Stephen and Franc to ensure guards were posted around the clock. If that was what it took to keep his mate safe then it would be done. He had been touched by the kindness several of his people had shown Tammy. Maybe in time they would all come to love her as he did. He pulled her into his arms and she went willingly.

"I'm sorry," he said.

Tammy looked up at him, weariness reflected in her eyes. "Don't be. I trusted Bryant. When he said you sent him I didn't think twice. I have no one to blame but myself."

"I should have never left you."

"It's over. I need a bath to wash the stench off me."

The stairs creaked beneath their feet as they climbed. Quietly they opened the door to their bedroom to not disturb Donne, but the vampire stood by the fireplace, gazing into the flickering flames. He turned, his face bathed in shadows. He opened his arms and Tammy ran into them. Roark left them to run the bath water.

Sitting on the side of the tub, water cascading to splash on the bottom, Roark thought of the triangle that existed between them. Donne loved Tammy. She was the link between them, but they were from different worlds—leaders with responsibilities for their people. Were they kidding themselves that this screwed-up arrangement would work?

Lost in his wonderings, he didn't hear Tammy approach. He raised his head with her touch. She was gloriously naked. Only faded lines and bruises noted the injuries she incurred. He thought of her skin marred, and anger assaulted him.

"It's over." Tammy moved to stand between his thighs before she threaded her fingers through his hair and massaged. He pressed his cheek to her abdomen, thought of his children, and knew he could never let her go.

She stepped back and he stood to help her into the bathtub. Steam snaked off the surface as he turned the knobs and stopped the flow. A look of pleasure softened her face when she eased into the depths until her shoulders were covered. An audible breath released. She closed her eyes.

"Do you want me to wash your back?"

"Thank you, but I just want to lie here."

241

Roark started to undress, removing his coat and shirt. He'd shower while she soaked. Toeing off his boots, he jerked his socks off and pushed his jeans and shorts to the floor. His bare feet padded across the cool wood floor. The glass door creaked as he opened it and entered. A twist of knobs and ice cold water pelted him. He cringed, gritting his teeth until the temperature warmed and he could relax. Slowly he began to wash the events of the night away, praying that he'd never face another like it again.

Chapter Twenty

Nothing could be better than to wake sandwiched between two men, except the knowledge that each of them loved her. Tammy gazed down at the mass of black and auburn hair resting on her naked chest. They were different as day and night—yet so alike. Strong. Dependable. Sexy. She didn't need light in the darkened room to see Roark's palm lay upon her abdomen, Marcellus's hand atop his. Loving them both felt as natural as breathing.

Tammy inhaled their masculine scents, feeling the first sign of arousal sting her breasts. When she thought of their mouths and tongues so close to her peaks, the temptress inside her rose to the surface. She tried to quiet the siren, but a purr slipped from her mouth. Roark and Marcellus stirred, at the same time opening their eyes to stare up at her. While Marcellus was the picture of perfection, not one hair out of place, Roark's hair was sleep tousled, his eyelids heavy.

Damn, they were gorgeous.

"How are you feeling?" Roark asked, bending the arm he lay on to prop a palm against his head.

Marcellus slid his hand along her midsection to cup her breast. He squeezed several times. "She feels good." Flashing a devilish grin, he leaned forward to take her nipple into his hot, wet mouth. The suction and swirl of his tongue was exquisite.

She arched into his caress.

Roark watched Marcellus intently, his eyes pools of gold. Tammy wanted him to touch her.

When Marcellus's mouth popped, releasing her, he blew a stream of air over the nub, causing the area around the puckered flesh to bead. "She tastes good too."

"Mmmm...maybe I need to find out for myself." Roark dipped his head and captured her other nipple between his lips. In seconds, both men suckled, pulling and tugging, sending white-hot energy straight to her core.

Tammy whimpered. Talk about erotic. Two men pleasuring her at once sent her libido soaring. She threw back her head and cried out.

They answered her need by taking turns to smooth a hand between her thighs as they continued to lavish her breasts. While one parted her folds and buried a finger deep, the other found the bundle of nerves throbbing for attention. A featherlight touched teased her clit. The other penetrated her nice and slow. Her hips rose off the bed to meet each thrust.

Breathy sounds pushed from her mouth as her inner muscles contracted and her skin hummed with desire. Together Roark and Marcellus worked her into a sexual frenzy. Over and over again they played with her until Tammy thought she'd scream in frustration. Several times they carried her to the brink, her body a mass of sensation, only to ease their pace and bring her back down.

It was hell—it was heaven, and she wanted more.

When another spasm rippled through her body, Tammy arched groaning, "*Oui.*"

"That's it, baby," Roark whispered against her skin. "Give it to us."

Marcellus pinched her nipple between his teeth, scraping and nipping her flesh with his fangs. Anticipation built, waiting for him to take her.

In a whirlwind of strokes and caresses they continued to heighten her arousal until the blood in her veins turn to molten lava. She was burning up. When Marcellus finally pierced the flesh around her areola and began to suck, her mind spun out of control. Lightning flashed, radiating throughout her body. Like a match to a fuse, her climax exploded in all directions, undulating over her in waves that rose into a crescendo before crashing down upon her. Intermittently, her body firmed and released. It went on and on, wringing a cry from her very soul. When the last spasm freed, she lay in quiet bliss.

"You were magnificent." Roark covered her mouth with his. His kiss was hungry, his tongue seeking as he drank from her lips. She loved the taste of him, the way he pulled her into his arms and deepened the caress.

Marcellus spooned her from the behind, his cock nestled against her ass as he trailed his lips and tongue along the hollow of her shoulder and neck. It tickled. She flinched and erupted into giggles, breaking the kiss. Her laughter died as she stared into Roark's eyes. Raw emotion reflected in their depths, warming her as thoroughly as any fire could. Tammy had never felt as good as she did that moment. It was unbelievable that not one, but two men could make her feel like she was walking on air, but Roark and Marcellus did just that.

"*Je t'aime*," slipped from her mouth.

"Him?" Marcellus asked, at the same time Roark said, "Me?"

Happiness bubbled up inside her. "Both of you. I love you both."

"Let me have her," Marcellus growled, yanking her out of

Roark's embrace into his. Again she laughed until his eyes met hers. "*Je t'aime aussi.*" His voice was tight with emotion. He licked his lips. "I thought I'd lost you."

Tammy ran her fingers through his hair. She kissed him tenderly. "I'm here. Everything will be okay."

Marcellus shook his head as if he didn't believe her. "Lanier, what's the arrangement here? I can't leave my people and you can't abandon yours. Where do we go from here?"

The air around Tammy grew tense. Beneath her palms Marcellus's muscles bunched. He held her a fraction closer, a little tighter. The strained expression on Roark's face, his clenched jaws, revealed he was in no better condition.

An uncomfortable silence lingered, until Roark said, "Donne, she carries my children." The space between them seemed too grow with his words.

The pain in Marcellus's eyes stole Tammy's breath. In the next heartbeat, his features hardened. "I won't let her go." There was a haunting almost dangerous drop in his tone. His shadowy gaze was ice cold.

She glanced at Roark. No way could she choose between these two men or see them fight over her. Tammy could not live being the wedge between them.

Roark knew a wrong move could be deadly. It was in the way Donne's predatory glare followed him as he approached. He had known Donne for some time and the vampire had always been the effigy of control. Yet last evening he had seen Donne falter because of his deep feelings for Tammy. Feelings Roark also shared.

When he placed a hand on the vampire's shoulder, Roark felt a series of tremors erupt through him. Thin lips held back the snarl that rumbled low in Donne's throat. Roark wished he could erase the fear on Tammy's face, but until they came to an agreement, they were at an impasse.

"My friend, we are bound by this woman. No decision either of us makes will change that." Roark look at Tammy and felt so much love it squeezed his chest. "She holds our hearts in her hands. I can't take her from you any more than you can take her from me." He paused, thinking through his next choice of words. "Here she has developed friendships, people who care about her, while your clan has yet to accept her."

"But how can they if she doesn't walk among them?" The truth in Donne's statement wasn't something Roark wanted to hear. The same could be said about his people, but he left it unspoken.

"Perhaps now is not the time to make lifelong decisions." Roark knew it was a cop-out. He didn't have an answer for their dilemma. It wasn't as if they could all move in together and live happily ever after.

Tammy cupped Donne's face. "Please understand." She nibbled on her bottom lip. "Here I don't feel the anger and fear as strongly." Her brows furrowed as she fought the burning behind her eyelids. "I need time to adjust, to come to grips with what and who I am. It doesn't mean I love you less and it doesn't mean in time that our dreams of vampire and werewolf walking in unity won't materialize."

Donne laid his forehead against hers, his eyes closing. Roark felt when Donne's resolve melted. The tension beneath his palm dissolved as well as the electricity in the air.

When Donne opened his eyes again, his lashes were moist. "I can't bear not waking with you each evening. The last couple of nights without you have been miserable." His lips hovered over hers.

Dammit. The vampire was breaking Roark's heart. Yet

silently he shared the same fear.

"I've missed you too," Tammy whispered.

Marcellus's throat tightened as he released her. "So what?" He paused, before continuing, "I get you on weekends, every other holiday, and two weeks during the summer?" His words were jovial, but his tone lacked its usual spark. He had a feeling this arrangement was not to his benefit. Yet she was happy here—something he couldn't give her right now at his home, with his people. There was still work to be done. "What about the children?" The tendons in his neck grew taut. They snaked across his shoulders as he braced himself. Every since he discovered Tamanen was pregnant, he prayed that he would be included. "Will they be able to join her? I want to be a part of their lives—" He tipped his head back struggling to hold onto his control and find the words that he had been wanting to speak for some time. His chest heaved as he leveled his sights on Lanier. "—a part of your life." There he said it. His feelings for the wolf were known.

Lanier's eyes widened with surprise. Marcellus felt the beast inside the lycanthrope stir.

Marcellus quickly added, "I won't ask for more than you can give." He walked a delicate path here. Yet he would take whatever Lanier would allow. In truth, Marcellus wanted a true ménage a trios. He wanted to touch and be touched by Lanier. He needed to feel like a partner in their relationship and not the odd-man out. Tamanen carried the wolf's children. What did Marcellus have to offer her, but his love?

Lanier appeared speechless. Marcellus held his breath until Lanier said, "We'll work things out."

Air pushed from Marcellus's lungs in a single gush. He felt emotion prick his eyelids. "Okay. She stays with you, but if one hair on her head is harmed—" He didn't finished his sentence. Instead, he pulled Tamanen to him, ravishing her mouth before taking her down upon the bed.

"God, I love you." His voice was shaky.

Lanier moved quietly off the bed and headed toward the door.

"Don't go." Marcellus looked up and extended the lycanthrope his hand.

Lanier's back was to Marcellus, but he could see the man tense. His fingers curl into fists. When he turned around an array of emotions flicker across Lanier's face, his first step toward the bed was hesitant. He flexed his fingers, and then crossed the room. The squeaking of the mattress as he climbed upon it was the sweetest sound Marcellus ever heard.

Lanier pressed his body against Tamanen's back and she wiggled against him. His gaze met Marcellus's. There was a moment when time seemed to stand still, before he felt the pull between them—it was magnetic drawing him closer. Marcellus leaned inward and Lanier closed the distance, their lips meeting. It was everything he knew it would be. Strong and masculine and pure heaven.

"Ummm... You guys didn't forget about me?" Tamanen's chest rose and fell rapidly, clearly affected by their kiss. Her incisors had dropped. He could see the passion in her eyes as she moved her body between them.

"Never," Lanier growled as he ground his hips against her ass. His hand smoothed along Marcellus's thigh, sending his pulse racing. This was how it should be. Marcellus draped his arm over the two people that meant the most to him—his lifemates.

Epilogue

One Year Later

A steaming-mincemeat pie in each hand, Tammy pushed the kitchen door open with her hip and entered the spacious Town Hall. The meeting place had been converted into a wonderland of twinkling red, green, blue, and orange lights, a variety of glass bulbs hung from the ceiling, and pine garland align each door way. Evergreen mingled with nutmeg as she passed beneath the festoon. Along with several artificial trees spotted around the room, a beautifully decorated Blue Spruce stood off to the side. Numerous wrapped packages, big and small, draped in colorful ribbons and bows lay at its base. Already a host of the town's children had arrived surrounding the tree. Busily they picked up one package and then another, shaking each one for hints of what lay within.

Laughter caught her attention as Terry and Sue Ellen burst through the front door, their eyes brightened when they caught sight of the other children. A flurry of snow swooped in behind them, snowflakes dancing about the floor until Laura and Franc entered and pulled the door close. Tammy's heart melted when Franc looked at Laura with love in his eyes. The two of them had finally admitted their feelings. Tammy wouldn't be surprised if there was a wedding in store for the couple. She released a deep sigh.

Life had certainly changed.

As Tammy sat the pies upon the banquet table, leaving the potholders beneath them, a fussy infant's cry touched her ears. Justin was giving his father the once over, while his brother Jeremy slept peacefully in Marcellus's arms. Tammy's breath hitched. Tears burned her eyes. She loved them so much.

"The babies are growing leaps and bounds." Betty stepped beside Tammy. The older woman smiled sitting a dish of yams covered in melted marshmallows on the table. "It won't be long before they're sitting front row in my classroom."

"I can't believe how time flies." The last year had been a cyclone of events. Including a wedding in which she had taken not one, but two husbands. Their life together hadn't been a bed of roses. During one of her visits to be with Marcellus, Darta had made an attempt on her life. Her husband would not go into details but he had eliminated any further threat.

It hadn't been much easier here at home. Layton was a constant thorn in her paw. The man refused to accept her, though many of the wolves and vampires had done just that. It was a testament to have them together this holiday.

"This is your doings," Betty said with awe as she scanned the room, harmony lingered about. "You have made it possible that on this night we come together. It is a worthy celebration. You should be proud."

Several lycanthropes and undead chatted as if they had participated in the holiday together a million times throughout the years. They had truly made strides toward peace and unity. Yet Tammy wasn't fooling herself. There were those that fought them. Those who believed their race was superior. Still it was a start—she couldn't ask for anything more.

Not only was Tammy proud of their people, but Roark and Marcellus who appeared at ease sitting side by side on the small love seat, their thighs touching. Damn. They were gorgeous. Her heart stuttered. Life had definitely been a trial, but she wouldn't change it for anything in the world. She had two men who loved her, a family, and a future ahead of her.

Plus Tammy was constantly amazed with her growing power and abilities. The beast and temptress were under her control now. Occasionally, she found herself at odds with her hunger, especially during sex. With Marcellus it wasn't a problem, but she had to be careful with Roark. It took time for him to replenish his supply. Stephen had stepped in during emergencies, but that didn't go well with Roark or Marcellus. The fix was to ensure fresh blood was delivered to her weekly from the city when she couldn't make the trip.

From across the room her eldest son by two minutes hit a new time high with a piercing cry. Roark lunged to his feet, frantically bouncing Justin in his arms as he flashed Tammy a panicked look.

Betty chuckled. "You better save your husband. Looks like the little guy needs his mommy."

Before Tammy could reach them, Martin took the baby from Roark's arms and pressed him to his shoulder. He patted Justin several times on the back. A burp was the result. The baby released a shuddering sigh and spoke not a peep more.

Roark's eyes widened with surprise. "That was it? He needed burping?"

"Colic." Martin pressed his lips to Justin's forehead. "Grady had it for the first year of his life."

Tammy extended her arms. "Do you want me to take him?"

The tenderness in Martin's eyes touched Tammy. "Nah. It's Grandpa's turn to hold the rascal." She swallowed the emotion knotting her throat. Martin had never lost faith in her. He had been beside her from the beginning, her biggest supporter. It was because of him and Roark that many of the lycanthropes had embraced her.

Although at times, Tammy saw Martin's sadness, the pain of losing his son. Roark had sent several of their people in search of what had happened to Grady. It remained a quandary. Of course, there was the other mystery of how she came to be. The lycanthrope law of not turning humans was still in effect, but Tammy couldn't help wondering if she was the only Lamia, the only half werewolf and vampire who roamed this earth.

A sudden outburst from all the children made her turn around. Jolly Ol' St. Nicholas had arrived—or should she say Stephen, who didn't look all that jolly. The man had fought to the bitter end not to be the one donning the red suit, but she had won. As numerous children surrounded him, he pierced her with a look that said, "Paybacks are a bitch."

Roark's arms snaked around Tammy, pulling her back against his chest. "I'll save you from his retribution." He nibbled on her neck making her breasts ache with need. "You know you deserve it."

Tammy shot a glance over her shoulder and tried to feign innocence. "Me? I just thought he'd be the best Santa."

"You just wanted to see him squirm," Roark corrected, but she heard laughter creep into his voice. "I don't know what I'm going to do with the two of you." He hugged her closer. "I love you."

"I'd like a little bit of that." Marcellus had given Jeremy to Betty. She sat beside Martin on the love seat, each one of them the picture of contentment. Marcellus stood before Tammy. Roark released her and she went into his arms. He kissed her soundly. "I've missed you." His eyes were dark with desire, but that would have to wait.

"I've missed you too." The arrangement hadn't been ideal. The three of them stole what time they could, but the problem remained. As leaders of the lycanthropes and vampires, Roark and Marcellus had duties which required them to live individual lives. The funny thing was that it made their time together even sweeter. Every minute cherished, like this evening. Tonight they were hers and she planned to make the most of it. Even now her body tightened in anticipation. Moisture dampened her thighs.

Roark's hugged her back so that she was sandwiched between them. "Mmmm...your musk is driving me crazy."

Uneasy laughter slipped from her mouth. "Uh, fellows. This isn't the place—room full of children."

"When?" Marcellus breath whispered across her ear as he released her.

"Yeah. When?" Roark nibbled her neck, again sending chills up her back, before he moved away.

Tammy's legs felt like jelly. "You're killing me here." She wanted nothing more than to haul both of them out the door and home. Of course, there were the boys and the party. It was times like this that she was thankful for her newly found control. She beckoned the temptress back into the shadows. "The gifts haven't been distributed." Justin yawned, making a soft sound as his eyelids drifted close. "Besides, I have to get the babies to bed."

"Dear, we'll take care of the little ones," Betty offered.

"I'd say there was no time like the present to escape. Your rough and tough bodyguard has everyone preoccupied." Two children sat on Stephen's lap, one jerking on his bread. When Tammy looked back at Martin, he winked. "You've got an hour and then we'll bring the boys home."

An hour? That sounded heavenly to Tammy.

"Baby, you haven't had anything to eat." Roark pampered her something terrible during her pregnancy and now that the children were born it was getting worse. Too cold? Too hot? He kept checking on her comfort, even though she could easily regulate her temperature. Not to mention, if she ate every time he offered her something she'd be as big as a house. He brushed his palm up her arm—love shimmered in his eyes. You'd thought she'd given him the world. She gazed down upon her two boys sleeping peacefully. Maybe she had given him the world. Roark and Marcellus had certainly given her a life beyond her wildest dreams.

"I'm not hungry." Tammy wagged her brows. "Let's go."

In a blink of an eye they made it to the door, grabbing their coats as they slipped outside. Snow fell lightly. She tipped her face up and let the icy flakes land on her face.

"Happy?" Marcellus asked as he slipped his hand in hers. Roark took her other one.

"More than you can imagine." When she looked at each of them, her chest swelled with love.

"Race you to the house." In a flash Marcellus was gone. Not to be outdone, Roark used preternatural speed to follow him.

Tammy paused for only a moment to breathe in the air and surrounding beauty, and then disappeared, materializing on the porch of the cabin. She stomped her feet and wiped her boots on a rug lying before the door, before she pushed it open and entered. A fire crackled in the hearth. The Christmas tree was aglow in the corner. Tomorrow was Christmas Day and they would wait until the evening when Marcellus could join them to open their gifts.

Tammy padded up the stairs. When she opened the door Marcellus and Roark were naked, sprawled across the bed like Adonises. She couldn't help the grin that slid across her face.

Handsome and sexy, they looked good enough to eat—and they were all hers.

The door creaked as she shut it. With just a thought she shed her clothing, eagerly approaching until Marcellus folded his fingers around Roark's semi-hard cock. He didn't flinch, just sucked in a shuddering breath before he did the same to Marcellus. Strong hands stroked from base to tip and back again.

The image was so hot, Tammy's pulse sped. She loved it when they touched each other. There was something about these two men pressed close together that sent her desire soaring. The proof was in her rapid pulse and release of moisture between her thighs.

Roark bent a knee giving Marcellus access to his scrotum. Marcellus fondled the sac gently, before he said, "Join us, my pet."

When she climbed upon the bed and slipped between the two of them Tammy knew this was going to be the best Christmas Eve. Releasing a sigh, she closed her eyes and let Roark and Marcellus carry her to heaven.

About the Author

A taste of the erotic, a measure of daring and a hint of laughter describe Mackenzie McKade's novels. She sizzles the pages with scorching sex, fantasy and deep emotion that will touch you and keep you immersed until the end. Whether her stories are contemporaries, futuristics or fantasies, this Arizona native thrives on giving you the ultimate erotic adventure.

When not traveling through her vivid imagination, she's spending time with three beautiful daughters, three devilishly handsome grandsons, and the man of her dreams. She loves to write, enjoys reading, and can't wait 'til summer. Boating and jet skiing are top on her list of activities. Add to that laughter and if mischief is in order—Mackenzie's your gal!

To learn more about Mackenzie, please visit www.mackenziemckade.com. Send an email to Mackenzie at mackenzie@mackenziemckade.com or sign onto her Yahoo! group to join in the fun with other readers and authors as well as Mackenzie!

http://groups.yahoo.com/group/wicked_writers/

*An abused woman has the power to unite werefolk, fey and
vampire against an evil that would see them all
dead—if she can learn to love again.*

Sweeter Than Wine
© 2007 Bianca D'Arc

Christy lies near death after a brutal beating by her
estranged husband. Her preternatural friends reach a desperate
conclusion: The only way to save her is to turn her. Sebastian
steps forward to take on the burden of being her Maker.

For him it's no burden at all. She draws him as no other
woman has for centuries. With the help of a werecougar friend,
Sebastian teaches Christy about her new life and abilities,
making certain she is as strong as he can make her. Only then
can she face her abusive ex-husband and put her old life
behind her. But Christy's ex-husband is involved in something
more dangerous than any of them had guessed.

Vampire, were, and even a fey knight must work together to
put an end to the threatening evil. To overcome her past, help
keep the darkness at bay, and fight for a new life with
Sebastian, Christy must draw on all of her new-found strength.

Will it be enough?

*Warning, this title contains explicit sex, graphic language,
ménage a trois, hot neck biting and werecougar stroking.*

Available now in ebook and print from Samhain Publishing.

Enjoy the following excerpt from Sweeter Than Wine...

Christina woke in slow increments, like a kitten just learning about the world around it. Sebastian watched her from the side of the large bed, waiting for the moment when she'd realize she wasn't alone.

"I bet you're hungry." He was enchanted by the sleepy look in her eyes as she met his gaze. Rubbing her tummy, she looked like she was considering his words.

"I feel strange."

He nodded and moved closer, sitting on the edge of the bed. "That's to be expected when you're newly turned."

"Then it wasn't a dream?"

"No, my dear. It was most certainly real." He dipped his head closer, smiling so she could see his fangs. He was hungry too, it seemed. "You've been deep in healing sleep for more than two days. That's longer than most of the newly turned, but you were gravely injured, so I encouraged your sleep." He tugged at the sheet that covered her, inching it away. "I've decided on a course of action some might consider reckless." He paused. "Do you trust me?"

She seemed to think that one over before answering. "I think so."

"What I'm going to ask of you will seem strange, but I need you to believe it is for your own welfare that I've even considered this." He pulled the sheet a little lower.

"Now you're frightening me, Sebastian."

"That's not my intent. But I need you to know that what comes next is necessary for your future. I want you to be strong enough to deal with Jeff Kinsey on your own. I believe standing up to him—and winning—is the only way to face the rest of your years, now that you are immortal. If you let him win, even the smallest confrontation, it will set a tone for your new life that could prove disastrous."

"Did I mention you'd already scared me enough?"

Sebastian was glad to see a spark of humor in her wary eyes. It made him feel a little better about what he was about to do, though other aspects of his plan still made him uneasy. There was jealousy for one thing. It was likely to eat him alive before long. Good thing the task could be accomplished quickly. He knew he couldn't take too much of this.

"I'm sorry, Christina. What I propose will not hurt. On the contrary, it will bring you great pleasure, but it is somewhat...risqué. I know from your friends that you've never been very adventurous sexually. That will have to change."

She looked wary, but receptive. "What exactly are you talking about?"

"Your body is fully healed now, and its chemistry forever altered. Now it's time for your lessons to begin."

"Lessons?"

"I promised to teach you everything you need to know to survive in your changed state. Those lessons begin now, with our most basic needs—blood and lust. You need to feed." He dipped his head, kissing her savagely. He didn't mean to do it, but her soft lips were so close, so inviting, he couldn't resist.

Sebastian reveled in the sweet taste of her, delving deep with his tongue as her petite fangs began to emerge. He ran his tongue over them, encouraging their arrival. He'd forgotten how it felt to kiss one of his own kind. It was beyond erotic. It was nearly orgasmic in itself.

When she jumped, he pulled back, looking past her beautiful, bare body to see what had scared her. Sebastian understood her alarm when he saw Matt. He'd come in and prowled right up to the bed, taking a seat near the foot as if he belonged there, while Sebastian had been distracted. It was a shock to realize he'd been so lost in her kiss, he hadn't even sensed Matt's arrival. Matt's knowing wink didn't go a long way to soothe Sebastian's self-recrimination, but it did make him smile. The lad was audacious, but Christina needed a little nudge to guide her on this path. Before the night was through, Sebastian knew she'd need to put all her inhibitions behind her and Matt Redstone was just the creature to help her do it.

"I invited a mortal friend to help you learn how to feed both bodily and psychically." He waved one hand toward Matt, releasing her slowly. "He is *were*. You might note the difference in his scent from ordinary mortals. He'll make an excellent first feeding for you to grow strong and he's agreed to let us use him as our guinea pig for this evening. It's a rare honor. You should be thankful."

Christy looked at the gorgeous, muscular man who sat on the edge of her bed and began stroking her legs. "Um, thank you?"

She didn't know what to think. On the one hand, she'd never slept around. On the other, she'd never been this horny in her life. It had to do with whatever Sebastian had done to save her life. She felt different in startling ways. Liquid fire raced through her veins and straight to her womb, making her yearn in a way she never had before.

Cunning topaz eyes smiled up at her. "You're very welcome, sweet thing. It's been a long time since I had vampire pussy." He licked his lips, daring to smack them at her. She liked the sparkle in his gaze and could tell right away this handsome stranger was a bit of a tease. He drew her, but at the same time she was afraid of her own response. She didn't know this man.

Was Sebastian going to sit by and let him touch her—perhaps even take her—just like that?

"Sebastian?" Her voice rose along with her distress.

Reassuring hands stroked her back, helping her sit up. "Don't fear anything that will happen here this night. A vampire's first feeding is one of the most important of her existence. That Matt has agreed to let you feed from him tonight is no small thing. A portion of his inherent cunning, agility, and strength will forever be passed on to you. Like I said, it's a great honor."

"But is he going to um..." she felt heat stain her cheeks, "...will he want to have sex with me?"

Matt shifted to sit between her legs. "I'm going to fuck your brains out, sweetheart, and eat this pretty pussy 'til you come in my mouth."

"Sebastian!" The objection came out on a shocked gasp.

To be honest, though, she had to admit the new hunger wasn't only for the blood she could actually hear coursing through this strange, savage man's veins. He was handsome and muscular in a way she'd never seen in person. His golden hair practically invited her fingers to run through it, and he had the most gorgeous, bright, inquisitive eyes.

"It's all right, Christina." Sebastian's hypnotic voice soothed her. "It's only fair that Matt gain something from giving you his blood. By lapping your fluids, he will temporarily attain some of our healing and regenerative abilities to augment his own. It's a fair exchange."

"Who is he?" She was upset both at Sebastian's cavalier attitude and his assumptions about her willingness to sleep with a complete stranger. But even more upsetting was her body's response. She wanted to know how that muscular body would feel over her—inside her—fucking her. The thought was deliciously forbidden and altogether shocking. She shook her head, but clarity refused to come. So she appealed to Sebastian—her lifeline in this world gone wild. "How do you expect me to be intimate with someone I don't even know? That may be normal for you, but it's not for me. Not by a long shot!"

"Sorry, ma'am." Matt grinned and held out one hand for her to shake, still sitting between her thighs. "I'm Matt Redstone. Like Sebastian said, I'm *were*, and the youngest brother of the leader of the cougar clan."

She shook his hand as if in a trance. This was probably the strangest situation she'd ever been in. Bar none.

"What is *were*? What does that mean?"

Matt Redstone shot an amused look up at Sebastian. "She doesn't know anything yet, does she?"

GREAT
CHEAP
FUN

Discover eBooks!
THE FASTEST WAY TO GET THE HOTTEST NAMES

Get your favorite authors on your favorite reader, long before they're
out in print! Ebooks from Samhain go wherever you go, and work with
whatever you carry—Palm, PDF, Mobi, and more.

Samhain
publishing, Ltd

WWW.SAMHAINPUBLISHING.COM